ONE
SIDE
LAUGHING

ONE SIDE LAUGHING

Stories Unlike

Other Stories

DAMON KNIGHT

ST. MARTIN'S PRESS
NEW YORK

Design by Judith Stagnitto

Library of Congress Cataloging-in-Publication Data

Knight, Damon Francis
      One side laughing : stories unlike other stories / Damon Knight
          p.   cm.
      ISBN 0-312-05939-6
   1. Science fiction, American.   I. Title.
PS3561.N4405   1991
813'.54—dc20   90-29151
                                                          CIP

First edition: July 1991

10   9   8   7   6   5   4   3   2   1

For GORDON VAN GELDER

CONTENTS

INTRODUCTION

Some stories are written because the author wants to pay the rent, others because they swarm around demanding to be written. The stories in this volume are all of the second kind.

Writing fiction, which was agonizingly difficult when I started to learn it, is now and has been for many years the greatest pleasure of my life. I tell you this to encourage those who are in the painful stage. Trust me: the pleasure is worth the pain a thousand times over.

DAMON KNIGHT

P.S.   A moment ago I went to the mailbox and found in it a catalog advertising for sale, among other curious and useful objects, a Limoges golf ball, warranted to be in every way identical to a real one except for being made of china.

As you read these stories, I ask you to remember that if I had invented *that*, I would have been accused of having an overactive and probably unhealthy imagination.

D.K.

STRANGERS ON PARADISE

Gordon Van Gelder, to whom this book is dedicated, is not much more than a third my age, but I believe him to be one of the most intelligent and perceptive editors I have ever known—and, of course, the fact that you are holding this book in your hand demonstrates that I am right.

My reason for telling you this, apart from my natural desire to flatter Mr. Van Gelder into publishing more of my books, is that he coaxed me very gently to write individual introductions to the stories in this one.

Knowing Van Gelder as I do, I was sure this was no idle whim. He had to have a good reason, and I think I have ferreted out what it is.

Van Gelder believes that you are now standing in a bookstore leafing through this book to see if you might like it, and that if any of the introductions strike your fancy, you may say to yourself, "This is just the kind of fellow I like, and therefore I will probably like his stories too."

And besides, it is convenient to tell you this here, because the real introduction to this first story is at the end, where it will not spoil your surprise unless you peek.

Paradise was the name of the planet. Once it had been called something else, but nobody knew what.

From this distance, it was a warm blue cloud-speckled globe turning in darkness. Selby viewed it in a holotube, not directly, because there was no porthole in the isolation room, but he thought he knew how the first settlers had felt a century ago, seeing it for the first time after their long voyage. He felt much the same way himself; he had been in medical isolation on the entryport satellite for three months, waiting to get to the place he had dreamed of with hopeless longing all his life: a place without disease, without violence, a world that had never known the sin of Cain.

Selby (Howard W., Ph.D.) was a slender, balding man in his forties, an Irishman, a reformed drunkard, an unsuccessful poet, a professor of English literature at the University of Toronto. One of his particular interests was the work of Eleanor Petryk, the expatriate lyric poet who had lived on Paradise for thirty years, the last ten of them silent. After Petryk's death in 2156, he had applied for a grant from the International Endowment to write a definitive critical biography of Petryk, and in two years of negotiation he had succeeded in gaining entry to Paradise. It was, he knew, going to be the peak experience of his life.

The Paradisans had pumped out his blood and replaced it with something that, they assured him, was just as efficient at carrying oxygen but was not an appetizing medium for microbes. They had taken samples of his body fluids and snippets of his flesh from here and there. He had been scanned by a dozen machines, and they had given him injections for twenty diseases and parasites they said he was carrying. Their faces, in the holotubes, had smiled pityingly when he told them he had had a clean bill of health when he was checked out in Houston.

It was like being in a hospital, except that only machines touched him, and he saw human faces only in the holotube. He had spent the time reading and watching canned information films of happy, healthy people working and playing in the golden sunlight. Their faces were smooth, their eyes bright. The burden of the films was always the same: how happy the Paradisans were, how fulfilling their lives, how proud of the world they were building.

The books were a little more informative. The planet had two large continents, one inhabited, the other desert (although from space it looked much like the other), plus a few rocky, uninhabitable island chains. The axial tilt was seven degrees. The seasons were mild. The planet was geologically inactive; there were no volcanoes, and earthquakes were unknown. The low, rounded hills offered no impediment to the global circulation of air. The soil was rich. And there was no disease.

This morning, after his hospital breakfast of orange juice, oatmeal, and toast, they had told him he would be released at noon. And that was like a hospital, too; it was almost two o'clock now, and he was still here.

"Mr. Selby."

He turned, saw the woman's smiling face in the holotube. "Yes?"

"We are ready for you now. Will you walk into the anteroom?"

"With the greatest of pleasure."

The door swung open. Selby entered; the door closed behind him. The clothes he had been wearing when he arrived were on a rack; they were newly cleaned and, doubtless, disinfected. Watched by an eye on the wall, he took off his pajamas and dressed. He felt like an invalid after a long illness; the shoes and belt were unfamiliar objects.

The outer door opened. Beyond stood the nurse in her green cap and bright smile; behind her was a man in a yellow jumpsuit.

"Mr. Selby, I'm John Ledbitter. I'll be taking you groundside as soon as you're thumbed out."

There were three forms to thumbprint, with multiple copies. "Thank you, Mr. Selby," said the nurse. "It's been a pleasure to have you with us. We hope you will enjoy your stay on Paradise."

"Thank you."

"Please." That was what they said instead of "You're welcome"; it was short for "Please don't mention it," but it was hard to get used to.

"This way." He followed Ledbitter down a long corridor in which they met no one. They got into an elevator. "Hang on, please." Selby put his arms through the straps. The elevator fell away; when it stopped, they were floating, weightless.

Ledbitter took his arm to help him out of the elevator. Alarm bells were ringing somewhere. "This way." They pulled themselves along a cord to the jump box, a cubicle as big as Selby's hospital room. "Please lie down here."

The lay side by side on narrow cots. Ledbitter put up the padded rails. "Legs and arms apart, please, head straight. Make sure you are comfortable. Are you ready?"

"Yes."

Ledbitter opened the control box by his side, watching the instruments in the ceiling. "On my three," he said. "One ... two ..."

Selby felt a sudden increase in weight as the satellite decelerated to match the speed of the planetary surface. After a long time the control lights blinked; the cot sprang up against him. They were on Paradise.

The jump boxes, more properly Henderson-Rosenberg devices, had made interplanetary and interstellar travel almost instantaneous—not quite, because vectors at sending and receiving stations had to be matched, but near enough. The hitch was that you couldn't get anywhere by jump box unless someone had been there before and brought a receiving station. That meant that interstellar exploration had to proceed by conventional means: the Taylor Drive at first, then impulse engines; round trips, even to nearby stars, took twenty years or more. Paradise, colonized in 2054 by a Geneite sect from the United States, had been the first Earthlike planet to be discovered; it was still the only one, and it was off-limits to Earthlings except on special occasions. There was not much the governments of Earth could do about that.

A uniformed woman, who said she had been assigned as his guide, took him in tow. Her name was Helga Sonnstein. She was magnificently built, clear-skinned and rosy, like all the other Paradisans he had seen so far.

They walked to the hotel on clean streets, under monorails that swooped gracefully overhead. The passersby were beautifully dressed; some of them glanced curiously at Selby. The air was so pure and fresh that simply breathing was a pleasure. The sky over the white buildings was a robin's-egg blue. The disorientation Selby felt was somehow less than he had expected.

In his room, he looked up Karen McMorrow's code. Her face in the holotube was pleasant, but she did not smile. "Welcome to Paradise, Mr. Selby. Are you enjoying your visit?"

"Very much, so far."

"Can you tell me when you would like to come to the Cottage?"

"Whenever it's convenient for you, Miss McMorrow."

"Unfortunately, there is a family business I must take care of. In two or three days?"

"That will be perfectly fine. I have a few other people to interview, and I'd like to see something of the city while I'm here."

"Until later, then. I'm sorry for this delay."

"Please," said Selby.

That afternoon Miss Sonnstein took him around the city. And it was all true. The Paradisans were happy, healthy, energetic, and cheerful. He had never seen so many unlined faces, so many clear eyes and bright smiles. Even the patients in the hospital looked healthy. They were accident victims for the most part—broken legs, cuts. He was just beginning to understand what it was like to live on a world where there was no infectious disease and never had been.

He liked the Paradisans—they were immensely friendly, warm, outgoing people. It was impossible not to like them. And at the same time he envied and resented them. He understood why, but he couldn't stop.

On his second day he talked to Petryk's editor at the state

publishing house, an amiable man named Truro, who took him to lunch and gave him a handsomely bound copy of Petryk's *Collected Poems*.

During lunch—lake trout, apparently as much a delicacy here as it was in North America—Truro drew him out about his academic background, his publications, his plans for the future. "We would certainly like to publish your book about Eleanor," he said. "In fact, if it were possible, we would be even happier to publish it here first."

Selby explained his arrangements with Macmillan Schuster. Truro said, "But there's no contract yet?"

Selby, intrigued by the direction the conversation was taking, admitted that there was none.

"Well, let's see how things turn out," said Truro. Back in the office, he showed Selby photos of Petryk taken after the famous one, the only one that had appeared on Earth. She was a thin-faced woman, fragile-looking. Her hair was a little grayer, the face more lined—sadder, perhaps.

"Is there any unpublished work?" Selby asked.

"None that she wanted to preserve. She was very selective, and of course her poems sold quite well here—not as much as on Earth, but she made a comfortable living."

"What about the silence—the last ten years?"

"It was her choice. She no longer wanted to write poems. She turned to sculpture instead—wood carvings, mostly. You'll see when you go out to the Cottage."

Afterward Truro arranged for him to see Potter Hargrove, Petryk's divorced husband. Hargrove was in his seventies, white-haired and red-faced. He was the official in charge of what they called the New Lands Program: satellite cities were being built by teams of young volunteers—the ground cleared and sterilized, terrestrial plantings made. Hargrove had a great deal to say about this.

With some difficulty, Selby turned the conversation to Eleanor Petryk. "How did she happen to get permission to live on Paradise, Mr. Hargrove? I've always been curious."

"It's been our policy to admit occasional immigrants, when we think they have something we lack. *Very* occasional. We don't publicize it. I'm sure you understand."

"Yes, of course." Selby collected his thoughts. "What was she like, those last ten years?"

"I don't know. We were divorced five years before that. I remarried. Afterward, Eleanor became rather isolated."

When Selby stood up to leave, Hargrove said, "Have you an hour or so? I'd like to show you something."

They got into a comfortable four-seat runabout and drove north, through the commercial district, then suburban streets. Hargrove parked the runabout, and they walked down a dirt road past a cluster of farm buildings. The sky was an innocent blue; the sun was warm. An insect buzzed past Selby's ear; he turned and saw that it was a honeybee. Ahead was a field of corn.

The waves of green rolled away from them to the horizon, rippling in the wind. Every stalk, every leaf, was perfect.

"No weeds," said Selby.

Hargrove smiled with satisfaction. "That's the beautiful part," he said. "No weeds, because any Earth plant poisons the soil for them. Not only that, but no pests, rusts, blights. The native organisms are incompatible. We can't eat them, and they can't eat us."

"It seems very antiseptic," Selby said.

"Well, that may seem strange to you, but the word comes from the Greek *sepsis,* which means 'putrid.' I don't think we have to apologize for being against putrefaction. We came here without bringing any Earth diseases or parasites with us, and that means there is *nothing* that can attack us. It will take hundreds of thousands of years for the local organisms to adapt to us, if they ever do."

"And then?"

Hargrove shrugged. "Maybe we'll find another planet."

"What if there aren't any other suitable planets within reach? Wasn't it just luck that you found this one?"

"Not luck. It was God's will, Mr. Selby."

Hargrove had given him the names of four old friends of Petryk's who were still alive. After some parleying on the holo, Selby arranged to meet them together in the home of the Mark Andrevon, a novelist well known on Paradise in the seventies. (The present year, by Paradisan reckoning, was A.L. 102.) The others were Theodore Bonwait, a painter; Alice Orr, a poet and ceramicist; and Ruth-Joan Wellman, another poet.

At the beginning of the evening, Andrevon was pugnacious about what he termed his neglect in the English-Speaking Union; he told Selby in considerable detail about his literary honors and the editions of his works. This was familiar talk to Selby; he gathered that Andrevon was now little read even here. He managed to soothe the disgruntled author and turn the conversation to Petryk's early years on Paradise.

"Poets don't actually like each other much, I'm sure you know that, Mr. Selby," said Ruth-Joan Wellman. "We got along fairly well, though—we were all young and unheard-of then, and we used to get together and cook spaghetti, that sort of thing. Then Ellie got married, and . . ."

"Mr. Hargrove didn't care for her friends?"

"Something like that," said Theodore Bonwait. "Well, there were more demands on her time, too. It was a rather strong attachment at first. We saw them occasionally, at parties and openings, that sort of thing."

"What was she like then, can you tell me? What was your impression?"

They thought about it. Talented, they agreed, a little vague about practical matters ("which was why it seemed so lucky for her to marry Potter," said Alice Orr, "but it didn't work out"), very charming sometimes, but a sharp-tongued critic. Selby took notes. He got them to tell him where they had all lived, where they had met, in what years. Three of them admitted that they had some of Petryk's letters, and promised to send him copies.

After another day or so, Truro called him and asked him to come to the office. Selby felt that something was in the wind.

"Mr. Selby," Truro said, "you know visitors like yourself are so rare that we feel we have to take as much advantage of them as we can. This is a young world, we haven't paid as much attention as we might to literary and artistic matters. I wonder if you have ever thought of staying with us?"

Selby's heart gave a jolt. "Do you mean permanently?" he said. "I didn't think there was any chance—"

"Well, I've been talking to Potter Hargrove, and he thinks something might be arranged. This is all in confidence, of course, and I don't want you to make up your mind hurriedly. Think it over."

"I really don't know what to say. I'm surprised—I mean, I was sure I had offended Mr. Hargrove."

"Oh, no, he was favorably impressed. He likes your spice."

"I'm sorry?"

"Don't you have that expression? Your, how shall I say it, ability to stand up for yourself. He's the older generation, you know—son of a pioneer. They respect someone who speaks his mind."

Selby, out on the street, felt an incredulous joy. Of all the billions on Earth, how many would ever be offered such a prize?

Later, with Helga Sonnstein, he visited an elementary school. "Did you ever have a cold?" a serious eight-year-old girl asked him.

"Yes, many times."

"What was it like?"

"Well, your nose runs, you cough and sneeze a lot, and your head feels stuffy. Sometimes you have a little fever, and your bones ache."

"That's *awful*," she said, and her small face expressed something between commiseration and disbelief.

Well, it *was* awful, and a cold was the least of it— "no worse than a bad cold," people used to say about syphilis. Thank God she had not asked about that.

He felt healthy himself, and in fact he was healthy—even before the Paradisan treatments, he had always considered himself healthy. But his medical history, he knew, would have looked like a catalog of horrors to these people—influenza, mumps, cerebrospinal meningitis once, various rashes, dysentery several times (something you had to expect if you traveled). You took it for granted—all those swellings and oozings—it was part of the game. What would it be like to go back to that now?

Miss Sonnstein took him to the university, introduced him to several people, and left him there for the afternoon. Selby talked to the head of the English department, a vaguely hearty man named Quincy; nothing was said to suggest that he might be offered a job if he decided to remain, but Selby's instinct told him that he was being inspected with that end in view.

Afterward he visited the natural history museum and talked to a professor named Morrison, who was a specialist in native life forms.

The plants and animals of Paradise were unlike anything on Earth. The "trees" were scaly, bulbous-bottomed things, some with lacy fronds waving sixty feet overhead, others with cup-shaped leaves that tilted individually to follow the sun. There were no large predators, Morrison assured him; it would be perfectly safe to go into the boonies, providing he did not run out of food. There were slender, active animals with bucket-shaped noses climbing in the forests or burrowing in the ground, and there were things that were not exactly insects; one species had a fixed wing like a maple seedpod—it spiraled down from the treetops, eating other airborne creatures on the way, and then climbed up again.

Of the dominant species, the aborigines, Morrison's department had only bones, not even reconstructions. They had been upright, about five feet tall, large-skulled, possibly mammalian. The eyeholes of their skulls were canted. The bones of their feet were peculiar, bent like the footbones of horses or cattle. "I wonder what they looked like," Selby said.

Morrison smiled. He was a little man with a bushy black

mustache. "Not very attractive, I'm afraid. We do have their stone carvings, and some wall pictures and inscriptions." He showed Selby an album of photographs. The carvings, of what looked like weathered granite, showed angular creatures with blunt muzzles. The paintings were the same, but the expression of the eyes was startlingly human. Around some of the paintings were columns of written characters that looked like clusters of tiny hoofprints.

"You can't translate these?"

"Not without a Rosetta Stone. That's the pity of it—if only we'd gotten here just a little earlier."

"How long ago did they die off?"

"Probably not more than a few centuries. We find their skeletons buried in the trunks of trees. Very well preserved. About what happened, there are various theories. The likeliest thing is plague, but some people think there was a climatic change."

Then Selby saw the genetics laboratory. They were working on some alterations in the immune system, they said, which they hoped in thirty years would make it possible to abandon the allergy treatments that all children now got from the cradle up. "Here's something else that's quite interesting," said the head of the department, a blond woman named Reynolds. She showed him white rabbits in a row of cages. Sunlight came through the open door; beyond was a loading dock, where a man with a Y-lift was hoisting up a bale of feed.

"These are Lyman Whites, a standard strain," said Miss Reynolds. "Do you notice anything unusual about them?"

"They look very healthy," said Selby.

"Nothing else?"

"No."

She smiled. "These rabbits were bred from genetic material spliced with bits of DNA from native organisms. The object was to see if we could enable them to digest native proteins. That has been only partly successful, but something completely unexpected happened. We seem to have interrupted a series of cues that turns on the aging process. The rabbits do not age past maturity. This pair, and those in the next cage, are twenty-one years old."

"Immortal rabbits?"

"No, we can't say that. All we can say is that they have lived twenty-one years. That is three times their normal span. Let's see what happens in another fifty or a hundred years."

As they left the room, Selby asked, "Are you thinking of applying this discovery to human beings?"

"It has been discussed. We don't know enough yet. We have tried to replicate the effect in rhesus monkeys, but so far without success."

"If you should find that this procedure is possible in human beings, do you think it would be wise?"

She stopped and faced him. "Yes, why not? If you are miserable and ill, I can understand why you would not want to live a long time. But if you are happy and productive, why not? Why should people have to grow old and die?"

She seemed to want his approval. Selby said, "But, if nobody ever died, you'd have to stop having children. The world wouldn't be big enough."

She smiled again. "This is a very big world, Mr. Selby."

Selby had seen in Claire Reynolds' eyes a certain guarded interest; he had seen it before in Paradisan women, including Helga Sonnstein. He did not know how to account for it. He was shorter than the average Paradisan male, not as robust; he had had to be purged of a dozen or two loathsome diseases before he could set foot on Paradise. Perhaps that was it: perhaps he was interesting to women because he was unlike all the other men they knew.

He called the next day and asked Miss Reynolds to dinner. Her face in the tube looked surprised, then pleased. "Yes, that would be very nice," she said.

An hour later he had a call from Karen McMorrow; she was free now to welcome him to the Cottage, and would be glad to see him that afternoon. Selby recognized the workings of that law of the universe that tends to bring about a desired result at the least convenient time; he called the laboratory, left a message of regret, and boarded the intercity tube for the town where Eleanor Petryk had lived and died.

The tube, a transparent cylinder suspended from pylons, ran up and over the rolling hills. The crystal windows were open; sweet flower scents drifted in, and behind them darker smells, unfamiliar and disturbing. Selby felt a thrill of excitement when he realized that he was looking at the countryside with new eyes, not as a tourist but as someone who might make this strange land his home.

They passed mile after mile of growing crops—corn, soybeans, then acres of beans, squash, peas; then fallow fields and grazing land in which the traceries of buried ruins could be seen.

After a while the cultivated fields began to thin out, and Selby saw the boonies for the first time. The tall fronded plants looked like anachronisms from the Carboniferous. The forests stopped at the borders of the fields as if they had been cut with a knife.

Provo was now a town of about a hundred thousand; when Eleanor Petryk had first lived there, it had been only a crossroads at the edge of the boonies. Selby got off the tube in late afternoon. A woman in blue stepped forward. "Mr. Selby."

"Yes."

"I'm Karen McMorrow. Was your trip pleasant?"

"Very pleasant."

She was a little older than she had looked on the holotube, in her late fifties, perhaps. "Come with me, please." No monorails here; she had a little impulse-powered runabout. They swung off the main street onto a blacktop road that ran between rows of tall maples.

"You were Miss Petryk's companion during her later years?"

"Secretary. Amanuensis." She smiled briefly.

"Did she have many friends in Provo?"

"No. None. She was a very private person. Here we are." She

stopped the runabout; they were in a narrow lane with hollyhocks on either side.

The house was a low white-painted wooden building half-hidden by evergreens. Miss McMorrow opened the door and ushered him in. There was a cool, stale odor, the smell of a house unlived in.

The sitting room was dominated by a massive coffee table apparently carved from the cross section of a tree. In the middle of it, in a hollow space, was a stone bowl, and in the bowl, three carved bones.

"Is this native wood?" Selby asked, stooping to run his hand over the polished grain.

"Yes. Redwood, we call it, but it is nothing like the Earth tree. It is not really a tree at all. This was the first piece she carved; there are others in the workroom, through there."

The workroom, a shed attached to the house, was cluttered with wood carvings, some taller than Selby, others small enough to be held in the palm of the hand. The larger ones were curiously tormented shapes, half human and half tree. The smaller ones were animals and children.

"We knew nothing about this," Selby said. "Only that she had gone silent. She never explained?"

"It was her choice."

They went into Petryk's study. Books were in glass-fronted cases, and there were shelves of books and record cubes. A vase with sprays of cherry blossoms was on a windowsill.

"This is where she wrote?"

"Yes. Always in longhand, here, at the table. She wrote in pencil, on yellow paper. She said poems could not be made on machines."

"And all her papers are here?"

"Yes, in these cabinets. Thirty years of work. You will want to look through them?"

"Yes. I'm very grateful."

"Let me show you first where you will eat and sleep, then

you can begin. I will come out once a day to see how you are getting on."

In the cabinets were thousands of pages of manuscript—treasures, including ten drafts of the famous poem *Walking the River*. Selby went through them methodically one by one, making copious notes. He worked until he could not see the pages, and fell into bed exhausted every night.

On the third day, Miss McMorrow took him on a trip into the boonies. Dark scents were all around them. The dirt road, such as it was, ended after half a mile; then they walked. "Eleanor often came out here, camping," she said. "Sometimes for a week or more. She liked the solitude." In the gloom of the tall shapes that were not trees, the ground was covered with not-grass and not-ferns. The silence was deep. Faint trails ran off in both directions. "Are these animal runs?" Selby asked.

"No. She made them. They are growing back now. There are no large animals on Paradise."

"I haven't even seen any small ones."

Through the undergrowth he glimpsed a mound of stone on a hill. "What is that?"

"Aborigine ruins. They are all through the boonies."

She followed him as he climbed up to it. The cut stones formed a complex hundreds of yards across. Selby stooped to peer through a doorway. The aborigines had been a small people.

At one corner of the ruins was a toppled stone figure, thirty feet long. The weeds had grown over it, but he could see that the face had been broken away, as if by blows of a hammer.

"What they could have taught us," Selby said.

"What could they have taught us?"

"What it is to be human, perhaps."

"I think we have to decide that for ourselves."

Six weeks went by. Selby was conscious that he now knew more about Eleanor Petryk than anyone on Earth, and also that he did not understand her at all. In the evenings he sometimes went into the workroom and looked at the tormented carved figures. Obviously she had turned to them because she had to do something, and because she could no longer write. But why the silence?

Toward the end, at the back of the last cabinet, Selby found a curious poem.

XC

> Tremble at the coming of the light,
> Hear the rings rustle on the trees.
> Every creature runs away in fright;
> Years will pass before the end of night;
> Woe to them who drift upon the seas.
> Erebus above hears not their pleas;
> Repentance he has none upon his height—
> Earth will always take what she can seize.
>
> Knights of the sky, throw down your shining spears.
> In luxury enjoy your stolen prize.
> Let those who will respond to what I write,
> Lest all of us forget to count the years.
> Empty are the voices, and the eyes
> Dead in the coming of that night.

Selby looked at it in puzzlement. It was a sonnet of sorts, a form that had lapsed into obscurity centuries ago, and one that, to his knowledge, Petryk had never used before in her life. What was more curious was that it was an awkward poem, almost a jingle. Petryk could not possibly have been guilty of it, and yet here it was in her handwriting.

With a sudden thrill of understanding, he looked at the initial letters of the lines. The poem was an acrostic, another forgotten form. It concealed a message, and that was why the poem was awkward—deliberately so, perhaps.

He read the poem again. Its meaning was incredible but clear.

They had bombed the planet—probably the other continent, the one that was said to be covered with desert. No doubt it was, now. Blast and radiation would have done for any aborigines there, and a brief nuclear winter would have taken care of the rest. And the title, "XC"—Roman numerals, another forgotten art. Ninety years.

In his anguish, there was one curious phrase that he still did not understand—"Hear the rings rustle," where the expected words was "leaves." Why rings?

Suddenly he thought he knew. He went into the other room and looked at the coffee table. In the hollow, the stone bowl with its carved bones. Around it, the rings. There was a scar where the tree had been cut into, hollowed out; but it had been a big tree even then. He counted the rings outside the scar: the first one was narrow, almost invisible, but it was there. Altogether there were ninety.

The natives had buried their dead in chambers cut from the wood of living trees. Petryk must have found this one on one of her expeditions. And she had left the evidence here, where anyone could see it.

That night Selby thought of Eleanor Petryk, lying sleepless in this house. What could one do with such knowledge? Her answer had been silence: ten years of silence, until she died. But she had left the message behind her, because she could not bear the silence. He cursed her for her frailty; had she never guessed what a burden she had laid on the man who was to read her message, the man who by sheer perverse bad fortune was himself?

In the morning he called Miss McMorrow and told her he was ready to leave. She said good-bye to him at the tube, and he rode back to the city, looking out with bitter hatred at the scars the aborigines had left in the valleys.

He made the rounds to say good-bye to the people he had met. At the genetics laboratory, a pleasant young man told him that Miss Reynolds was not in. "She may have left for the weekend, but I'm not sure. If you'll wait here a few minutes, I'll see if I can find out."

It was a fine day, and the back door was open. Outside stood an impulse-powered pickup, empty.

Selby looked at the rabbits in their cages. He was thinking of something he had run across in one of Eleanor Petryk's old books, a work on mathematics. "Fibonacci numbers were invented by the thirteenth-century Italian mathematician to furnish a model of population growth in rabbits. His assumptions were: 1) it takes rabbits one month from birth to reach maturity; 2) one month after reaching maturity, and every month thereafter, each pair of rabbits will produce another pair of rabbits; and 3) rabbits never die."

As if in a dream, Selby unlatched the cages and took out two rabbits, one a buck, the other a doe heavy with young. He put them under his arms, warm and quivering. He got into the pickup with them and drove northward, past the fields of corn, until he reached the edge of the cultivated land. He walked through the undergrowth to a clearing where tender shoots grew. He put the rabbits down. They snuffed around suspiciously. One hopped, then the other. Presently they were out of sight.

Selby felt as if his blood were fizzing; he was elated and horrified all at once. He drove the pickup to the highway, and parked it just outside town. Now he was frozen and did not feel anything at all.

From the hotel he made arrangements for his departure. Miss Sonnstein accompanied him to the jump terminal. "Good-bye, Mr. Selby. I hope you have had a pleasant visit."

"It has been most enlightening, thank you."

"Please," she said.

It was raining in Houston, where Selby bought, for sentimental reasons, a bottle of Old Space Ranger. The shuttle was crowded and smelly; three people were coughing as if their lungs would burst. Black snow was falling in Toronto. Selby let himself into his apartment, feeling as if he had never been away. He got the bottle out of his luggage, filled a glass, and sat for a while looking at it. His notes and the copies of Petryk's papers, were in his suitcase, monuments to a book that he now knew would never be written. The doggerel of "XC" ran through his head. Two lines of it, actually, were not so bad:

> *Empty are the voices, and the eyes*
> *Dead in the coming of that night.*

AUTHOR'S NOTE

A couple of editors told me I should not have written this story (I am paraphrasing and distorting a little to make a point.) One said, more or less, "There are too many stories about how bad we are; if I published them the magazine wouldn't be any fun." The other, "Come on, Damon, you live in the Pacific Northwest where something just about like this happened, and how often do you feel a twinge?"

I admit the strength of those arguments, but it seems to me that they leave something out. It is true that all of us are the beneficiaries of crimes committed by our ancestors, and it is true that nothing can be done about that now because the victims are dead and the survivors are innocent. These are good reasons for keeping our mouths shut about the past: but tell me, what are our reasons for silence about atrocities still to come?

POINT OF
VIEW

Here is a story that I remember with fondness for two reasons. The first is that Playboy bought it and paid me an absurdly large amount for such a short story (and hid a clue to it in the centerfold, in the last issue in which that act of deception was possible).

The second reason is that I wrote it in the best possible way: having formed a vague idea of the story, I said to myself in the shower one morning, "I'm going to write that sucker today"; and I sat down and did it.

He awakened in a place that was not a room but a cosmos. At first he recognized nothing, not even his own mountainous body. Because he was not a man now, shapes no longer had the same meaning; he could not tell the ceiling from the floor.

He had expected all this, and yet nothing was what he had expected. It was evident that he had made a serious, fundamental error; luckily it was one that would be easy to correct next time.

He moved dizzily around the room, found the rabbit's water dish and drank, tasted its food; he even walked over the body that had been his own, and peered with one eye into its nostril where the hairs fluttered with barely perceptible breathing.

He had no idea how much time had passed before the voices

began. They came through wires into the room: slow, booming sounds that vibrated the air like flapping dishcloths.

"The theory is that if the brain is alive but not functioning, the consciousness has got to go somewhere."

"All right, but where?"

"That's what he wanted to find out. He did it to a dog, you know, and left it in a Faraday cage with a frog."

"Frog and dog. That's funny. Why the Faraday cage?"

"He hoped it would restrict the movement of consciousness to whatever animal he put in the cage. He wanted to make sure it didn't just drift away to god knows where."

"I see. And?"

"Well, the frog didn't move for a while. Then it hopped over to the dog's dish and tried to eat dog food."

That voice must be Mathews, his assistant; the other he didn't know. He located the rabbit's dishes again in the enormous space and went there under the eye of the television camera. Surely they must notice. But the voices went on.

"I see. So then he decided to try it on himself?"

"Yes, because that's the whole point—to experience the world through the sensorium of another animal. If it works, it will be a tremendous breakthrough—something we always thought belonged to metaphysics."

"But it doesn't seem to be working."

"We don't know that."

"The rabbit was supposed to do something with those alphabet charts?"

"That was our hope, but there are all kinds of reasons why it might not be possible. Anyway, we'll find out soon enough."

"If he comes out of this."

"Yes."

Hearing these words, he darted toward the giant square things that must be alphabet charts, pressed his nose to one, then another. The shapes of them were meaningless to him; he was more aware of their smell. But surely they would see that he was trying?

"Hot for this time of year."

"Yes. It's almost time. We might as well go in."

Booming footsteps in the corridor, squeak of wheels on the trolley. A straight line of darkness opened from the floor upward, and widened. Then the vast foreshortened shapes were moving around him.

"When you turn off the current, his cortical activity will resume?"

"Yes."

One of the men was bending to look at the rabbit. "Do you suppose he's in there?" The rabbit hopped and sat still.

He flew at the man, hovered in front of his cratered face. *Here I am, here! Not the rabbit—me!*

"Hold on a minute."

"What's the matter?"

"Before we do anything else, I'm going to swat this blasted fly."

Help, it's me. Whack.

AZIMUTH

1 , 2 , 3 . . .

I have disguised the real identity of the central figure in this story, but not so well, I'm afraid, that an assiduous reader cannot find it out. (Actually, I had two people in mind, neither one of whom is or ever was named Azimuth Backfiler.)

The story is one of my favorites because of its good-humored malice toward an old friend, and also because, like certain works of Jorge Luis Borges, it is a review of an imaginary book.

The recently published memoirs of Azimuth Backfiler provide a fascinating glimpse into the life of a little-known genius. The son of an eccentric experimental educator, Azimuth graduated from MIT at the age of seven and obtained his first doctorate when he was nine. While still in his teens, he invented the steam-powered crossbow, the three-hundred-and-sixty-day calendar, and the edible typewriter.

At the age of thirty, having solved the riddles of the Philosopher's Stone, the elixir of life, and the unified field theory to his own satisfaction, Backfiler turned his attention to time.

"Consider time," he told himself. "According to conventional theory, it is a dimension along which we travel at a fixed rate, and as we travel, the whole physical universe continually comes into being and ceases to exist again behind us, a wasteful and highly improbable process.

"Is it not more likely," he went on, "that the universe exists in its perfect completeness both in time and in space, and that the movement through time which we experience is merely an artifact of consciousness? But, if so, why should it be impossible to travel backward in time? Evidently our experience of duration is conditioned by an increase of entropy in the direction of travel; if, therefore, I could discover or create a local system in which there was a decrease in entropy, I would necessarily experience a movement through time in the opposite direction."

Backfiler accordingly built a large shielded chamber and filled it entirely with living organisms of various kinds—trees, shrubs, insects, worms, snails, and bacteria—for it is well known that living things do not obey the law of entropy. Entropy is defined by physicists as an increase in disorder, as, for example, in reducing an automobile to a pile of junk; every living organism, however, is an example of the contrary tendency, which might be described as a junk pile growing into an automobile.

By a clever application of unified-field mechanics, which he had worked out during an idle evening, he shielded the chamber from all outside influences whatsoever, and made up his mind to enter the chamber, wearing a self-contained suit of his own design, exactly one week from the day the chamber was completed. Therefore he was not surprised to see himself emerge from the chamber, wearing this very suit, a moment after he had formed the decision.

The second Azimuth, having discarded the suit, handed him a copy of the *Wall Street Journal* dated one week in the future; he then sat down in Azimuth's favorite chair, crossed his legs and lit Azimuth's favorite pipe. Azimuth 1, as we had better call him, turned at once to the financial section, noted the rise of certain stocks, and telephoned orders to his broker.

Our philosopher's purpose in this was not to increase his already vast fortune, but to investigate certain paralogical consequences of his successful reversal of time. Leaving Azimuth 2 to

his own devices, he retired to one of his several laboratories
where he spent six days in drawing plans for a perpetual motion
machine, an automatic novel-writer, and an engine designed to
run on chicken fat.

On the seventh day he returned to the chamber carrying a
copy of the *Wall Street Journal* containing a financial section which
he had had especially printed for the purpose, and in which
certain stocks which had actually risen were shown as having
declined, whereas certain others which had really declined were
shown as having risen.

Wearing his life-support suit, he entered the chamber, where
he was so closely surrounded by greenery that for the next seven
days it was impossible for him to do anything but meditate on the
curvature of space and the origin of the Big Bang. This he accordingly did, and by the end of the week had developed and
committed to memory a new theory of transcendental functions
expressed by a novel system of notation. When the week was up,
he emerged from the chamber and was interested to discover that
there were already two Azimuths awaiting him.

One of these, whom we had better call Azimuth 3, had just
taken off his suit and was handing a copy of the *Journal* to Azimuth 2. Our philosopher in turn divested himself of his heavy
garment and handed a copy of the *Journal* to his counterpart,
whereupon still another Azimuth emerged from the chamber.
Azimuth 3, taking advantage of the confusion, had already seized
the favorite chair and favorite pipe, but within a few minutes the
room was crowded with so many Azimuths, all of whom hated to
be jostled, that those nearest the door were forced out into the
corridor, and thence to other rooms which also rapidly filled up,
with the result that in half an hour Azimuths were spilling out
onto the grounds and through the gate into the public road.
Since, as has been said, the time chamber was shielded from all
outside influences whatsoever, it was useless to contemplate de-
stroying it, even if it had been possible for the Azimuths outside
to make their way through the press of others emerging.

More than thirty Azimuths were waiting for the next airport

bus, the others having correctly calculated that there would be no room for them; these latter were dispersed along the streets, attempting to flag down taxicabs or hitch a ride. By various such means, approximately three thousand Azimuths had reached the Boston airport by early afternoon and had booked seats, using three thousand identical credit cards, on the earliest flights in every direction. Other thousands packed the railway station and caused a traffic jam in the streets outside. While waiting, each Azimuth scribbled calculations, supporting his papers on the back of the Azimuth ahead. It quickly became clear to all of them that they, or rather their predecessor Azimuth 1, had made a serious blunder: by handing a doctored copy of the *Wall Street Journal* to Azimuth 2, he had created a conditional loop in which the Azimuths were part of an infinite series.

Assuming that the Azimuths were emerging at the rate of approximately one every three seconds, at the end of a day there would be 28,800, not counting the original Azimuth, and at the end of the first week there would be 201,600. The world could well support that number of universal geniuses and might even benefit from their existence, but at the end of a year, if nothing were done to halt the influx, there would be 10,512,000, causing a severe strain on food supplies, not to mention housing and laboratory facilities.

Interviewed in the Boston airport by a representative of the press, one of the Azimuths said, "The problem is a rather challenging one, because it is impossible *a priori* to intervene in the time loop, and equally impossible to reach a period before the beginning of the loop by the method I used, since the latter depends on the construction of a chamber which I did not construct before I constructed it.

"Is that clear so far? Now, it follows that the only way out of our dilemma is to discover a second method of reversing the flow of time, perhaps by the use of an artificial worm-hole. Even if this turns out to be possible, it will be difficult to create such a worm-hole on the surface of the planet without severe disruptions of the superficial layers of the crust, and therefore I conclude that this research may take as much as a year or perhaps even longer. However, as soon as the project is completed, of course—"

At this moment he vanished with a pop, and so did all the other Azimuths except the original one, who, before the beginning of his ill-fated experiment, had received a visit from still another Azimuth warning him not to attempt it. This Azimuth, whom we may refer to as Azimuth 10,512,000, then popped back into his worm-hole and returned to his own time a year in the future, with the result that none of the catastrophic consequences of Azimuth 1's blunder ever happened, and accordingly that the world never knew of it until it was revealed by the charmingly modest scientist himself in his memoirs, which we thoroughly recommend to your attention.

O

....
....
....
....

I have always been fascinated by the alphabet, by the shapes of the letters as well as by their saunds, and wan day I began ta wander, what wauld it be like if there were anly twenty-five instead ef twenty-six?

One day everybody in the world whose name began with the letter O abruptly disappeared. Marina Oswald, who was then living in Chevy Chase, went away and never came back; so did Mr. and Mrs. Robert F. Otto, of Binghamton, New York, and all their children; so did Barry Outka and Lynn Overall, both of Austin, Texas; so did Aram Ouzounian of the Armenian S.S.R. and Jean-Luc Ouellette of France and Tetsu Okuma of Japan. All the O'Haras, O'Gradys, O'Flahertys and O'Keefes vanished like smoke, along with the Owens, the Ortegas and the Oppenheims.

A good deal of real estate came on the market, especially in Ireland. Suddenly there was elbow room in cities that had been overcrowded. The tempo of life relaxed; people had time to smile at each other on the street.

The next thing that happened was that all animals, birds, fish, and reptiles whose names began with the letter *o* disappeared: ocelots, octopuses, okapis, opossums, orang-utans, orioles, ostriches, otters, owls, and oxen, together with whole orders and suborders such as the ophidia, the orthoptera, and the ostracods. As a general thing, nobody missed them.

Oak trees, oats, okra, olives, oranges, and other plants also vanished, but there were lots of substitutes: barley, for instance, pickles, and tangerines.

So far, so good, but when whole cities, states, and other geographical features turned up missing, there was widespread unease. Ohio, Oklahoma, and Oregon were gone, no one knew where; so were Omaha, Omsk, Ontario, Osaka, Oshkosh, Oslo, and Oxford, along with a host of lesser-known places such as Oconomowoc, Odendaalrust, Opa-locka, Opp, and Ouagadougou. The United Nations appointed a Commission of Inquiry into the Disappearance of Inhabited Places, but it bogged down because nobody could remember the names of the towns they were looking for.

On the whole, most people thought the changes were improvements. There was nothing between Toronto and Rochester but a large grassy plain, suitable for agriculture or grazing. The main island of Hawaii was gone, but it had been all built up in condominiums anyway. The space between Indiana and Pennsylvania had closed up somehow, and Kansas was now bounded on the south by Texas.

A curious result was that people began to feel superstitious about using words that began with the missing letter. "Ah, shit," they said, and "Unlatch the door." Children, when they wanted to write something dirty on a wall, simply drew circles. Custodians went around behind them changing the circles into figure 8s.

Mathematicians began to use the symbol z for a zero, thus: "The national debt amounts to \$156,zzz,zzz,zzz." Multiples of one thousand became "zizzes," as in "We've got to come up with a megazizz in new funding by the end of January."

In dictianaries and in camman usage, the letter a ar e was used as a substitute far the missing and naw unspeakable letter. Ane spake ef gaing ta "the men's rum," ar "the tailet." The ultimate insult was "yeu asshale."

Manufacturers had ta change many ef their brand names, at great expense and sametimes with unfartunate results. Marlbara and Xerex were all right, but Caca-Cala suffered a nasedive in papularity.

The publishing industry was buming, and sign painters had mare wark than they cauld handle. In spite ef the glut ef hausing, canstructian warkers were busy tu, tearing dawn traffic circles and turning them inta squares. Eyeglasses were square, and sa were cups and saucers, drinking glasses and battles, resulting in great ecanamies in shipping and starage. A labaratary in Califarnia perfected a chicken that laid square eggs. A few peaple tuk the wheels aff their cars, replacing them with skids ar runners, but mast falks were cantent ta caver the wheels with ruffled skirts.

As the new century dawned, peaple surveyed their warld and faund it gud. Fram pale ta pale, the square-shauldered earth was cavered with the rectilinear warks ef man: square buildings, square intersecting streets, square traffic exchanges, square lakes and square mauntains. Children blew square seap-bubbles. Even peaple's faces were becaming square. Set free ef all their circularity and canfusian, faur-square ta the sunrise, the peaple ef the warld cauld well say, with the paet Alexander Pape,

> Let us, since life can little mare supply
> Than just ta luk abaut us, and ta die,
> Expatiate free a'er all this scene ef man;
> A mighty maze! but nat withaut a plan.

THE GOD

MACHINE

This story is a byproduct of the research I did in 1983 for The Man
in the Tree, *a novel in which I undertook to explain the miracles performed by Jesus Christ (or "allegedly performed," if you are a skeptic like
me) by writing the story of a man with similar powers, born in Oregon
in this century.*

*In the course of my Bible reading, I ran across the perplexing story
of Uzzah, who was smitten by God because he laid his hand on the ark.
For people who have not consulted their Bibles lately, I had better explain
that this was not Noah's Ark but the ark of God, a box made to house
the two stone tablets that Moses brought down from Mt. Sinai.*

*God's directions for the ark are found in Exodus 25: 10–22. The
box was to be made of shittim wood, two and a half cubits long, one and
a half cubits broad and one and a half cubits high. The ark was to be
overlaid with gold inside and out, and on top of it was to be placed a
"mercy seat" of pure gold, with a golden cherub at each end.*

*This is the last we hear of the ark until II Samuel 6:2–7, where we
read:*

> And David arose, and went with all the people that
> *were* with him from Baale of Judah, to bring from thence
> the ark of God, whose name is called by the name of the
> LORD of hosts that dwelleth *between* the Cherubims.

And they set the ark of God upon a new cart, and brought it out of the house of Abinadab that *was* in Gibeah, accompanying the ark of God; and Uzzah and Ahio, the sons of Abinadab, drave the new cart. [. . .]

And when they came to Nachon's threshingfloor, Uzzah put forth *his hand* to the ark of God, and took hold of it; for the oxen shook it.

And the anger of the LORD was kindled against Uzzah; and God smote him there for his *error; and there he died by the ark of God.*

Is that all clear so far? Now we skip about three thousand years. . . .

Not a good morning. Bunny is on the rampage again. Three people in the art department are out with AIDS. Heavy smog. At ten o'clock Terry is called in to Olly's office. Terry is the Creative Director. Olly is the President. Handlebar mustache, striped T-shirt, Adidas. Beside Olly's desk sits a little man with a suitcase in his lap. Plastic suitcase. Undistinguished haircut.

"Terry," says Olly, "I want you to meet Bill Sonntag. He's here to show us the marketing miracle of nineteen eighty-five. The client is Universal Electric. They want a presentation for a ten-mil all-media campaign starting in September."

"What is the product, Bill?" Terry inquires.

"It's, like, God in a box," says Bill.

"How's that for a slogan?" asks Olly, popping a pill. "Not bad, eh, Terry?"

"Terrific, just terrific, Olly. What does it do?"

"I'm going to let Bill explain that. Take him back to your office, and, Terry, lock your door."

They go to Terry's office. Terry moves a Teddy bear to make room for Bill to sit down. "What is your position with U.E., Bill?" he asks.

"I'm not with them, I'm the inventor. One of the inventors. They sent me because nobody else seems to be able to explain it."

Terry nods several times. "Excuse me." He takes two aspirins. "Well, so it's God in a box? What does that mean, exactly?"

"Okay," says Bill. "The basic idea is, is that God is immanent in certain objects, like, for instance, the best example is the Ark of the Covenant. I don't know if you're familiar with the story of Uzzah, in the second book of Samuel?"

"Remind me."

"Maybe I better start further back? See, the Ark was like a box made of wood, about four feet by two by two. It was supposed to have the tablets of the Law in it, you know, the ones that God gave to Moses."

"Oh, yeah."

"You saw the movie, right? Okay, that makes it a little easier. Well, the story goes, they're moving the Ark in a cart, and this Uzzah sees it's about to tip over, so he puts his hand on it, like to steady it? And he gets a charge of something that kills him."

"This box is something that kills people, Bill?" Terry asks. He takes two more aspirins.

"No, no, that's only if you get too big a jolt. Like electricity? Anyway, what got us thinking, it says in the Bible the Ark was covered inside and out with gold. Now there could be two reasons for that. One, gold is a precious metal, okay?"

"You're right there, Bill. What's the other reason?"

"The other reason is"—Bill leans forward confidentially— "gold is a good conductor. Not just a good conductor, a *great* conductor. So we said, what if there *is* something in holy objects that could be electronically enhanced, or, you know, throttled down if it's too strong. The first thing we tried was a really old set of the scrolls, the Torah. Bingo. Furthermore, we found out you can transfer this energy, immanence, we call it, by leaving your holy object in a lead-lined container with some other object. For a relic, like a piece of bone, say, we use bone. Lamb is the best."

"That's unbelievable, Bill."

"I know. That's the problem. All I can do is, is I can let you try it yourself. May I ask what your religion is, Terry?"

"I'm a Presbyterian."

"Okay, you get the Protestant model. For that, we had to go to old Bibles—we bought a Gutenberg, and maybe you think that didn't cost. We found out later the Wyclif is just as good." Bill is taking a small black box out of the suitcase. He lays it on the desk, and Terry looks at it. On the left is a dial and on the right, inset in the box, a disk of some off-white material. Bill plugs it in; a red light comes on.

"Now what you do is, is you just relax and put your fingers on this ceramic plate, and then slowly turn up the gain. This is a low-immanence circuit, so you don't have to worry. Go ahead."

Terry does as he is told. The ceramic plate is cool and slick under his fingers. He turns the dial with his other hand. "I don't feel a thing."

"You got it all the way up? That's funny." Bill pulls the box toward him. "Let's try the theometer." He takes a bright little instrument from among the ballpoint pens in his shirt pocket, lays it across the ceramic plate. The digital readout stays at "0."

"Dead," says Bill. He opens the case and peers inside. "Okay, here's the trouble—it blew a resistor." He pulls out a little cylinder and shows it to Terry. In the box, nestled among wires and ugly electrical parts, is a Gideon Bible.

"This is a prototype," Bill says. "Still a few bugs in it. The production model will have all printed circuits." He gropes in his suitcase, finds another resistor and puts it in, closes the case. "Try it again."

Terry puts his fingers on the ceramic plate, turns the dial up. Almost at once, a feeling of indescribable peace comes over him. He no longer cares about Bill's haircut or Olly's T-shirts. The throbbing at the back of his head goes away.

"See? See?" says Bill, exposing his mediocre dentistry.

Bill leaves the machine with Terry. Terry calls in Lori and Reggie and swears them to silence. Over the next three days they rough out a campaign. It is terrific. The client is impressed. Terry gets a bonus.

The fall campaign is a success. "HOLINEX for instant tranquility—the peace that passes understanding at the touch of a button, in the privacy of your own home!" Hospitals buy the professional model at $1,795. Psychiatrists buy it. The home models retail for $695 plus tax. People line up for it in department stores. It comes in Protestant, Catholic, Orthodox and Reformed versions. For the overseas market, Buddhist, Moslem and Hindu versions are on the drawing boards.

Church and synagogue attendance zooms, then nosedives, until pastors begin allowing worshipers to bring their Holinexes. An enterprising minister in the West Village announces plans to build them into the backs of pews. A pirated Soviet version is rumored, using relics of Lenin. Labor unrest is down. Gross national product is up.

Bunny is happy. Olly is happy. Terry is not happy. There are persistent rumors that Bill's partner, the other inventor, is confined to a mental institution, where he performs miracles of healing but has to be anchored to a bed to keep him from floating away.

Yesterday, the day before Christmas, Terry saw a black man levitating up the stairway of the IRT at 50th street. A week ago, he found himself speaking in Japanese, a language he does not know, to a Puerto Rican waiter in a restaurant. For the last several days Terry has been bleeding slightly from the palms of his hands. This morning, when he left the apartment, his wife asked him, "When will you be home?"

"Verily, I know not," Terry answered.

Now he is up on the parapet of the agency building, looking down at Third Avenue, from which the strains of "Away in a Manger" arise. He knows that in a moment he will spread his arms and step off. Will he fly?

TARCAN OF
THE HOBOES

I was driving with my son Jonathan one day in late December when he noticed two hoboes with a Christmas tree beside the tracks. That started me thinking about hobo jungles, and from that it was only a step to this impudent and reprehensible retelling of Edgar Rice Burroughs.

In the spring of the year 19—, John Clayton and his pregnant young wife set out on a journey by railroad from Boston to Los Angeles, where Clayton had been offered a post as manager of an orange plantation. Clayton's father, the banker Cyrus T. Clayton, was a millionaire many times over, but it was his wish that his son earn his own way in the world rather than become a playboy or ne'er-do-well; therefore Clayton and his bride were poor, but their hopes were high. On the third day, as Clayton was taking the air in the vestibule, he happened to observe the conductor and a porter standing close together just inside the next car. Words were exchanged which Clayton could not hear; then the conductor, whose face was empurpled with rage, struck the porter and knocked him down.

Clayton stepped across to the vestibule of the next car and opened the door. The porter, with blood on his lip, was trying to rise, and the conductor had drawn back his foot to kick him.

"Look here," said Clayton quietly, removing his pipe from his mouth, "this won't do, you know."

The conductor turned to him with a foul oath. "You're only a d——d passenger," he said. "Keep out of this, if you know what's good for you, Mr. Clayton."

The porter, meanwhile, got to his feet and slunk away, casting a malevolent glance back over his shoulder at the conductor.

"I may be only a passenger, as you say," Clayton said, "but if I observe any such conduct again, I shall report you."

The conductor, who was obviously drunk, stared at him sullenly with his reddened eyes, then turned with another oath and stalked away.

At breakfast the following morning, Clayton saw a little knot of waiters in close conversation at the end of the car. As Clayton and his wife were rising to leave, one of the waiters approached them casually and murmured in Clayton's ear, "Black Bart says, you keep in your compartment today."

"What did that man say, dear?" inquired Alice. "Is anything wrong?"

"No, it's nothing," said Clayton lightly, but once they were in their compartment he took her hands and said earnestly, "Dearest, I'm afraid there's going to be trouble on the train. Don't lose heart. We must just wait and·trust in God's mercy."

"I'm going to be brave," said Alice, and they sat down together, with hands clutched tightly. After an hour had passed, they heard a loud report from the forward end of the train; then another, then a fusillade, followed by deathly silence.

The Claytons waited, with straining ears and beating hearts. At last the door was flung open, and in the aperture appeared a porter with a revolver in his hand. "Wanted in the rear," he said. He would not reply to their anxious questions, but herded them down the corridor. When they reached the dining car, a terrible sight met their eyes. All the other passengers were there, crowded between the tables, with their hands bound behind them, while two waiters rifled their pockets, throwing wallets, watches and coins into a bag held by a third ruffian.

"What is the meaning of this?" Clayton cried, turning to the porter who had escorted them. "Where is the conductor?"

The man's face split in an evil grin. "The *meaning* is, we've took the train, see? We've threw the conductor off, *and* the engineer and the fireman, see? So stand right there and keep your d——d traps shut, or it'll be the worse for you."

Clayton put his arm around his trembling wife and they watched as the porters, having finished their thievery, began to herd the bound passengers toward the farther end of the car. At first they did not understand the dreadful thing that was about to take place; then they heard a chorus of shrieks, and, turning to look out the window, saw three passengers tumbling down the embankment as the train hurtled on. The grisly scene was repeated, again and again, until the last passenger was gone: only the Claytons remained.

Toward them now came the man Clayton had seen knocked down by the conductor. Beside him was the man with the bag of stolen valuables.

"Give me your wallet," said the porter, holding out his hand. "You won't need it."

"This is an outrage," said Clayton, but he handed over his watch and wallet.

"Speak polite when Black Bart talks to you," said the man with the bag. "Now the lady—purse and rings." Alice gave him the articles he requested, but when he pointed to the locket she wore on a chain around her neck, she shrank away. "No, please not that," she protested. "It is the dearest thing I own—a present from my husband. It has no value to you, but to me it is worth more than gold or diamonds."

"Give it to him, dear, you must," said Clayton, but Black Bart pushed the bagman aside. "Keep the locket," he said gruffly to Alice, and pulled the emergency cord. After a moment they heard the squeal of brakes, and the car rocked as the train slowed down.

"Bring their luggage," said Black Bart, and a porter scurried away.

"What do you intend doing with us?" Clayton demanded.

"Putting you off the train, but you'll land soft, not like them others. You done me a good turn once, and Black Bart don't forget."

"I don't like it," said another man, shouldering forward. "I say tie their hands and shove them over the side like the rest." There was a murmur of agreement from the other mutineers.

"What's this?" said Bart, turning slowly around. There was a revolver in his hand. "You boys elected me conductor, didn't you? Well, I'm the conductor, and what I say goes."

"Maybe it don't. Suppose we unelect you, Bart, and throw you over too?"

Bart's expression did not change, but his fist shot out and cracked against the other man's jaw. The ruffian fell without a sound and sprawled senseless on the floor.

"Anybody else?" demanded Bart, glaring around. The mutineers were silent.

"Now listen," said Bart, bringing his unshaven face close to Clayton's. "When we stop, get off quick, because I can't keep this scum in line forever. You'll have your luggage, and you'll find some tools in one of the suitcases. I'm giving you a chance, and that's the best I can do."

"But my God, man," cried Clayton, glancing at the desolate landscape outside, "this is murder."

The porter appeared with their bags just as the train ground to a halt. "Quick now, or I won't answer for it," said Black Bart.

Herded by a gun in the porter's hands, Clayton and his bride stumbled down onto the rough grade of the railway. Their luggage lay in the weeds below, where the porter had thrown it. No sooner were they clear of the train than it began to move again, gathering speed so quickly that in a few moments the caboose was rushing by them; then the train dwindled in the distance. They watched it until it was only a spot on the horizon.

The Claytons looked about them. They were in the middle of a great wilderness, the heartland of the continent. Not far off there was a little stream, around which trees grew thickly; except for these, and a few other wooded spots, and the railway track itself, there was nothing to break the vast immensity.

"Dearest, what are we to do?" asked Alice.

"Never mind, my dear," said Clayton, although his heart was sinking within him. "We have our luggage, after all, and we have each other."

In one of the suitcases, as Black Bart had promised, he found a set of tools, some nails, screws, and hinges, together with a long-barreled revolver and a box of cartridges, an American flag, some fishing lines and hooks, and other useful things. With the tools, Clayton built a rude shelter in a tree, covering it with blankets draped over branches, and there he and Alice spent their first shivering, lonely night in the wilderness.

On the following day a freight train came hurtling out of the west; Clayton took off his shirt and tried to flag it down, but it roared past and was gone in a cloud of cinders. He knew that Alice's time must be near and that it would be dangerous for her to travel afoot. That day he began the construction of a sturdier house in the tree, and in the intervals of his labor he showed Alice how to catch grasshoppers for bait and fish in the stream.

Clayton finished the cabin before the end of the week, and none too soon, for he had glimpsed a cougar in the distance. The next night they heard the beast prowling around their tree, and although Clayton tried to calm her, Alice's courage broke when the forest animal climbed the trunk and clawed at the door. That night she bore her child, a boy, while the cougar snarled and snuffled outside.

Alice never recovered completely from the shock of bearing a child in these rude surroundings; she grew steadily weaker and her lucid moments farther apart. At last, three weeks after the birth of the child, she died.

Clayton buried her under a willow beside the stream. Her locket, which contained miniature portraits of herself and John, he kept to remember her by, and he tried to calm the child by swinging the pretty thing back and forth over his crib.

Miles away, in a hobo jungle along the tracks where the freights slowed to climb a steep grade, another boy-child had been born. The mother was Fat Karla, and the father was Big Jim Korchak, who called himself King of the Hoboes. There were others who claimed the title, but wherever Korchak was, he was king. Six feet four and broad in proportion, hairy, dirty, and foul-tempered, Korchak enforced his rule by the weight of his hamlike fists.

He and a half-dozen of his followers had encamped in this desolate place when Karla's time came upon her; now the victuals were running short, and so was Korchak's temper.

From the hills they had seen a thread of smoke arising far out on the plain, day after day. "Where there's smoke there's folks," said Korchak, "and where there's folks there's grub." So the little band set out, with Korchak at the head as usual, and Karla in the rear carrying her little bundle. The child was fretful, and Karla lagged behind to nurse him. At last Korchak lost his patience; whirling on her, and scattering the other 'boes with his fists, he snarled, "Rotten little brat, what's the use of him anyway?" He plucked the child from its mother's arms and flung it down on the tracks. With a moan, Karla snatched the pitiful bundle up again, but it was too late: the child was dead.

All the rest of that day Karla stumbled along like one demented, clutching the poor little body to her breast. She never spoke, but if any of the other 'boes came near her she backed away snarling, and even Korchak did not approach her again to try to take the child away.

Toward evening they came to the forest by the little stream where John Clayton had built his hut. Softly the men crept up to the tree. They listened but heard nothing. Korchak swung himself up through the branches, followed by the others.

John Clayton raised his head from his arms just in time to see the giant hobo fling the door open and rush in. He rose to defend himself, but one terrific blow felled him. He lay on the floor, his neck broken.

The other 'boes were hurrying about the room, ransacking it of its pitiful possessions, but Karla leaped to the crib where the infant, awakened by the struggle, was beginning to wail. She snatched it up, dropping her own dead infant as she did so, and rushed out of the house. The others caught up with her a little way down the track, but Karla would not suffer any of them to come near her. She had another child now, and she would keep it.

In hobo jungles from Natchez to Point Barrow, the boy grew up sturdy and strong. Because of his habit of sitting bare-bottomed on railroad ties, the 'boes called him "Tarcan." He learned to use a knife and a slingshot with such deadly accuracy that even the biggest 'boes dared not challenge him; he learned to board a freight at a grade crossing and how to leap from a moving train without injury; he learned which bulls to avoid, and which jails were the warmest in winter. The locket that had been his mother's he wore always under his dirty shirt; he did not know who the pictured people were, but he thought the man looked kind, and the woman was beautiful.

When Tarcan was sixteen, Karla died, a used-up old woman; Korchak had wandered away long since. Tarcan went on alone.

Every year or two his wanderings brought him back to the place where he had been born. On one of these occasions, roaming the forest beside the track, he stumbled over the abandoned tree house and went in. Marauding animals had scattered the bones of two skeletons, one of a full-grown man and the other of an infant. Mice and squirrels had done their work with blankets, papers, and the few scraps of worn-out clothing the 'boes had left, but in a closed cabinet Tarcan found a diary, which he could not read, and a children's book, grimed with the prints of tiny fingers. With the packrat instinct of the hobo, he put both books away in his bindle; he ransacked the little cabin for anything else of value, but found nothing except a tiny leather-bound folder.

Later, crouched by his fire in the jungle, he pored over the children's book with its faded pictures. Tarcan could read, after a fashion: he knew "RR Xing," and "Café," "City Limits," and a few

more words, but this was the first book he had ever tried to read.
Although he was untaught, his keen intelligence enabled him to
make rapid progress. Soon he was able to read such sentences as
"The boy runs after the spotted dog." Next he turned his attention
to the leather folder, and after a few attempts discovered the
secret of its metal clasp and opened it. Inside were two photographs, one of a man, the other of a woman: and he knew their
faces. With leaping heart, Tarcan withdrew the locket which he
wore around his neck and compared the pictured faces: they were
the same.

Karla had told him nothing about his birth except that his
father had been a gent, and that the locket had belonged to him.
Was the man who had died in the lonely tree house, then, Tarcan's father? How had he died, and why had his bones been left
for marauding bobcats and coyotes?

Perhaps the other book would give some clue. He opened it
eagerly, but it was written in an angular script which at first
defeated him. Gradually he began to realize that the letters, unfamiliar as they were, were distorted forms of the printed alphabet. Slowly, sentence by sentence, he puzzled out the diary and
read its pathetic story.

When he had done so, he was more bewildered than before.
He, Tarcan, could not be the infant the diary spoke of, for its
bones were scattered on the floor of the cabin along with its
father's. There was no mention of another child, or of Karla.

Many times, after that, he came back to the deserted cabin
and sat there to brood, reading the diary over and over again and
hoping that somehow it would disclose its secret. One day, as he
sat thus pensive, he heard the hoot of an approaching express,
then a terrific crash. Running outside, he beheld an appalling
sight: the train had been derailed and its cars lay buckled and
overturned up and down the right of way.

On a fine summer evening, Charles Clayton, nephew of Cyrus
T. Clayton and heir to the Clayton banking millions, sat comfortably in his private train en route from San Francisco to Boston.

With him as his guests were Professor Archimedes Q. Potter and his daughter Jane, and a young French naval officer, Paul D'Arnot. D'Arnot, on Clayton's advice, had converted his personal fortune into gold, obtained at the San Francisco mint; the bullion, in a sealed chest, was locked in the baggage compartment.

After a supper of roast pheasant under glass prepared by Clayton's personal chef, the party were preparing to retire to their luxurious compartments for the night when there was a tremendous crash; the car toppled over on its side as if struck by a giant hammer, and the stunned occupants lay dazed on the floor.

Clayton was the first to regain his senses. Struggling to his feet, he ascertained that D'Arnot and the Potters were uninjured; then the two young men succeeded in opening a window and helping the others out. By climbing down the undercarriage of the toppled car, they were able to reach the track.

The sight that met their eyes was daunting. The engine and the coal car were still on the tracks, but the sleeping and dining cars, the saloon and the baggage car lay overturned like a child's toys. All around them lay a vast wasteland, the heart of America.

"My heavens!" ejaculated Professor Potter, fumbling for his glasses, which he had lost in the crash. "What has occurred? Why is the train no longer upright?"

"We have had a crash, Professor," responded Clayton. "Miss Potter, are you sure you are all right?"

"Yes," said the girl faintly, pressing her hand to her brow, "only a little dizzy, I think."

"Sit down here, please, and you, too, Professor, while Paul and I see if the others need help." Clayton and D'Arnot started off toward the engine, but at this moment the engineer and the fireman dropped to the cinders and came toward them. "What happened, McTaggart?" Clayton called.

"I don't know, sir," responded the engineer, a gruff Scot. "It looks to me as if the roadbed gave way, sir, just after the engine passed over it. The maintenance of this line is something shocking, sir, saving your presence."

It was decided that the engineer and fireman would proceed

to the nearest station and get help. "There is no room for anyone else in the cab," Clayton explained, "and you, Miss Potter, cannot ride in a coal car." Accordingly, when the engine and the coal car had been uncoupled, the fireman got up steam and the engine moved rapidly off into the distance.

Tarcan watched from the trees as the little party entered the forest and began exploring. Presently they stumbled over the cabin in the tree, and excited shouts rang back and forth. Water was brought from the stream, and the chef began to prepare a late snack. Jane was to sleep in the cabin, while the men wrapped themselves in blankets on the ground. There were five: Clayton, Professor Potter, D'Arnot, the chef, and a rat-faced baggageman.

That night, as he lay in his sleeping bag watching the cabin, Tarcan saw a flicker of movement near the train; a pale glint of light showed between the trees. His curiosity aroused, he crept closer. Down toward the stream a human figure was moving, dim in the starlight: a faint ray of light, as if from a shielded flashlight, preceded it. As Tarcan noiselessly approached, he saw that it was the baggageman, carrying some bulky object in his arms. The man stumbled over a root with a muffled curse, regained his balance, and at last set his burden down. Presently Tarcan heard the clink of a spade. He crept as near as he dared, and saw the man digging a hole at the foot of a great tree. When he was done, he lowered a brass-bound chest into the hole, covered it with dirt, then with leaves and branches. Having done so, and rested a moment from his exertions, the baggageman retreated toward the camp.

Tarcan waited until he was gone, then dug up the chest and filled the hole with rocks and earth. The chest was locked; he could not tell what was in it, but from its weight he knew it must be valuable. He carried it deeper into the forest and buried it again.

On the following afternoon, while the men were busy gathering firewood, he saw the golden-haired girl leave the cabin and stroll off through the woods. He pursued her, at a distance. He saw her dip her fingers in the little stream; he saw her pause to examine a patch of forget-me-nots and press the blossoms against her cheek. She wandered to the edge of the woods and strolled out into the meadow beyond. The air was balmy, and she took off her sun-hat and let it trail in her fingers. Tarcan followed, crouching low, ready to drop and conceal himself in the grasses, but she seemed oblivious of his presence.

They came to a low hill, and Jane went on into the valley beyond. Hastening to catch up, Tarcan beheld a horrifying sight. Jane Potter was standing in the open, transfixed with terror, while a tawny cougar crept toward her.

Tarcan leaped forward, shouting, "Run!" For a moment she hesitated, half-turning toward him; then, too late, she began to move. The cougar was hurtling after her, a steak of golden fur.

Tarcan's slingshot was in his hand; he fitted a stone to it without pausing in his career, and let fly. The missile struck the cougar's shoulder and bowled it over, but it was up at once, snarling. Out of the corner of his eye he saw that Jane had tripped and fallen, but he had no time to spare for her: the cougar, with a scream of rage, was springing directly toward him. Another man might have lost his nerve and fled before that juggernaut of feline fury, but Tarcan coolly stood his ground. He took another stone from his pocket, fitted it into the slingshot, took deliberate aim. The stone struck the charging animal squarely in the forehead, and it rolled over, dead, almost at his feet.

Only then did he turn his attention to the prostrate girl. She was sitting up, her face pale. "You've saved my life," she breathed as he came closer. "How can I ever thank you?"

"Can you walk?"

"I think so." She took his hand and struggled up to her feet, only to collapse again with a little moan. Tarcan's strong arm went around her, holding her up. "It's my ankle," she said; "I think I must have sprained it."

Tarcan said nothing, but picked her up in his arms as lightly as if she were a child. He crossed the little valley, climbed the hill beyond. At first she was tense with alarm, but after a time she relaxed and let her golden head fall against his shoulder. With the hill behind them, she could not see the railroad tracks, and did not know that he was carrying her in the opposite direction. The sun, dipping toward the western horizon, might have warned her that something was wrong, but Jane Potter, the daughter of an absent-minded Boston professor, was not schooled in the ways of the wilderness.

For a long time they did not speak. Then, "I don't even know your name," she said.

"They call me Tarcan."

"How odd! Is that your real name?"

"Yes." He carried her to the next little stand of trees, and past it to another. Jane raised her head and looked around. "Surely this isn't the right place," she said. "Are we lost?"

Tarcan, who was never lost, said nothing. In the next patch of forest, where a little tributary stream ran, he carried her by a forest trail to a secluded clearing and set her down. It was dark now in the woods; the light was almost gone.

The girl shrank against the bole of a tree and watched as Tarcan opened the bindle he carried on his back. He withdrew a scrap of cloth and tore it into strips with his strong fingers. How strange he was, this silent forest man! Yet she sensed deep within her that he meant her no harm.

With gentle fingers he probed her injured ankle. It was slightly swollen, and painful, but no bones were broken. He bound it with the cloth, then stood up. "You're not leaving?" she asked in alarm.

"Just a minute," he said curtly, and disappeared into the trees.

In a few moments he was back, carrying a heap of branches in his arms. With the smaller twigs he built a tiny fire, and with the longer ones he began to construct a rude shelter, leaning the branches together and tying them with twine. When the little fire had died to embers, he opened two cans of pork and beans and heated them. They ate in silence; then Tarcan drew a waterproof poncho from his bindle and draped it across the shelter for a roof. "Time for bed," he said.

The girl hesitated, for she was alone in the wilderness with an unknown man. Tarcan seemed to sense what she was thinking; he took out his clasp knife, opened it and handed it to her, handle first. She crept into the rude shelter, where Tarcan had made a bed of fragrant leaves, and saw him stretch out on the ground in his sleeping bag.

When the men at camp realized that Jane was missing, they ran about calling her name futilely until the cook discovered a clue: Jane's dainty handkerchief, dropped beside the trail. They gathered to look at the little scrap of cloth, mute witness to a tragedy. "Give me some food, please, in a knapsack or suitcase," said old Professor Potter sadly. "I shall go into the wilderness after my daughter, and if I do not find her I shall not return."

"Professor, pardon me, that will not do," said Paul D'Arnot. "You have lost your glasses and cannot see even a foot in front of your face. It is I who shall go, and I promise that I shall bring your daughter home safely."

"And I, too," cried Clayton.

"*Mon ami*, a word in your ear," said the Frenchman quietly, and drew Clayton aside. "If we should both go, who will guard the Professor from harm? There are savage animals here, and besides, to be frank, I do not like the look of your baggageman."

After some discussion, it was agreed that D'Arnot would go in search of the missing girl, and that if he did not return in two days, the rest would go in search of him; meanwhile, if Jane should return, Clayton would fire a pistol in order to alert him. D'Arnot, with a few provisions hastily thrust into a traveling case, slipped into the forest.

D'Arnot guessed that the girl had followed the path beside the stream, but he did not see the traces where she had wandered away from it; he pursued the stream, therefore, and at nightfall he made camp miles distant from the place where Tarcan and Jane lay.

On the following day he pressed on into the wilderness, heavy of heart, for he did not believe that Jane would ever be found. The sun was low when, in a little clearing, he stopped short. Facing him across the greensward, motionless and menacing, was a gigantic coyote. Seeing his hesitation, the beast bared its fangs and charged.

D'Arnot was a brave man, but he was unarmed. He turned and sprang for the nearest tree and scrambled up it. Then, in a moment of horror, he realized that a branch to which he had trusted his weight was rotten; it parted with a sickening crack and D'Arnot plummeted to the ground. His head struck a stone, and he knew no more.

In the morning Tarcan examined the girl's ankle and found it still swollen; he picked her up again and started back toward the camp. Jane lay in his arms with a feeling of perfect trust, glancing up now and then through her lashes at his strong, soiled face. She fell into a daydream; she wished the journey might last forever.

All too soon, she saw that they were approaching the camp. Tarcan set her down gently and said, "You'll be all right now."

"Jane!" came a joyful shout, and she saw the little group hurrying toward her. "We've all been so worried," cried Clayton, "but here you are safe and sound!"

"Yes, thanks to Mr.—" She turned to introduce Tarcan, but he was gone.

The others gathered around her, and old Professor Potter pressed her to his trembling breast, murmuring, "My child! My child!"

"But where is D'Arnot?" Clayton said suddenly.

"I don't understand—isn't Monsieur D'Arnot here?"

In a few words they explained what had happened, and Clayton, recollecting himself with a start, drew out his pistol and fired it repeatedly into the air. The echoes of the reports died away into silence. "He will hear the signal and come," said Clayton.

"But what if he does not? Suppose something dreadful has happened to him? Oh, dear, and it would be my fault!"

Tarcan, who had been listening in the shelter of the trees, turned and walked away from the camp. He did not know this D'Arnot, but Jane was concerned about him, and that was enough.

He found the Frenchman's footprints quickly, in the soft earth along the stream, and followed them. He saw where Jane had turned aside, and how the Frenchman, missing the almost imperceptible traces of her passage, had continued along the bank. By late afternoon, moving more swiftly and surely than D'Arnot had, he had found the latter's dead campfire. Pausing only to eat a can of beans, he pressed on. The sun was low when he stepped into a clearing and beheld an appalling sight. The man he sought was in the act of toppling from a tree, while a slavering coyote advanced toward him.

With Tarcan, to think was to act. As he ran forward, he drew his clasp knife from his pocket and opened the deadly blade. The great beast turned at his approach and launched itself in a snarling attack. The impact bowled Tarcan over, but even as he fell beneath the weight of the ferocious beast, his knife drank deep. With a shuddering convulsion, the coyote fell dead.

He found D'Arnot unconscious beneath the tree, with a great bloody welt on his forehead. Tarcan dragged him out of the underbrush carefully, and made sure he had no broken bones; but the blow to his head was injury enough, and it was plain that the man was in no condition to be moved. Tarcan made a bed of branches for the wounded man, built a rude shelter over him, and laid a cold compress on his head. As evening fell, he butchered the coyote and cooked some of the meat in a tin can; it would make a nourishing stew. The rest of the carcass he carried several hundred yards downstream and tossed into the undergrowth, lest it attract other predators.

That night, indeed, other coyotes found the carcass, tore it apart and dragged the remnants away, so that on the following afternoon, when Clayton and his party reached the spot, they saw that D'Arnot's footprints led to a great bloody smear in the shrubbery. Sadly they returned to their camp, and sadly, two days later, they boarded the rescue train which had been sent by McTaggart.

Meanwhile, D'Arnot lay for two days in delirium while Tarcan patiently nursed him. It was three weeks before the Frenchman was strong enough to travel, and during that time the two men became fast friends. Tarcan showed D'Arnot his treasures, including the locket, the folder with its two photographs, the journal and the children's book. D'Arnot read them with fascination. "But, *mon dieu*," he exclaimed, "this means that you yourself, and not Clayton, are the heir to millions!"

"That can't be," said Tarcan. "The baby's bones were there."

"Let me see," said the Frenchman, taking the children's book again. "Here are the fingerprints of that baby. Now let us examine yours." Taking a sheet of paper from his pocket, he pressed Tarcan's fingerprints upon it one after another. There was no need for ink; Tarcan's fingers were grimy enough. When the task was done, the Frenchman minutely compared the prints with the aid of a pocket magnifying glass. "It is possible," he muttered. "But we must be sure—too much is at stake. Let me borrow this book, my friend, and when we get back to civilization I will show it to a policeman that I know. He will tell us."

A few days later Tarcan pronounced D'Arnot fit to travel, and the two friends retraced their steps to the lonely cabin beside the railroad track. It was empty, but on the desk Tarcan found an envelope bearing his name in a feminine hand. Tearing it open, he read:

> Dear Tarcan,
>
> We all wanted to thank you for your kindness, but the rescue train has arrived and we must go. If you are ever in Boston, please call on me.
>
>   Jane Potter

He showed the note to D'Arnot. "And will you accept the invitation?" the Frenchman inquired.

Tarcan shook his head. "She's rich, and I'm a 'bo."

"My friend, once I was rich too, and if only I had the chest which was stolen from me, there would be plenty for both of us; but, alas—"

"What chest is that?" Tarcan asked abruptly. D'Arnot explained about the chest of gold that had mysteriously disappeared from the train. Tarcan, in turn, told him of the scene he had witnessed. "I dug the chest up and buried it again, like a packrat," he said. "We'll get it, and then you'll be rich."

"*We* shall be rich, *mon ami*! Do you think I spoke in jest? No, half of all I have is yours."

Tarcan dug up the chest and they set out along the track until they reached the grade, several miles away, where the fast freights slowed down. They boarded the first train and rode it as far as the nearest station, where D'Arnot paid for the rest of their passage to Boston, and also bought a full set of clothing and luggage for each of them. Bathed, shaved, and dressed in the fashion, Tarcan was, D'Arnot declared, the picture of a gentleman; but his manners left something to be desired.

"*Mon dieu!*" the Frenchman remarked, "you must not eat pork chops in your fingers, Tarcan! Do as I do." Tarcan copied him patiently, and soon learned to eat as daintily as any aristocrat.

Arriving in Boston, they found that the Potters had left for their summer cottage in Brattleboro. D'Arnot had business in the city, including a visit to the policeman he had mentioned, but Tarcan could not wait; he hired a car and set out for Vermont.

Jane Potter was in a quandary. Clayton, who had accompanied them to the summer cottage, had been increasingly attentive of late, and she knew, with the intuition of womankind, that he was about to propose. Clayton loved her; he was young, handsome, rich, and he would do his best to make her happy: but her heart was with the strange forest man who had borne her off into the wilderness.

"Dear Jane," Clayton said to her when they were alone that afternoon. "—I may call you Jane, mayn't I? You must know, dear, how I feel about you. I want you to marry me. Won't you say yes?"

Jane hesitated. After all, what hope could she have of ever seeing again the strange, vibrant man who had come so briefly into her life?

"Yes," she said.

Afterward, pleading a headache, she retired to her room and

waited until the others had gone off on their various errands; then she strolled out of the house into a little wood that ran along the railroad track. The scene reminded her of her forest love, and she wandered deeper into the trees, unaware of the black cloud that hung ominously on the horizon.

When at last she smelled the smoke and saw it drifting through the trees, it was too late. She stumbled away from the oncoming flames, only to find another line of fire racing across her path. Suddenly she heard her name called; a tall stranger was running toward her. Without a word he caught her up in his arms and bounded back the way he had come.

On the railroad track, a little distance away, stood a small handcar. The stranger deposited her on it without ceremony, climbed aboard himself, and began to pump. It was only then that Jane saw his face clearly. "You!" she said.

"Yes, me, Tarcan."

"And you've saved my life again!" she marveled.

"Not yet," said Tarcan grimly. On both sides of the railway, trees were blazing fiercely; flaming bits of debris rained upon them, and they were blinded by smoke. Then, little by little, the flames receded, and they were hurtling down the track in clear air again.

Near the cottage, Tarcan brought the handcar to a halt and handed Jane down. In a moment he had clasped her in his strong arms. "I love you, Jane," he said. "I want you to be my wife."

Her eyes were downcast. "I am promised to another," she said.

"Clayton?"

"Yes."

"And do you love him?"

"Please don't ask me that."

Back at the cottage, Clayton and Professor Potter received Jane joyfully. They were wonderstruck when Jane introduced Tarcan as the mysterious forest wanderer who had rescued her in the wilderness. Professor Potter stammered his gratitude, and Clayton offered him a cigar.

Shortly thereafter a messenger came to the door with a telegram. "Why, it's for you," said the Professor in surprise. "Dear me, how did they know you were here?"

"Pardon me," said Tarcan, and ripped the envelope open. The message read:

FINGERPRINTS PROVE YOU CLAYTON HEIR.
D'ARNOT

Tarcan glanced at his cousin, who was pouring himself a whiskey and soda at the sideboard. Clayton was handsome, well-groomed, and soft; he had never boarded a moving freight in his life, or faced the charge of an enraged coyote. With a word, Tarcan could take away his fortune, and his woman as well.

"I say," Clayton smiled, crossing the room to him, "this is all very extraordinary, you know. How did you come to be in that wilderness in the first place, if you don't mind my asking?"

Tarcan folded the telegram and put it in his pocket. "I was born there," he said deliberately. "My mother was a giant hobo; I never knew my father."

I SEE YOU

I am fond of this one because it embodies a wish-fulfillment fantasy. I would give anything to have the experiences the people in the story have; the next best thing is to have them vividly stimulated by my own prose.

I don't reread this story very often, but I remember it a lot.

You are five, hiding in a place only you know. You are covered with bark dust, scratched by twigs, sweaty and hot. A wind sighs in the aspen leaves. A faint steady hiss comes from the viewer you hold in your hands; then a voice: "Lorie, I see you—under the barn, eating an apple!" A silence. "Lorie, come on out, I see you." Another voice. "That's right, she's in there." After a moment, sulkily: "Oh, all right."

You squirm around, raising the viewer to aim it down the hill. As you turn the knob with your thumb, the bright image races toward you, trees hurling themselves into red darkness and vanishing, then the houses in the compound, and now you see Bruce standing beside the corral, looking into his viewer, slowly turning. His back is to you, so you know you are safe, and you sit up. A jay passes with a whir of wings, settles on a branch. With your own eyes now you can see Bruce, only a dot of blue beyond the gray shake walls of the houses. In the viewer, he is turning toward you, and you duck again. Another voice: "Children, come in and get washed for dinner now." "Aw, Aunt Ellie!" "Mom, we're playing hide and seek. Can't we just stay fifteen minutes more?"

"Please, Aunt Ellie!" "No, come on in now—you'll have plenty of time after dinner." And Bruce: "Aw, okay. All out's in free." And once more they have not found you; your secret place is yours alone.

Call him Smith. He was the president of a company that bore his name and which held more than a hundred patents in the scientific instrument field. He was sixty, a widower. His only daughter and her husband had been killed in a plane crash in 1968. He had a partner who handled the business operations now; Smith spent most of his time in his own lab. In the spring of 1990 he was working on an image intensification device that was puzzling because it was too good. He had it on his bench now, aimed at a deep shadow box across the room; at the back of the box was a card ruled with black, green, red and blue lines. The only source of illumination was a single ten-watt bulb hung behind the shadow box; the light reflected from the card did not even register on his meter, and yet the image in the screen of his device was sharp and bright. When he varied the voltage and amperage beyond certain limits, the bright image vanished and was replaced by shadows, like the ghost of another image. He had monitored every television channel, had shielded the device against radio frequencies, and the ghosts remained. Increasing the illumination did not make them clearer. They were vaguely rectilinear shapes without any coherent pattern. Occasionally a moving blur traveled slowly across them.

Smith made a disgusted sound. He opened the clamps that held the device and picked it up, reaching for the power switch with his other hand. He never touched it. As he moved the device, the ghost images had shifted; they were dancing now with the faint movements of his hand. Smith stared at them without breathing for a moment. Holding the flex, he turned slowly. The ghost images whirled, vanished, reappeared. He turned the other way; they whirled back.

Smith set the device down on the bench with care. His hands were shaking. He had had the device clamped down on the bench all the time until now. "Christ almighty, how dumb can one man get?" he asked the empty room.

You are six, almost seven, and you are being allowed to use the big viewer for the first time. You are perched on a cushion in the leather chair, at the console; your brother, who has been showing you the controls with a bored and superior air, has just left the room saying, "All right, if you know so much, do it yourself."

In fact, the controls on this machine are unfamiliar; the little viewers you have used all your life have only one knob, for nearer or farther—to move up/down, or left/right, you just point the viewer where you want to see. This machine has dials and little windows with numbers in them, and switches and pushbuttons most of which you don't understand, but you know they are for special purposes and don't matter. The main control is a metal rod, right in front of you, with a gray plastic knob on the top. The knob is dull from years of handling; it feels warm and a little greasy in your hand. The console has a funny electric smell, but the big screen, taller than you are, is silent and dark. You can feel your heart beating against your breastbone. You grip the knob harder, push it forward just a little. The screen lights, and you are drifting across the next room as if on huge silent wheels, chairs and end tables turning into reddish silhouettes that shrink, twist and disappear as you pass through them, and for a moment you feel dizzy, because when you notice the red numbers jumping in the console to your left, it is as if the whole house were passing massively and vertiginously through itself: then you are floating out the window with the same slow and steady motion, on across the sunlit pasture where two saddle horses stand with their heads up, sniffing the wind; then a stubbled field, dropping away, and now below you the co-op road shines like a silver-gray stream. You press the knob down to get closer, and drop with a giddy swoop; now you are rushing along the road, overtaking and passing a silent yellow truck, turning the knob to steer. At first you blunder into the dark trees on either side, and once the earth surges up over you in a chaos of writhing red shapes, but now you are learning, and you soar down past the crossroads, up the farther hill, and now, now you are on the big road, flying eastward, passing all the cars, rushing toward the great world where you long to be.

It took Smith six weeks to increase the efficiency of the image intensifier enough to bring up the ghost pictures clearly. When he succeeded, the image on the screen was instantly recognizable. It was a view of Jack McCranie's office; the picture was still dim, but sharp enough that Smith could see the expression on Jack's face. He was leaning back in his chair, hands behind his head. Beside him stood Peg Spatola in a purple dress, with her hand on an open folder. She was talking, and McCranie was listening. That was wrong, because Peg was not supposed to be back from Cleveland until next week.

Smith reached for the phone and punched McCranie's number. After a moment the little screen lighted up. McCranie, wearing a different necktie and with his jacket on, said, "Yes, Tom?"

"Jack, is Peg in there?"

"Why, no—she's in Cleveland, Tom."

"Oh, yes."

McCranie looked puzzled. "Is anything the matter?" In the other screen, he had swiveled his chair and was talking to Peg, gesturing with short, choppy motions of his arm.

"No, nothing," said Smith. "That's all right, Jack, thank you." He broke the connection. After a moment he turned to the breadboard controls of the device and changed one setting slightly. In the screen, Peg turned and walked backward out of the office. When he turned the knob the other way, she repeated these actions in reverse. Smith tinkered with the other controls until he got a view of the calendar on Jack's desk. It was Friday, June 15th—last week.

Smith locked up the device and all his notes, went home and spent the rest of the day thinking.

By the end of July he had refined and miniaturized the device and had extended its sensitivity range into the infrared. He spent most of August, when he should have been on vacation, trying various methods of detecting sound through the device. By focusing on the interior of a speaker's larynx and using infrared, he was able to convert the visible vibrations of the vocal cords into sound of fair quality, but that did not satisfy him. He worked for a while on vibrations picked up from panes of glass in windows and on framed pictures, and he experimented briefly with the diaphragms in speaker systems, intercoms and telephones. He kept on into October without stopping, and finally achieved a device that would give tinny but recognizable sound from any vibrating surface—a wall, a floor, even the speaker's own cheek or forehead. He redesigned the whole device, built a prototype and tested it, tore it down, redesigned, built another. It was Christmas before he was done. Once more he locked up the device and all his plans, drawings and notes.

At home, he spent the holidays experimenting with commercial adhesives in various strengths. He applied these to coated paper, let them dry, and cut the paper into rectangles. He numbered these rectangles, pasted them onto letter envelopes, some of which he stacked loose; others he bundled together and secured with rubber bands. He opened the stacks and bundles and examined them at regular intervals. Some of the labels curled up and detached themselves after twenty-six hours without leaving any conspicuous trace. He made up another batch of these, typed his home address on six of them. On each of six envelopes he typed his office address, then covered it with one of the labels. He stamped the envelopes and dropped them into a mailbox. All six were delivered to the office three days later.

Just after New Year's, he told his partner that he wanted to sell out and retire. They discussed it in general terms.

Using an assumed name and a post office box number which was not his, Smith wrote to a commission agent in Boston with whom he had never had any previous dealings. He mailed the letter, with the agent's address covered by one of his labels on which he had typed his own address. The label detached itself in transit; the letter was delivered. When the agent replied, Smith was watching and read the letter as a secretary typed it. The agent followed his instructions to mail his reply in an envelope without return address. The owner of the post office box turned it in marked "Not here"; it went to the Dead Letter Office and was returned in due time, but meanwhile Smith had acknowledged the letter and had mailed, in the same way, a large amount of cash. In subsequent letters he instructed the agent to take bids for components, plans for which he enclosed, from electronics manufacturers, for plastic casings from another, and for assembly and shipping from still another company. Through a second commission agent in New York, to whom he wrote in the same way, he contracted for ten thousand copies of an instruction booklet in four colors.

Late in February he bought a house and an electronics dealership in a small town in the Adirondacks. In March he signed over his interest in the company to his partner, cleaned out his lab and left. He sold his co-op apartment in Manhattan and his summer house in Connecticut, moved to his new home and became anonymous.

You are thirteen, chasing a fox with the big kids for the first time. They have put you in the north field, the worst place, but you know better than to leave it.

"He's in the glen."

"I see him, he's in the brook, going upstream."

You turn the viewer, racing forward through dappled shade, a brilliance of leaves: there is the glen, and now you see the fox, trotting through the shallows, blossoms of bright water at its feet.

"Ken and Nell, you come down ahead of him by the spring-house. Wanda, you and Tim and Jean stay where you are. Everybody else come upstream, but stay back till I tell you."

That's Leigh, the oldest. You turn the viewer, catch a glimpse of Bobby running downhill through the woods, his long hair flying. Then back to the glen: the fox is gone.

"He's heading up past the corn-crib!"

"Okay, keep spread out on both sides, everybody. Jim, can you and Edie head him off before he gets to the woods?"

"We'll try. There he is!"

And the chase is going away from you, as you knew it would, but soon you will be older, as old as Nell and Jim; then you will be in the middle of things, and life will begin.

By trial and error, Smith has found the settings for Dallas, November 22, 1963: Dealey Plaza, 12:25 P.M. He sees the Presidential motorcade making the turn onto Elm Street. Kennedy slumps forward, raising his hands to his throat. Smith presses a button to hold the moment in time. He scans behind the motorcade, finds the sixth floor of the Book Depository Building, finds the window. There is no one behind the barricade of cartons; the room is empty. He scans the nearby rooms, finds nothing. He tries the floor below. At an open window a man kneels, holding a high-powered rifle. Smith photographs him. He returns to the motorcade, watches as the second shot strikes the President. He freezes time again, scans the surrounding buildings, finds a second marksman on the roof of one of them, photographs him. Back to the motorcade. A third and fourth shot, the last blowing off the side of the President's head. Smith freezes the action again, finds two gunmen on the grassy knoll, one aiming across the top of a station wagon, one kneeling in the shrubbery. He photographs them. He turns off the power, sits for a moment, then goes to the washroom, kneels beside the toilet and vomits.

The viewer is your babysitter, your television, your telephone (the telephone lines are still up, but they are used only as signaling devices; when you know that somebody wants to talk to you, you focus your viewer on him), your library, your school. Before puberty you watch other people having sex, but even then your curiosity is easily satisfied; after an older cousin initiates you at fourteen, you are much more interested in doing it yourself. The co-op teacher monitors your studies, sometimes makes suggestions, but more and more, as you grow older, leaves you to your own devices. You are intensely interested in African prehistory, in European theater, and in the ant-civilization of Epsilon Eridani IV. Soon you will have to choose.

New York Harbor, November 4, 1872—a cold, blustery day. A two-masted ship rides at anchor; on her stern is lettered: MARY CELESTE. Smith advances the time control. A flicker of darkness, light again, and the ship is gone. He turns back again until he finds it standing out under light canvas past Sandy Hook. Manipulating time and space controls at once, he follows it eastward through a flickering of storm and sun—loses it, finds it again, counting days as he goes. The farther eastward, the more he has to tilt the device downward, while the image of the ship tilts correspondingly away from him. Because of the angle, he can no longer keep the ship in view from any distance but must track it closely. November 21 and 22, violent storms: the ship is dashed upward by waves, falls again, visible only intermittently; it takes him five hours to pass through two days of real time. The 23rd is calmer, but on the 24th another storm blows up. Smith rubs his eyes, loses the ship, finds it again after a ten-minute search. The gale blows itself out on the morning of the 26th. The sun is bright, the sea almost dead calm. Smith is able to catch glimpses of figures on deck, tilted above dark cross-sections of the hull. A sailor is splicing a rope in the stern, two others lowering a triangular sail between the foremast and the bowsprit, and a fourth is at the helm. A little group stands leaning on the starboard rail; one of them is a woman. The next glimpse he has is of a running figure who advances into the screen and disappears. Now the men are lowering a boat over the side; the rail has been removed and lies on the deck. The men drop into the boat and row away. He hears them shouting to each other but cannot make out the words. Smith turns to the ship again: the deck is empty. He dips below to look at the hold, filled with casks, then the cabin, then the forecastle. There is no sign of anything wrong—no explosion, no fire, no traces of violence. When he looks up again, he sees the sails flapping, then bellying out full. The sea is rising. He looks for the boat, but now too much time has passed and he cannot find it. He returns to the ship, and now reverses the time control, tracks it backward until the men are again in their places on deck. He looks again at the group standing at the rail; now he sees that the woman has a child in her arms. The child struggles, drops over the rail. Smith hears the woman shriek. In a moment she is over the rail and falling into the sea.

He watches the men running, sees them launch the boat. As they pull away, he is able to keep the focus near enough to see their faces and hear what they say. One calls, "My God, who's at the helm?" Another, a bearded man with a face gone tallow-color, replies, "Never mind—row!" They are staring down into the sea. After a moment one looks up, then another. The *Mary Celeste*, with three of the four sails on her foremast set, is gliding away, slowly, now faster; now she is gone.

Smith does not run through the scene again to watch the child and her mother drown; but others do.

The production model was ready for shipping in September. It was a simplified version of the prototype, with only two controls, one for space, one for time. The range of the device was limited to one thousand miles. Nowhere on the casing of the device or in the instruction booklet was a patent number or a pending patent mentioned. Smith had called the device "Ozo," perhaps because he thought it sounded vaguely Japanese. The booklet described the device as a distant viewer and gave clear, simple instructions for its use. One sentence read cryptically: "Keep Time Control set at zero." It was like "Wet Paint—Do Not Touch."

During the week of September 23, seven thousand devices were shipped to domestic and Canadian addresses supplied by Smith: five hundred to electronics manufacturers and suppliers, six thousand, thirty to a carton, marked "On Consignment," to TV outlets in major cities, and the rest to people chosen at random. The instruction booklets were in sealed envelopes packed with each device. Three thousand more went to Europe, South and Central America, and the Middle East.

A few of the outlets which received the cartons opened them the same day, tried the devices out, and put them on sale at prices ranging from $49.95 to $126. By the following day the word was beginning to spread, and by the close of business on the third day every store was sold out. Most people who got them, either through the mail or by purchase, used them to spy on their neighbors and on people in hotels.

In a house in Cleveland, a man is watching his brother-in-law in the next room, who is watching his wife getting out of a taxi. She pays the driver, goes into the lobby of an apartment building. The husband watches as she gets into the elevator, rides to the fourth floor. She rings the bell beside a door marked "410." The door opens; a dark-haired man takes her in his arms; they kiss.

The brother-in-law meets him in the hall. "Don't do it, Charlie."

"Get out of my way."

"I'm not going to get out of your way, and I tell you, don't do it. Not now and not later."

"Why the hell shouldn't I?"

"Because if you do I'll kill you. If you want a divorce, OK, get a divorce. But don't lay a hand on her or I'll find you the farthest place you can go."

A surgeon is using the Ozo with a camera attachment to photograph a series of perfect sections of his patient's abdominal cavity: better than computerized X rays, they have depth and full detail, he can look into the living body. There is the tumor, it is operable. And tears are running down his cheeks.

Smith got his consignment of Ozos early in the week, took one home and left it to his store manager to put a price on the rest. He did not bother to use the production model, but began at once to build another prototype. It had controls calibrated to one-hundredth of a second and one millimeter, and a timer that would allow him to stop a scene, or advance or regress it at any desired rate. He ordered some clockwork from an astronomical supply house.

A high-ranking officer in Army Intelligence, watching the first demonstration of the Ozo in the Pentagon, exclaimed, "My God, with this we could dismantle half the establishment—all we've got to do is launch interceptors when we see them push the button."

"It's a good thing Senator Burkhart can't hear you say that," said another officer. But by the next afternoon everybody had heard it.

The first Ozo was smuggled into the Soviet Union from West Germany by Katerina Belov, a member of a dissident group in Moscow, who used it to document illegal government actions. The device was seized on December 13 by the KGB; Belov and two other members of the group were arrested, imprisoned and tortured. By that time over forty other Ozos were in the hands of dissidents.

You are watching an old movie, *Bob and Carol and Ted and Alice.* The humor seems infantile and unimaginative to you; you are not interested in the actresses' occasional seminudity. What strikes you as hilarious is the coyness, the sidelong glances, smiles, grimaces hinting at things that will never be shown on the screen. You realize that these people have never seen anyone but their most intimate friends without clothing, have never seen any adult shit or piss, and would be embarrassed or disgusted if they did. Why did children say "pee-pee" and "poo-poo," and then giggle? You have read scholarly books about taboos on "bodily functions," but why was shitting worse than sneezing?

Cora Zickwolfe, who lived in a remote rural area of Arizona and whose husband commuted to Tucson, arranged with her nearest neighbor, Phyllis Mell, for each of them to keep an Ozo focused on the bulletin board in the other's kitchen. On the bulletin board was a note that said "OK." If there was any trouble and she couldn't get to the phone, she would take down the note, or if she had time, write another.

In April, 1992, about the time her husband usually got home, an intruder broke into the house and seized Mrs. Zickwolfe before she had time to get to the bulletin board. He dragged her into the bedroom and forced her to disrobe. The state troopers got there in fifteen minutes, and Cora never spoke to her friend Phyllis again.

Between 1992 and 2002 more than six hundred improvements and supplements to the Ozo were recorded. The most important of these was the power system created by focusing the Ozo at a narrow aperture on the interior of the Sun. Others included the system of satellite repeaters in stationary orbits, and a computerized tracer device which would keep the Ozo focused on any object.

Using the tracer, an entomologist in Mexico City is following the ancestral line of a honey bee. The images bloom and expire, ten every second: the tracer is following each queen back to the egg, then the egg to the queen that laid it, then that queen to the egg. Tens of thousands of generations have passed; in two thousand hours, beginning with a Paleocene bee, he has traveled back into the Cretaceous. He stops at intervals to follow the bee in real time, then accelerates again. The hive is growing smaller, more primitive. Now it is only a cluster of round cells, and the bee is different, more like a wasp. His year's labor is coming to fruition. He watches, forgetting to eat, almost to breathe.

In your mother's study after she dies you find an elaborate chart of her ancestors and your father's. You retrieve the program for it, punch it in, and idly watch a random sampling, back into time, first the female line, then the male . . . a teacher of biology in Boston, a suffragette, a corn merchant, a singer, a Dutch farmer in New York, a British sailor, a German musician. Their faces glow in the screen, bright-eyed, cheeks flushed with life, unaware that they are dead. Someday you too will be only a series of images in a screen.

Smith is watching the planet Mars. It is his ninth visit, and the clockwork which turns the Ozo to follow the planet, even when it is below the horizon, makes it possible for him to focus instantly on the surface, but he never does this. He takes up his position hundreds of thousands of miles away, then slowly approaches, in order to see the red spark grow to a disk, then to a yellow sunlit ball hanging in space. Now he can make out the surface features: Syrtis Major and Thoth-Nepenthes leading in a long gooseneck to Utopia and the frostcap.

The image as it swells hypnotically toward him is clear and sharp, without tremor or atmospheric distortion. It is summer in the northern hemisphere: Utopia is wide and dark. The planet fills the screen, and now he turns northward, over the cratered desert still hundreds of miles away. A dust storm, like a yellow veil, obscures the curved neck of Thoth-Nepenthes; then he is beyond it, drifting down to the edge of the frostcap. The limb of the planet reappears; he floats like a glider over the dark area tinted with rose and violet-gray; now he can see its nubbly texture; now he can make out individual plants. He is drifting among their gnarled gray stems, their leaves of violet horn; he sees the curious misshapen growths that may be air bladders or some grotesque analogue of blossoms. Now, at the edge of the screen, something black and spindling leaps. He follows it instantly, finds it, brings it hugely magnified into the center of the screen: a thing like a hairy beetle, its body covered with thick black hairs or spines: it stands on six jointed legs, waving its antennae, its mouth parts busy. And its four bright eyes stare into his across forty million miles.

Smith's hair got whiter and thinner. Before the 1992 Crash, he made heavy contributions to the International Red Cross and to volunteer organizations in Europe, Asia and Africa. He got drunk periodically, but always alone. From 1993 to 1996 he stopped reading newspapers. At intervals while dressing or looking into the bathroom mirror, he stared as if into an invisible camera and raised one finger. In his last years he wrote some poems, which are on file in a few libraries, but there are few calls for their retrieval codes. Not many people read poetry or fiction anymore: reality is so much more interesting.

We know his name. Patient researchers, using advanced scanning techniques, followed his letters back through the postal system and found him, but by that time he was safely dead.

The whole world has been at peace for more than a generation. Crime is almost unheard of. Free energy has made the world rich, but the population is stable, even though early detection has wiped out most diseases. Everyone can do whatever he likes, providing his neighbors would not disapprove, and after all, their views are his own.

You are forty, a respected scholar, taking a few days out to review your life, as many people do at your age. You have watched your mother and father coupling on the night they conceived you, watched yourself growing in her womb, first a red tadpole, then a thing like an embryo chicken, then a big-headed baby kicking and squirming. You have seen yourself delivered, seen the first moment when your bloody head broke into the light. You have seen yourself staggering about the nursery in rompers, clutching a yellow plastic duck. Now you are watching yourself hiding behind the fallen tree on the hill, and you realize that there are no secret places. And beyond you in the ghostly future you know that someone is watching you as you watch, and beyond that watcher another, and beyond that another.

Forever.

ON THE WHEEL

....
....
....
....

This story makes use of some experiences I had on one of the infrequent occasions when I tried to get an honest job. The only time I ever got such a job, it was at an aircraft factory in Los Angeles, and I think they were hiring anybody who could see the application form. Luckily, when I declined to join the union they guessed that I was not planning to make file-clerking my career, and they laid me off after six weeks.

I made up the part about the seapigs.

From his perch in the foretop of the *Vlakengros*, Akim could see almost straight down into the cargo well of the old tub, where half a dozen trogs were still scrambling about. Nearby stood his father and the shipmaster, Hizoor Niarefh. Akim could see the tops of their turbaned heads and the bright shafts of their lances. The trogs, black and foreshortened, were like clumsy insects. Akim blew out his breath impatiently and lifted his eyes to the horizon. Westward, above the low hills of the mainland, the sun lay behind veils of purple and gold. A faint offshore breeze roughened the water. To the east, above the ocean, one of the moons had already risen. It was the end of his watch; another day was gone, wasted. Nothing ever happened on the *Vlakengros*.

At last there was a stirring, a distant shout. The trogs were climbing over the rail into their catamarans. Akim waited, twitching with impatience, until a figure stepped leisurely toward the foot of the mast and began to climb.

It was his brother Ogo, who had pimples and never smiled. "Pig," said Akim. He swung himself down the side of the lookout without waiting for Ogo to climb in; his toes caught the rope ladder and he started down. Ogo's dark head appeared above him. "Squid!" Akim shook his fist and kept on descending.

The deck trembled faintly under his feet as he crossed toward the forecastle; the auxiliaries were on, they were under way. Smells of cooking came from the galley. Akim ran down the companionway, snatched a meat pie from the table and was out again, followed by the curses of the cooks. Eating as he went, he reached his cubby and shut the door behind him. He tossed his fire lance into the rack, pulled off turban and robe, and sank down in his chair before the viewer. Now, at last!

He remembered exactly where he had left off, but he thumbed the rewind, listened to the tape squeal for a few moments, then punched "play." The screen lighted. There he was, Edward Robinson, opening the door at the end of the long hall. Still chewing, Akim settled lower into his chair, careful not to move his eyes a millimeter from the screen. The room was large but divided by frosted glass partitions into a jungle of smaller spaces. Behind one of these partitions, looking out through a hole in it, sat a girl with pink and white skin. Over her glossy brown hair she wore a telephone headset. Somewhere in the labyrinth behind her, close and yet invisible, a voice was raised in anger. She looked at Robinson with weary indifference. "Yes, can I help you?"

He advanced, straightening his thin shoulders, and took a folded paper out of his pocket. He unfolded it and laid it on the counter. "Central Employment sent me."

"All right, fill this out." She handed him a card. Along the wall to his right were straight chairs in which three young men sat. One was biting his pencil and scowling. Robinson sat down and began filling out his card. Name. Address. Sex. Age. Race (crossed out by a heavy black line). Education. Previous Employment (list your last three jobs, with dates, duties performed, and reason for leaving). Robinson made up the education, the dates, the reasons, and one of the jobs. While he was doing this, one of the other young men was called. He walked down the corridor between the glass partitions and disappeared. Robinson finished his card and gave it to the girl behind the partition, who was filing her nails. A typewriter clattered somewhere. The second young man was called. Robinson looked around, saw a copy of *Time* on the table beside him, and picked it up. He read an article about dynamic Eric Woolmason who at the age of forty-one was forging a new empire in Pacific Northwest public utilities. The third young man stood up suddenly and crumpled his card. His face was pink. He glanced sidelong at Robinson, then walked out. The girl at the window looked after him with a faint one-sided smile. "Well, good-bye," she murmured.

Robinson began to read the ads in the back of the magazine. He did not think about the coming interview, but his heart was thumping and his palms were moist. At last the girl's voice said, "Mr. Robinson." He stood up. She pointed with her pencil. "Straight down. End of the hall."

"All hands! All hands!" He sat up with a jerk, his heart racing. The room was dark except for the tiny lighted screen. The bellowing voice went on, "All hands to stations! All hands!"

Akim staggered out of the chair, painfully confused. He got into his robe somehow, snatched up the fire lance. Where was his turban? In the screen, a tiny Robinson was walking between the rows of frost-white partitions. He hit the "off" button angrily and lurched out of the room.

Abovedecks, searchlights and the jets of fire lances were wavering across the windy darkness. Something heavy fell to the deck and lay snapping and squealing. A half-naked sailor ran up and hit it with an axe. Akim kept on going. He could see that the foretop was crowded already—three lances were spitting up there. There was another shriek from the sky, a pause, then a splash near the bow. He ran to the quarterdeck rail and found a place between his brother Emmuz and his uncle's cousin Hudny. A searchlight in the bow probed the sky like a skeletal finger. Something appeared in it and was gone. The beam swung, caught it again. Half a dozen lance flames spitted it. It fell, trailing oily smoke.

There were more shrieks, splashes. Back toward the waist, there was a flurry of running feet, curses, shouts. Something was thrashing, tangled in the foremast shrouds. A voice screamed, "Don't shoot, you fool! Up the mast and chop it!"

Something came whistling through the darkness under the searchbeam. Akim crouched, raised his lance, fired. The flame illuminated a ferocious tusked head, a pink hairless body, leathery wings. There was a shriek and a stench, and the thing plopped down beyond him like a sack of wet meal. Someone hit it with an axe.

The noise died away. The searchlights continued to swing across the darkness. After a time, one of them picked up another bright shape, but it was far away, swinging wide around the ship, and the lance-flames missed it.

"Any more?" came a bellow from the deck.

"No, your worship," answered a voice from the foretop.

"All right then, secure."

Akim lingered glumly to watch the deckhands gather up the bodies and throw them over the side. Pigs were the only excitement in these latitudes; in the old days, it was said, ships had fought them for days with musket and cutlass. But now, not ten minutes since the first alarm, it was all over. A few sailors were swabbing the blood away with sea water, the rest were drifting back belowdecks.

Yawning, Akim went back to his cubby. He was tired, but too restless to go to bed. He wondered whether he was hungry and thought of going to the galley again, but it did not seem worth the effort. With a sigh, he sat in front of the viewer and switched it on.

There was Robinson, walking stiffly into a large area filled with desks cluttered with papers and typewriters. A heavy dark-haired man with black-rimmed glasses stood waiting. His white shirtsleeves were rolled to the elbow. "Robinson? I'm Mr. Beverly." At other desks, a few men glanced up, all pale, unsmiling. Beverly gave Robinson a brief, moist handshake and motioned to a chair. Robinson sat down and tried not to look self-conscious. Glancing at the card in his hand, Beverly said, "Not much experience in this line. Do you think you can handle it?"

Robinson said, "Yes, I think—well, I think I can handle it." He crossed his legs, then uncrossed them.

Beverly nodded, pursing his lips. He reached for a magazine on the desk, pushed it an inch closer. "You're familiar with this publication?"

The cover had a picture of a woman in a tramp's costume smoking a cigar, and a headline, "SMOKES TEN STOGIES A DAY." "Yes, I've seen it," Robinson answered. He tried to think of something else to say. "It's, uh, the kind of thing you read in barbershops, isn't it?"

Beverly nodded again, slowly. His expression did not change. Robinson crossed his legs. "Your job," Beverly said, "would involve choosing pictures for the magazine from photos like these." He pointed to the next desk; it was covered with disorderly heaps of photographs. "Do you think you could do that?"

Robinson stared at the topmost picture, which showed a young woman in what appeared to be a circus costume. He could see the powder caked on her dimpled face, and the beads of mascara on her eyelashes. "Yes, sure. I mean, I think I could handle it."

"Uh-huh. Okay, Robinson, thanks for coming in. We'll let you know. Go out that way, if you don't mind." He gave Robinson another handshake and turned away.

Robinson walked to the elevator. He knew he was not going to get the job, and even if he did get it, he would hate it. In the street, he turned west and walked against a tide of blank-eyed, gum-chewing faces. A taxi went over a manhole cover, clink-clank. Steam was rising from an excavation at the corner. The world was like a puzzle with half the pieces missing. What was the point of all these drab buildings, this dirty sky?

In his room, he made some hash and eggs and ate it, reading the *Daily News* and listening to the radio. Then he poured a cup of instant coffee and took it to the easy chair in the corner. On the table beside him lay a paperback book. The cover showed a half-naked red-skinned young man whose smooth muscles bulged as he struck with a scimitar at a monstrous flying boar. A maiden in metal breastplates cowered behind him, and there was ship's rigging in the background. Robinson found his place, bent the book's spine to flatten it, and began to read.

Sometime during the night (he read), the young crewman awoke with a start. He had fallen asleep in his chair, and his legs were cramped, his neck stiff. He got up and walked back and forth the few steps the cubby allowed, but it was not enough, and he went out into the passage. The ship was silent and dark. On an impulse, he climbed the companionway and emerged under a spectral sky. The deck was awash with moonlight. Up in the foretop, there was a wink of red as the lookout lighted his pipe. That would be Rilloj, his second cousin, a heavy, black-browed man who had the same ox-like face as his father, and his uncle Zanid, and all the rest. On the whole ship there was not one of them he could talk to, not one who understood his yearnings.

Hugging himself for warmth, he walked over to the lee rail. A few stars shone above the dim horizon. Up there, somewhere, unreachable and unknown, there must be worlds of mystery, worlds where a man could *live*. Gigantic cities thronged with people, exotic machines, ancient wisdom. . . .

And he was Akim, seventeen years old, a crewman on the *Vlakengros*. As he turned, he felt a queer loss of balance for an instant; the world seemed to split, and he had a glimpse of a ragged crack with grayness showing through it. Then it was gone, but it had frightened him. What could cause such a thing?

Back in his cubby, he sat down heavily in front of the screen. He would be sorry for it in a few hours, when the watch turned him out, but after all, what else was there? He turned on the machine. There was Robinson, reading in his chair. A cigarette beside him in the ashtray had burned to a long gray ash. The alarm clock read two-thirty. It was the gray turning point of the night, when the eyes are dry and the blood flows thin. Robinson yawned, read another line without interest, then shut the book and tossed it aside. He began to realize how tired he really was.

He shut off the viewer, pulled his bunk down out of the wall, stripped off his robe. He got up and headed for the bathroom, unbuttoning his shirt as he went. He brushed his teeth, wound the alarm clock (but did not set it), undressed and got in between the rumpled sheets. He went to the head, made sure his door was secure, then rolled into the bunk. As he lay there between sleep and waking, the events of the day got all mixed up somehow with the story he had been viewing. Tomorrow they would be at their next port of call, and he would pick up his unemployment check. Maybe he would get a job. The ship was rolling gently. Under the edge of the blind, the neons winked red-blue, red-green, red-blue. Good night, good night. Sleep tight, don't let the seapigs bite.

E A C H
P R I S O N E R
P E N T

This is one of my problem-solving stories. The problem is what we perceive as "crime." The proposed solution, I think, is a practical one, although it will never be adopted, because we prefer our present system of building more and more jails and handing down longer and longer sentences.

Remembering Ezra Pound's happy years in jail, I took care of the subsidiary problem—what to do with all those vacant cells—by putting artists in them.

The first thing he did, when he was eighteen, he split a man's skull with a pool cue in a Hamtramck bar. That was in 2010, and the judge gave him a Temporary ticket, good for a Super Mac and fries, a malt and fruit pie any time he wanted to walk in and put his ticket down.

There were three catches to it. The first one was that he had to spend every Friday night in jail. But it was a good jail, with private cells and holovision, and he made a lot of friends in there.

The second catch was that if he was ever convicted of another

A&B, after taking the ticket, it would mean the Social Work Organization Board or the Injection Chamber. And the third was that he had to wear a snitch around his wrist all the time. The monitor told Corrections where he was every minute, and whenever he passed a holo camera, the snitch would turn it on, so they would have a holo of his life whenever they wanted to look at it.

His parents had wanted him to go into construction, or service work taking care of the loonies in their prisons, but Scotty did not care for heavy labor, and service was for poindexters. Besides, all the guys he knew had tickets.

The Temporary was just the first step; then you had to decide what you wanted to go for. Scott waited until he was twenty, and then him and another guy broke into a house in Lincoln Park, killed the dogs and got out with a sack full of jewelry. Somebody turned them in, of course, and now he had a Permanent ticket, the white card they called it, good for apartment rental, retail purchases, and restaurants up to Class C. It wasn't a great living, but it was enough, and if he watched his budget he could even afford a few days' vacation twice a year in the Philippines or on the almost unspoiled beaches of Tierra del Fuego.

Once or twice his Dad gave him a hard time, but Scott said, "Look, I have a social conscience even if you don't. What did you ever do except be a drag to the community? You know what I'm doing? I'm saving the community forty big ones a year. That's right. If I would have kept on housebreaking, it would have cost them *twice* as much as they're paying me, for the salaries of cops, and the trial, and the cost of keeping me in the slammer. So you go ahead and collect your pension, but don't tell me what to do."

There were two hitches now: one was that he couldn't commit any felony without winding up in the SWOB or the Injection Chamber, and the other was that he didn't just have to go to jail every Friday, he had to spend the night in a canvas sling suspended over a latrine, with nothing but a narrow concrete ledge for his feet. It was pretty bad, but you could get used to anything, and he developed a scornful attitude to the punk kids he saw around, with their Temporaries and Super Macs.

In the spring of 2014 he met a man named Henry Martin in a night club. Martin was a big man in his fifties who smoked long Cuban cigars; you could tell by the way the waiters hovered around him that he was somebody important. "I like you, kid," he said. "You want to work for me? I need a gofer—you know, go for this, go for that? Get it?" He laughed heartily. "Come on home with me, see if you like my place." When they left the club, Scott saw him pay with a gold card: he knew that meant Murder One or better.

He took the job and moved into Martin's spacious condo. Three times a week, Scott drove him down to the Correctional Facility and picked him up bleary-eyed in the morning. The rest of the week, Martin lived like a prince; he had the best of everything, wines, food, women. Scott's duties were nothing much; Martin really just wanted somebody to be around, somebody to talk to if he woke up in the middle of the night.

One evening, in Martin's playroom, they watched an old flat-film about Chicago gangsters. Martin was vastly amused by the careening automobiles full of men spraying bullets from submachine guns. "Look at those suckers!" he said. "Look at the risk they're taking! You could get *killed* doing that!" And he liked this sentence so much that he kept saying it over: "You could get killed doing that!"

Then there was the time they drove out to Jackson and lectured to the loonies. It was the day after Martin's third night in the slammer that week, and he was feeling low. Martin did the talking. Scott stood behind him and tried to look mean. The loonies were gray-haired men and women in bathrobes, most of them writers and poets—a few water-color artists and like that, but the big painters and sculptors were somewheres else, it was too crowded for them here.

Martin talked about his first and only crime, the killing of a man named Friedrichs in Detroit twenty-five years ago. "You got to understand," he said, "I seen what the choice was. I could of gone for something easy, something simple, like jacking a freight. Lots of guys went that route, I'm not saying nothing against them.

They're comfortable, they don't never get the finer things in life, but they're where they want to be. Me, I wanted the best. That was my choice." He paused. "Yeah? You in the front there."

"How did you commit the act?" asked the old guy who had raised his hand.

"I done it with a carpenter's hammer," said Martin proudly. "Twenty ounces of steel with a twelve-inch handle. I had it up my sleeve, see, and I waited my chance. I waited till he was just lifting his drink, and I made like I was getting up to go to the donniker, and then I just let that hammer slide down my sleeve like this— and I went *whock* like that, right in the back of his head. Brains and blood all over my arm. He fell out of that chair, and he was dead. That was the end of that."

"How did you feel?" asked another of the loonies.

"I was sick to my stomach. What do you want, I had just taken the life of another human being. All right, I never liked Friedrichs. Who could like him, he was a son of a bitch. But he was a man, a grown man, forty-seven years old, and he was alive until I swung that hammer. The next day he was in the incinerator. I felt the jolt when the hammer hit his head. I'll never forget it. That will be with me till the day I die."

On the way home they stopped off at a Turkish bath, and Scott had a glimpse of Martin's naked body for the first time. Afterward Martin saw something in his expression. "You want to know why?" Martin looked at him curiously. "All right. Come here." He led Scott into another room and turned on the light. "Okay, look." He whipped away his towel and turned to show Scott his sagging buttocks and lower back stippled with red dots in a regular pattern.

Martin turned. "Enough? Now you know?"

"No, Henry, what is it?"

Martin put the towel around him again. "You couldn't handle it," he said around his cigar.

"Couldn't handle what? What, Henry?"

"Believe me, kid, in this life you pay for what you get. Those loonies we seen today, they get taken care of, right, they have all the time they want for their poetry or whatever, but they pay for it—they're locked up in there for their whole life. That's their decision. You want less, you pay less. You think you're a tough guy," Martin said. "They put you in a sling over a shithole, right? Well, get this, sonny. For me, they put nails in the sling."

"I could have been like you," Scott said after a moment.

"You made your choice. You made your choice. We can't all be alike. Remember that—you pay for what you get." He slapped the younger man on the shoulder. "Come on, let's get out of here. I'm tired. Let's go home."

THE OTHER
FOOT

....
....
....
....

With one exception, all the stories in this book are short; some might be
described as extremely short.

    The exception is "The Other Foot," which is quite long; in fact, it is
a novella. It is here for two very good reasons: the first is that if it were
not here the book would not be long enough, and the second is that it is
my darling.

    Other novellas of mine have been reprinted over and over, but this
one never, and I have been aching to get it back in print in its original
form, because I love it more than all the rest.

I

As the Flugbahn car began to slide away from the landing platform, the biped Fritz clutched the arms of his seat and looked
nervously down through the transparent wall.

    He was unused to travel. Except for the trip by spaceship to
Earth, which he hardly remembered, he had lived all his life in the
Hamburg Zoo. Although he was sure the suspended car would
not fall, the feeling of being so high, and surrounded by nothing
but glass, made him want to grip something for security.

    In the seat beside him, his keeper, a stupid man named Alleks,
was unfolding the crisp parchment sheets of the Berliner Zeitung.

The breath whistled in his hairy nostrils as he gazed cow-eyed at the headlines. Down the aisle, the other passengers were all staring at Fritz, but, being used to this, the biped hardly noticed it.

Below, Berlin was spread out in the morning sun like a richly faded quilt. Looking back, as the car began to fall with increasing speed, Fritz could see the high platform where the Hamburg rocket-copter had landed, and the long spidery cables of the other Flugbahnen radiating outward to the four quarters of the city.

The car swooped, rose, checked at a station platform. The doors opened and closed again, then they were falling once more. At the second stop, Alleks folded his paper and got up. "Come," he said.

Fritz followed him onto the platform, then into an elevator that dropped, in a dizzying fashion, through a transparent spiral tube, down, down and down, while the sunlit streets flowed massively upward. They got off into a bewildering crowd and a sharp chemical odor. Alleks, with a firm grip on the biped's arm, propelled him down the street, through a high open doorway, then into another elevator and finally into an office full of people.

"My dear young sir," said a red-faced fat man, advancing jovially, "come in, come in. Allow me to introduce myself, I am Herr Doktor Grück. And you are our new biped? Welcome, welcome!" He took the biped's three-fingered hand and shook it warmly, showing no distaste at the fact that it was covered with soft, feathery-feeling spines.

Other people were crowding around, some aiming cameras. "Sign," said Alleks, holding out a dog-eared notebook.

Dr. Grück took the notebook absently, scribbled, handed it back. Alleks turned indifferently and was gone. "Gentlemen and ladies," said Grück in a rich tenor, "I have the honor to introduce to you our newest acquisition, Fritz—our *second* Brecht Biped— and you see that he is a male!"

The biped darted nervous glances around the oak-paneled room, at the whirring cameras, the bookshelves, the massive chandelier, the people with their naked pink faces. His body was slight and supple, like that of a cat or a rooster. The grayish-green, cactus-like spines covered him all over, except for the pinkish sacs that swung between his thighs. His odd-shaped head was neither human, feline nor avian, but something like all three. Above the eyes, in the middle of his wide sloping forehead, was a round wrinkled organ of a dusty red-purple color, vaguely suggestive of a cock's comb, in shape more like a withered fruit.

"A word for the newscast!" called some of the people with cameras.

Obediently, as he had been taught, the biped recited, "How do you do, gentlemen and ladies? Fritz, the biped, at your service. I am happy to be here and I hope you will come to see me often at the Berlin Zoo." He finished with a little bow.

Three white-smocked men stepped forward; the first bowed, took the biped's hand. "Wenzl, head keeper." He was bony and pale, with a thin straight mouth. The next man advanced, bowed, shook hands. "Rausch, dietitian." He was blonder and ruddier than Grück, with eyelashes almost white in a round, serious face. The third: "Prinzmetal, veterinary surgeon." He was dark and had sunken cheeks.

Dr. Grück beamed, his red face as stretched and shiny as if cooked in oil. His round skull was almost bald, but the blond hair, cut rather long, still curled crisply above his ears. His little blue eyes gleamed behind the rimless glasses. His body, round and firm as a rubber ball under the wide brown waistcoat and the gold watch chain, radiated joy. "What a specimen!" he said, taking the biped's jaw in one hand to open the mouth. "See the dentition!" The biped's "teeth" were two solid pieces of cartilaginous tissue, with chisel-shaped cutting edges. He broke free nervously after a moment, clacking his wide jaws and shaking his head.

"Halt, Fritz!" said Grück, seizing him to turn him around. "See the musculature—perfect! The integument! The color! Never, I promise you, even on Brecht's Planet, would you find such a biped. And he is already sexually mature," said Grück, probing with his fat hand between Fritz's legs. "Perfect! You would like to meet a female biped, would you not, Fritz?"

The biped blinked and said haltingly, "My mother was a female biped, honored sir."

"Ha ha!" said Grück, full of good humor. "So she was! Correct, Fritz!" Rausch smiled; Prinzmetal smiled; even Wenzl almost smiled. "Come then, first we will show you your quarters, and afterward—perhaps a surprise!"

Picking up his shiny new valise, the biped followed Grück and the others out of the office, along a high, glass-walled corridor that overlooked the grounds with their scattered cages. People walking on the gravel paths looked up and began to point excitedly. Grück, in the lead, bowed and waved benignly down to them.

Inside, they emerged in an empty hall. Wenzl produced a magnetic key to open a heavy door with a small pane of wired glass set into it. Inside, they found themselves in a small but conveniently arranged room, with walls and floor of distempered concrete, a couch which could be used for sitting or sleeping, a chair and table, some utensils, a washbowl and toilet. "Here is the bedroom," said Dr. Grück with a sweeping gesture. "And here—" he led the way through a doorless opening— "your personal living room." The outer wall was of glass, through which, behind an iron railing, they saw a crowd of people. The room was larger and more nicely furnished than the one inside. The floor was tiled and polished. The walls were painted. There was a comfortable relaxing chair, a television, a little table with some magazines and newspapers on it, a large potted plant, even a shelf full of books.

"And now for the surprise!" cried Dr. Grück. Brushing the others aside, he led the way again through the bedroom, to another doorless opening in the far wall. The room beyond was much larger, with a concrete floor on which, however, some rubber mats had been laid, and two desks with business machines, filing cabinets, wire baskets, telephones, a pencil sharpener, a pneumatic conveyor and piles of documents.

Across the room, beside one of the filing cabinets which had an open drawer, someone turned and looked at them in surprise. It was another biped, smaller and more faintly colored than Fritz. Of the other differences, the most notable was the organ in the middle of her forehead, which, unlike Fritz's, was developed into a large, eggshaped red-purple ball or knob. "Now the surprise!" cried Dr. Grück. "Fritz, here stands Emma, your little wife!"

With a faint shriek, the other biped clapped her hands over her head and scurried out of the room, leaving a storm of dropped papers to settle behind her.

Fritz sat in his relaxing chair, staring disconsolately out through the glass at the darkening air of the Zoo grounds. It was late afternoon. The Zoo was about to close, and the paths were almost deserted.

"That takes time," Dr. Grück had said heartily, patting him on the shoulder. "Rest, get acquainted, tomorrow is better. Fritz, good afternoon!"

Left alone, curious and vaguely excited, he had poked all around the work room, examining papers and opening drawers, then had wandered over to the doorway of the room into which Emma had disappeared. But no sooner had he put his nose timidly inside than her voice piped, "Go away! Go away, go away, go *away!*"

Since then there had been silence from the room next to his. At feeding time Wenzl had come in with a cart, had left one tray for him, another for Emma. But although he listened intently, he had not heard a sound of knife or fork, or a glass set down.

It was exciting to think of having another biped to talk to. It was not right for her to refuse to talk to him. Why should she want to make him miserable?

As he stared through the window, his eye met that of a dark-haired young man who had paused outside. The man was carrying a camera and looked vaguely familiar. Perhaps he had been one of the reporters. He was slight and stooped, with very pale, clear skin and large soft eyes. As they looked wordlessly at each other, Fritz felt an abrupt slipping and sliding, the room whirled around him.

He struggled to get up from the floor. He could not understand what had happened to him, why it was suddenly so dark, why the room had grown so large. Then he squirmed up to hands and knees, and discovered that he was looking across an iron railing, through a window into a little lighted room in which a biped lay half sprawled in a chair, looking back at him with glazed eyes and making feeble motions with his arms.

The afternoon breeze was crisp and sibilant along the path. There were smells of damp earth and of animals. Gravel crunched beside him, and a courteous voice said, "Is anything wrong, good sir?"

The biped in the lighted room was floundering across the floor. Now he was beating with both hands on the glass, and his mouth opened and shut, opened and shut.

"You have dropped your camera," said the same voice. "Allow me." Someone's hands were patting him, with a curious muffled feeling, and he turned to glimpse a kindly, mustached face. Then something glittering was being thrust at him and he stared, with a kind of disbelieving wonder, as his hands closed automatically around the camera . . . his pink, hairy, five-fingered hands, with their pale fingernails.

II

Dr. Grück was alone in his office, with some preliminary budget figures spread out on his desk, and the greasy remains of a knackwurst dinner on a little table beside him. Wearing his reading spectacles, he looked like a rosy, good-humored old uncle out of Dickens. His little blue eyes blinked mildly behind the spectacles, and when he counted, his sausage-fat thumb and fingers went *eins, zwei, drei.*

Humming, he turned a paper over. The melody he was humming was *I Lost My Sock in Lauterbach.*

The paneled room was warm, comfortable and silent. "And without my sock, I won't go home," hummed the Director.

The little desk visiphone flickered to life suddenly, and the tiny face in the screen said, "Doctor, if you please—"

Grück frowned slightly, and pressed the stud. "Yes, Freda?"

"Herr Wenzl wishes to speak with you, he says it is urgent."

"Well then, if it's urgent, Freda, put him on."

"Thank you, Doctor."

The screen flickered again. Wenzl's pale, fanatical face appeared. "Trouble with the new biped," he began immediately.

Grück took his glasses off. "The mischief!" he said. "What sort of trouble, Wenzl?"

"Ten minutes ago," said the head keeper, "I was notified that Fritz was making a disturbance in his cage. I went there, and found he had been trying to break the window with a wooden chair."

"Terrible, but why?" cried Dr. Grück, his jowls wobbling.

"I endeavored to calm Fritz," continued Wenzl, "but he informed me that I was without authority over him, since he was not Fritz, but a journalist named Martin Naumchik."

Grück pursed his lips several times, unconsciously forming the syllable "Num." He found some papers under his hand, looked at them in surprise, then pushed them aside with hasty, abstracted motions.

"He also told me," said Wenzl, "that Fritz had gone off in his body, with his camera and all his clothes."

Grück put both palms on his cheeks and stared at Wenzl's image. In the little screen, Wenzl looked like a portrait doll made by someone with an unpleasant turn of fantasy. Full-sized, Wenzl was really not so bad. He had a mole, there were hairs in his nostrils, one saw his adam's apple move when he spoke. But at the size of a doll, he was unbearable.

"What steps have you taken?" Grück asked.

"Restraint," said Wenzl.

"And your opinion?"

"The animal is psychotic."

Grück closed his eyes, pinched the bridge of his nose between thumb and finger for a moment. He opened his eyes, settled himself before the desk. "Wenzl," he said, "the biped is not necessarily psychotic. In our ten years with Emma, we have also seen some little fits of nerves, not so? As for Fritz, possibly he is only frightened, being in a new Zoo. Perhaps he wants reassurance, to dramatize himself a little, who knows? Can you show me in the handbooks where it says a biped goes psychotic?"

Wenzl was silent and did not change expression.

"No," said Grück. "So let's not be hasty, Wenzl. Remember that Fritz at present is our most valuable animal. Kindness, that does more than harsh words and beatings. A little sympathy, perhaps a smile—" He smiled, showing his small, blunt teeth as far back as the molars. "So, Wenzl? Yes?"

"You are always right, Doctor," said the head keeper sourly.

"Good, then we shall see. Go and talk to him reasonably, Wenzl; take off the jacket, and if he is calm, bring him to me."

"I will give you five reasons why I am Martin Naumchik," said the biped in a high, furious voice. His naked, green-spined body looked slender and fragile in the dark wooden chair. He leaned over the table toward Wenzl and Dr. Grück; his eyes were pink-rimmed, and the wide lipless mouth kept opening and closing.

"First, I know Berlin, whereas your menagerie animal has never been here before, and certainly never had liberty to roam the streets. Ask me anything you like. Second, I can tell you the names of the editor, managing editor and all the rest of the staff of *Paris-Soir*; I can repeat my last dispatch to them word for word, or nearly. If you give me a typewriter I'll even write it out. Third—"

"But, my dear Fritz—" said Grück, spreading his fat pink hands, with an ingratiating smile.

"*Third*," repeated the biped angrily, "my girl-friend, Julia Schorr, will vouch for me. She lives at number forty-one, Heinrichstrasse, flat seventeen, her visi number is UNter den Linden 8-7403. I can also tell you that she keeps a Siamese cat named Maggie and that she cooks very good spaghetti. My God, if it comes to that, I can tell you what kind of underclothing she wears. Fourth, you can examine my yourselves; I took a degree at the Sorbonne in 1999—ask about literature, mathematics, history, whatever you like! Fifth and last, I *am* Martin Naumchik, I have always been Martin Naumchik, I never even saw this ridiculous biped of yours until today, and if you don't help me, I promise you, I'll make such a stench . . ."

He fell silent. "Well?"

Grück and Wenzl exchanged glances. "My dear young sir," said Grück, rumpling his untidy blond hair; his little eyes were squeezed together in a frown. "My dear young sir, you have convinced me, beyond any shadow of doubt—" the biped started eagerly—"that you believe yourself to be one Martin Naumchik, a human being, and a correspondent for *Paris-Soir*, and so on, and so on."

The biped said in a choked voice. "Believe! But I've *told* you—"

"Please!" Grück held up his hand. "Have the politeness to listen. I say that there is no doubt, no *possible* doubt, that you believe in what you say. Very good! Now. Allow me to ask you this question." He folded his hands over his paunch, and his rosy lips shaped themselves into a smile.

"Suppose that you *are* Martin Naumchik." He waved his hand generously. "Go on. Suppose it, I make no objection. Very well, now you are Martin Naumchik. What is the result?"

He leaned forward and stared earnestly at the biped. Wenzl, beside him, was grimly silent.

"Why, you release me," said the biped uncertainly. "You help me find that animal who has got into my body, and somehow—in some way—"

"Yes?" said Dr. Grück encouragingly. "Somehow—in some way—"

"There must be some way," said the biped miserably.

Grück leaned back, shaking his head. "To make you change around again? My dear young sir, reflect a moment on what you are saying. To put a man's mind back in his body after it has gone into the body of an animal? Let's not be children! The thing is impossible, to begin with! You know it as well as I do! Supposing that it has actually happened once, still it's just as impossible as before! My dear young sir! To put a man's mind back in his body? How? With a funnel?"

The biped was leaning his head on his green-spined hand. "If we could find out why it happened—" he muttered.

"Good, yes," said Grück sympathetically. "A very good suggestion: that is what we must do, by all means. Courage, Fritz, or Martin, as the case may be! This will take time, we must be prepared to wait. Patience and courage, eh, Fritz?"

The biped nodded, looking exhausted.

"Good, then it's understood," said Grück cheerfully, getting up. "We shall do everything we can, you may be quite sure of that, and in the meantime—" he motioned toward Wenzl, who had also risen, "a little cooperation, no trouble for poor Wenzl. Agreed, Fritz?"

"You're going to keep me here? On display?" cried the biped, stiffening again with indignation.

"For the present," said Grück soothingly. "After all, what choice have we got? To begin with, where would you go? How would you live? Slowly, we must go slowly, Fritz. Take an older man's advice, haste can be the ruin of everything. Slowly, slowly, Fritz, patience and courage—"

Wenzl took the biped's slender arm and began to guide him out of the room. "My name is Martin Naumchik," he muttered weakly as he disappeared.

The dim gray light of early morning flooded the outer rooms, illuminating everything but emphasizing nothing. For some reason—the biped had noticed it before—it made you see the undersides of things more than usual, the loose dingy cloth hanging under the seat of a chair, the grime and dust in corners, the ordinarily inconspicuous streaks, smears, scratches.

He prowled restlessly down the corridor, past the closed doorway of the next room—the female had apparently upended a table against it—into the fluorescent-lit office space with its hooded machines, then back again. In his own inner room he caught sight of an ugly face in the mirror—greenish and flat-muzzled, like an impossible hybrid of dog and cock—and for a horrible instant did not realize it was his own.

He clutched at the wall and began to weep. Strangled, inhuman sounds came out of his throat.

Ten hours, ten hours or more, it must be. Just around supper time it had happened, and now it was past dawn. Ten hours, and he still wasn't used to it, it was harder to bear than ever.

He had to get out.

The biped's little valise was standing on the floor of the inner room near the washbowl. He pounced on it, ripped it open, flung the contents around. Toothbrush, chess set, some cheap writing paper, a dog-eared paperbound book called *Brecht's Planet: Riddle of the Universe;* nothing useful. Weeping, he ran into the office room and snatched up the telephone receiver. The line was still dead. Probably it was not linked into the Zoo switchboard this early in the morning. What else?

He caught sight of one of the typewriters, stopped in surprise, then sat down before it and took the cover off.

There was paper in a drawer. He rolled a sheet into the platen, switched the machine on, and sat for a moment anxiously gripping his three-fingered hands together.

The words took shape in his mind: *My name is Martin Naumchik. I am being held prisoner in . . .*

His hands stabbed at the keyboard, and the type bars piled up against the guide with a clatter and a snarl; the carriage jumped over and the paper leaped up a space.

The pain of realization was so great that he instinctively tried to bite his lip. He felt the stiff flesh move numbly, sliding against his teeth. Biting his lip was one of the things he could not do now. And typing was another.

It was too much. He would never get used to it. He would always forget, and be snubbed up like an animal at the end of a chain . . .

After a moment, half-blinded by tears, he pried at the jammed

keys until they fell back. Then, painfully, picking out the letters
with one finger, he began again: "My name is M . . ."

In half an hour, he had finished his account of the facts. Next
it would be necessary to establish his identity. Perhaps that should
come first, or the story would never even be read. He took a fresh
sheet, and wrote:

M. Frédéric Stein
PARIS-SOIR
98, rue de la Victoire
Paris 9e (Seine)

Dear Frédéric:

You will know the enclosed is really from me by the
following: When I was last in Paris, you and I went to the
Rocking Horse and got tanked on mint whistles. There were
three greenies in the jug. You told me about certain troubles
with your wife, and we discussed your taking a correspondent's job in the Low Countries.

This is not a joke; I need your help—in God's name, do
whatever

He paused, and over the machine's hum was lucky enough to
hear the whisper of footsteps in the corridor. He had barely time
to turn off the machine, cover it and hide the typed pages in a
drawer.

A young keeper with a sullen, pimpled face came in, wheeling
a cart with two steaming trays. It was breakfast time.

His first day as a caged animal was about to begin.

III

Here in the middle of the city, the streets were as bright as if it
were day. Over the tesselated pavements people were wandering.

Music drifted seductively from an open doorway; all the scarlet blossoms of the Antarean airweed, clinging to the sides of the buildings, were open and exuding a fresh pungence.

In one of the brilliant display windows, as he passed, the young man saw a row of green creatures in glass cages—sluggish globular animals about the size of a tomato, with threads of limbs and great dull green eyes. They floated on the green-scummed surface of the shallow water in the cages, or climbed feebly on bits of wet bark. Over them was a streamer: TAKE A WOG HOME TO THE CHILDREN.

He passed on. The people around him, moving in groups and couples for the most part, were a different sort than he was used to seeing at the Zoo in Hamburg. They were better dressed, better fed, their skins were clearer and redder and they laughed more. The women were confections of white-blond hair and red cheeks, with sparkling white teeth and flashing nails, and they wore puffed, shining garments like the glittering paper around an expensive gift. The men were more austere in dark, dull reds and blues. Their feet were thinly shod in gleaming patent leather, and their hair shone with pomade. Their talk, in the unfamiliar Berlin accent, eddied around him: confident tones, good humor, barks of laughter.

Very faintly, beneath his feet, the star mosaic of the pavement shook to the passage of an express car underneath. Here above-ground everyone was on foot. There was no wheeled vehicle in sight, not even an aircar: only the bright thread of one of the Flugbahnen visible in the distance.

Around the corner, in a little square surrounding the heroic anodized aluminum figure of a man in spaceman's dress, helmet off, an exultant expression on his metal face, the young man saw a tall illuminated panel on the side of a building. Luminous words were shuddering slowly down the panel, line by line. The young man moved closer, through the loose crowd of bystanders, and read:

INTERPLANET LINER CRASHES ON MARS;
ALL BELIEVED DEAD
Passenger list to follow.

MOVING-MACHINE THIEVES COMMIT ANOTHER
OUTRAGE IN BERLIN
"Will be brought to justice," vows Funk

HIGH ASSEMBLY VOTES TO ANNEX
THIESSEN'S PLANET
Vote is 1150 for to 139 against

SPACE STOCKS CLOSE AT RECORD HIGH
Society for Spaceflight, I.C.S.S.A. lead advance

READ FULL DETAILS IN
THE BERLINER ZEITUNG

The letters drifted down, like tongues of cold flame, and were followed by an advertisement for Heineken's beer.

The young man turned away, having read all the headlines with appreciation but without any interest whatever; he walked further down the street and gazed in fascination at the marquee of a cinema, where through some illusion brightly colored ten-foot figures of men and women seemed to be dancing. Even here he could not give his full attention. He was bothered, and increasingly so, by certain demands of his body.

He had an insistent urge to tear off the muffling, unfamiliar garments he was wearing, but realized it would attract attention to himself, and besides, this bald body would probably be cold. He had not realized that a simple thing like this could become so difficult. At home in the Zoo he had had his own little w.c., and that was that. People must have theirs, but where? What did people do who were strangers in Berlin? He looked around. He did not see a policeman, but a woman who was passing with her escort paused, looking at him, and on an impulse he stepped forward and said politely, "Pardon me, madam, but can you direct me to the w.c.?"

Her face registered first surprise, then shock, and she turned to her companion, saying angrily, "Come on, he's drunk." They walked rapidly away, the man's scowling face turned over his shoulder. The word "Disgraceful!" floated back.

Surprised and hurt, the young man stood for a moment watching them out of sight; then he turned in the opposite direction.

The place he was passing now was called "Konstantin's Café." The sight of people sitting at tables, visible through the big window, reminded him that he was hungry and thirsty. After a moment's hesitation, he went in.

A slender red-jacketed waiter met him alertly in the foyer. "Yes, sir? A table for one?"

"Yes, if you like," said the young man. The waiter hesitated, glancing at him oddly, then turned through the archway. "Come this way, sir."

The young man gave his surcoat and camera to a girl who asked for them. Inside, waiters in red jackets were moving like ants among the snowy tabletops; the room was crowded with rich silks and velvets of all colors, flushed clean faces, smiling mouths; unfamiliar smells of food swam in the air. The thick carpet muffled all footsteps, but there was a heavy burden of voices, clattering silverware, and music from some invisible source.

A little intimidated by so much crowded luxury, the young man followed the waiter to a small table and sat down.

The waiter opened a stiff pasteboard folder with a snap and presented it; the young man took it automatically, and in a moment perceived that it was a list of foods.

"To begin with, an apéritif, sir?" asked the waiter. "Some hors-d'oeuvres? Or shall we say a salad?"

The young man blinked at the menu, then set it down. "No," he replied, "but—"

"Just the dinner, then, sir," said the waiter briskly. "If the

gentleman will permit, I recommend the truite au beurre cano-
péen, with a Moselle, very good, sir."

"All right," the young man said hesitantly, "but first—"

"Ah, an apéritif, after all?" asked the waiter, smiling with annoyance. "Some hors-d'oeuvres? Or—"

"No, I don't wish any of those, thank you," said the young
man, making a clumsy gesture and oversetting a goblet.

"But then, what is it that the gentleman wishes?" The waiter
righted the goblet, brushed at the tablecloth, stood back.

The young man blinked slowly. "I wish for you to direct me
to the w.c., if you would be so kind."

He half expected the waiter to react like the woman in the
street, but the man's keen face only closed expressionlessly, and
he leaned down to murmur, "The doorway behind the curtain at
the rear, sir."

"Thank you, you are very kind."

"Not at all, sir." The waiter went away. The young man got up
and went in the indicated direction. Although he tried to move
carefully, he was still very clumsy in his body, and sometimes
would forget and pause between steps to try to shake off one of
his shoes. When he did this, he noticed that some of the diners
looked at him strangely. He determined to break the habit as
soon as possible.

When he returned, after some trouble with the unfamiliar
fastenings, the waiter was just removing from a little silver cart a
covered platter, which he placed on the table and unveiled with
a flourish. The young man sat down. The waiter took a slender
bottle from the cart, uncorked it, poured a pale liquid into the
goblet and stood back expectantly.

The young man looked at his plate.

The food steamed gently; there were five or six different
things, each of its own color, beautifully arranged on the platter.
He had never seen any of them before, except possibly in magazines, and all the smells were unfamiliar. Nevertheless, he picked
up his fork and pried at the largest object, a roughly oval burnt-
brown mass which came away flakily, running with juices. He put

the fork in his mouth on the second try. The food was a moist, unpleasant lump on his tongue: the taste was so startling that he immediately turned his head and spat it out.

The waiter looked down at the carpet, then at the young man. Then he went away.

The young man was gingerly trying some light green strips, which he found unusual but palatable, when the waiter came back. "Sir, the manager would like to speak with you, if you please." He gestured toward the foyer.

"Oh? With me?" The young man stood up agreeably, upsetting the goblet again. The pale liquid ran over the tablecloth and began to drip onto the carpet. "I am so sorry," he said, and began to mop at it with his napkin.

"It's of no consequence," said the waiter grimly, and took the young man by the arm. "If you *please*, sir."

In the foyer they met another waiter, who took his other arm. Someone handed him his surcoat and camera. Together the two waiters began to propel him toward the exit.

The young man craned his head around. "The manager?" he asked.

"The manager," said the first waiter, "wishes you to leave quietly, without disturbance, sir."

"But I haven't yet paid for my food," said the young man.

"There is no charge, sir," said the waiter, and they were at the door. The two gave him a last push. He was in the street.

In the men's room of a pfennig gallery, a little later (at least he was becoming adept at finding w.c.'s), the young man was examining the contents of his pockets. He discovered that he was Martin Naumchik, European citizen, born Asnieres (Seine) 1976, complexion fair, eyes brown, hair brown, no arrest record, no curtailment of citizenship, no identifying marks or scars, employed by Paris-Soir, 98 rue de la Victoire, Paris (9e); that he had a driver's license, a Cordon Bleu diner's card, a press card in five languages and a notebook full of penciled scribbling which he could not read. In his billfold were forty marks, and in the pockets

of his trousers, jacket and surcoat some coins amounting to another two or three marks. That was all, except some ticket stubs,
a key on a gold ring, tissues, pocket lint, a half-empty pack of
cigarettes, and a crumpled envelope, addressed to Herr Martin
Naumchik, 67, Gastnerstrasse, Berlin.

The young man had partially satisfied his hunger with two
sausages on rolls, bought at a stall near the gallery, but he was
tired, lonely and bewildered. At that moment he would have been
glad to go back to the Zoo, but he had lost his directions and did
not know where it was. He left the gallery and moved on down
the street.

The cinema beckoned to him with the open wings of its lobby
and the gigantic displays on either side: figures of men and
women, glossy leaves, planets floating in a violet-gray sky. Illuminated signs announced:

Experience new sensations!
Unprecedented excitement!

UNDER SEVEN MOONS
Stella Pain—Willem DeGroot
"Indescribable!"—Tageblatt.

The price was two marks ten. The young man paid, took his
ticket and went in. A few people were standing about in the
anteroom, talking and smoking. There were exotic fruits and confections for sale at a long counter, and rows of automatic machines for drinks, candy, tissues. The young man gave his ticket
to the turnstile machine at the door, got a stub back and found
himself in a huge well of darkened seats, lit only by faint glimmers
from the distant walls. Here and there, around the vast bowl,
clumps of people were sitting. Three-quarters of the seats were
empty. There was very little noise, no one was talking or moving,
evidently the show had not yet begun. The young man groped his
way down the aisle, chose a seat and unfolded it. The instant he

settled down and put his hands on the armrests, sound and motion exploded around him.

He sprang up convulsively, into darkness and silence. The
huge almost empty bowl of the theater was just as it had been
before: the flashing phantom shapes he had seen were nowhere.

After a moment, cautiously, he touched one of the armrests
again. Nothing happened. The other armrest. Still nothing. Gingerly and with trepidation, he unfolded the seat and lowered
himself into it.

Again the sudden blast of light and sound. This time he
glimpsed figures, heard words spoken before he leaped upright
again.

All around him, the people were sitting in eerie, intent silence.
Then this must be how one saw a movie—not projected on a wall,
as he had always imagined, but somehow mysteriously existing
when one sat in the chair. Shaking with nervousness, but determined not to be a coward, he sat down once more and gripped
the armrests hard.

Light and sensation surrounded him. He was seeing the upper
portions of two gigantic humans, a female and a male, against a
violet sky in which two moons shone dimly. Simultaneously there
was a grinding, insistent roar of wind and the man's stentorian
voice bellowed out, "Gerda, you are mine!" His face stared into
hers, his strong brown hands gripped her bare arms while she
replied, "I know it, Friedrich." The words crashed into the young
man's eardrums like bombs. The two immense bodies were not far
away, at the end of the theater, but loomed before him almost
close enough to touch. They glowed with color, not a natural
color but something altogether different and arresting, luminous
pastel tones overlying shadows of glowing darkness, with a rather
disturbing suggestion of dead black in all the outlines, almost like
a colored engraving. They had depth but not reality, and yet they
were incredibly more than mere pictures. The young man realized, with a shock of surprise, that he could smell the cold salt air
and that without knowing in the least how, he was aware of the

very *texture* of the giant woman's skin—smooth and waxy, like a soft artificial fruit—and of the cat-smelling tawny softness of her long blond hair whipping in the wind, and the hard-edged glossy stiffness of the green leaves in the near background.

"Gerda!" roared the man.

"Friedrich!" she trumpeted sadly.

Then without moving a muscle the two of them vertiginously receded, as if an invisible car were drawing them rapidly away, and as they dwindled, standing and staring at one another, green-leaved shrubs gathered in to fill the space, and the sky somehow grew bigger—there were *three* moons drifting with a perceptible motion through the violet sky—and at that moment with a thunderous rushing sound, the rain began. Dry as he sat there, the young man could feel the streaming wetness pelting the leaves; it was lukewarm. Music skirled up in wild dissonances, lightning cracked the sky apart and thunder boomed.

It was too much.

The young man stood up, trembling all over. Sight, touch and sound vanished instantly. He was alone in the vast theater with the silent, motionless people who sat in darkness.

He moved shakily to the aisle and went out, grateful for the quiet and the sense of being alone in his skin again. He was sorry to have given up so quickly, but consoled himself with the thought that it was his first time. Later, perhaps, he would grow used to it.

At a kiosk in the middle of the street, newspapers and magazines were on sale in metal dispensers. Beside this stood a dirty small boy and an old gray woman, with a portable teleset tuned to a popular singer. The little boy was singing harmony with him, badly, in a strained soprano. There were coins scattered on the little folding table in front of the teleset. Farther along, two drunken and disheveled men were scuffing ineffectually, grabbing at each other's surcoats for balance. A brightly painted woman giggled, but most people paid no attention. Three dark young men walked by abreast, scowling, with identical dark long surcoats and oiled forelocks. Tall cold-light signs over the building blinked, MOBIL, TELEFUNKEN, KRUPP-FARBEN. The young man moved through the crowd, listening to the voices and the snatches of music from open doorways, looking at faces, pausing to stare at the glittering merchandise in shop windows.

When he had been walking in the same direction for some time, he came upon a store which seemed to fill an entire square of its own, with many busy entrances and rows of brilliantly lighted display windows. The name, in tall cold-light letters over each entrance, was "ELEKTRA." For want of any other direction, the young man drifted in with the crowd.

Inside, the store appeared to be one gigantic room, high-ceilinged, echoing, glittering everywhere with reflected lights. Banks of brightly illuminated display cases were ranged in parallel lines, leaving aisles between. In open spaces were statues, great flowering plants, constructions of golden and white metal. The murmuring of the crowd washed back from the distant ceiling: up there, the young man noticed, were fiery trails of light, red, green, blue, amber, that pulsed and seemed to travel along the ceiling like the exhausts of rockets. The air was heavy with women's mingled scents and with other, unidentifiable odors; there was quiet music in the background, and a faint, multiple clicking or clattering sound.

The young man went in tentatively, listening and watching. A woman and an older man were standing by the entrance to one of the aisles, arguing vehemently in low, crisp voices; the young man caught the words, "Twenty millions at the minimum." A child in a red coat was crying, being dragged along by an angry woman. A man in dark-blue uniform went hurrying by, the trousers snapping about his ankles.

There were signs in colored lights on the ceiling; a red one said "MEN'S WEAR" and a red trail went pulsing off from it; another, blue, said "WATCHES AND JEWELRY"; another, green, "CAMERAS."

The young man followed the green trail, fascinated. Lines of people, most of them women, were moving slowly along the row of showcases. Here and there, the young man saw someone put money into one of the cases, open the glass front and take out a blouse or an undergarment, a pair of stockings, a scarf.

The young man had never seen so many beautiful things in one place. Here he was now in a whole corridor lined with nothing but cameras, hundreds of cameras, all achingly polished and bright; the winking reflections from their round eyes of metal and glass followed him as he walked. He actually saw a man buy one: a huge thing, big as the man's head, with pale leather sides and a complexity of lens tubes, dials, meters. The man held it reverently in his hands, staring at it as if at a loved one's face. As the glass door closed, a mechanism slowly revolved and another camera, just like the first, descended to fill the empty case. As the customer walked away, the young man looked at the price on the chrome rim of the showcase: it was 700 marks. He looked again at the beautiful camera behind the glass door, then at the one which hung around his neck. It was smaller and the metal was not so bright; the black sides were worn in places, and it did not look so beautiful as it had before. The young man walked on, looking down at himself, and was aware that his dark surcoat was worn thin at the cuffs, his shoes needed polishing, there was lint and dust on his trousers.

So, then, it was not enough to be a human being! One must also have money. The young man vaguely supposed that if he had 700 marks, his head would not ache so, he would not have the uncomfortable feeling in his insides that was bothering him more and more, he would not be tired and irritable.

But he had not the least idea how people got money.

To make himself feel better, he stopped in the next section and bought a wristwatch with an expanding platinum band. He put a ten-mark bill into the slot. The mechanism hummed and gripped the ten marks, pulling it gradually inside until it was all gone; then there was a clatter in the receptacle underneath, and the glass door swung open. The young man took out his watch and admired it. The marvelous thing was already running, the

second hand sweeping silently around the black dial. He put it on
his wrist, first the wrong way around, then the right way. In the
receptacle were twenty-seven pfennigs in silver and copper. He
scooped them up. Above, the mechanism was revolving and another wristwatch came into view. The young man found that he
could not resist it. He put another ten marks into the machine,
receiving another wristwatch and another twenty-seven pfennigs
in change. He put the second watch on his other wrist. Now he
felt rich and handsome. He held out his arms stiffly, to make the
cuffs of his sleeves slide back so that he could admire his watches.
Both showed the identical time: 20 hours 13 minutes. Now he
would always be sure what time it was, because if the two watches
showed different times he would know one was wrong, but if the
same time, then they must be right.

Feeling pleased to have worked this out for himself, and to
have made so sound a purchase, he went on. In an open space at
the end of the aisle, he saw curved escalators rising in spirals past
the ceiling, and beyond them, banks of elevators with doors that
constantly opened and shut: click, a door was open, someone
stepped in, click, the door closed, and in an instant it had whisked
its passenger off and was open again.

Diagonally across the open space, he caught sight of another
group of illuminated trails on the ceiling, and it seemed to him
that one of them was labeled "Foods." He went that way eagerly,
and nearly knocked down a hatless man in blue uniform, who
frowned at him and said, "I beg your pardon, sir."

"No, I beg *your* pardon."

"Not at all, sir."

"It's very kind of you."

"An honor, sir."

They both bowed and went on their way. The young man
found that the sign did say "Foods." He followed its pink trail until
he came to a sunken area full of people with metal carts, the carts
loaded with packages. He went down the five or six steps, sniffing
the air, and found a new set of lighted trails that pointed to
"Canned Goods," "Perishables," "Meats" and so on. Passing

through "Canned Goods," he came upon a stout man in a plaid surcoat who was lifting a can out of an open case and putting it on top of three others just like it in a cart.

The young man paused to watch. The mechanism inside the case slowly revolved; another large, odd-shaped can came down into view, and now the young man could see that it was labeled "COPENHAGEN SMOKED HAM," with a picture of a slab of pink meat. The cover of the display case was still open. As soon as the mechanism stopped, the stout man reached in, took out the canned ham, and put it in his cart along with the other four. The mechanism began to revolve again. The stout buyer glanced over his shoulder at the young man, hesitated, then took out a sixth ham and put it with the other five. The mechanism revolved again. As far as the young man could make out, the stout man had not put in any money. Each time he removed a ham, the door swung down but did not latch. Then the stout man lifted it up again and reached for the next ham.

The buyer looked around again, glanced from side to side, and muttered, "Go on, get away, can't you see I'm busy?"

"I'm sorry," said the young man politely, "but I only wanted to be next for the hams."

The stout customer growled something, trying to look at the next ham and at the young man simultaneously.

"Pardon?"

"I said devil's dirt," the stout man growled more distinctly. The mechanism stopped; he reached in and took the seventh ham.

At that moment one of the blue-uniformed men appeared at the end of the aisle. The stout customer was holding the ham close to his chest. The blue-uniformed man turned toward them.

The stout customer wheeled abruptly, thrust the ham into the young man's arms, said petulantly, "Here, then," and walked rapidly away.

"One moment, please!" called the approaching blue-uniformed man.

Still moving rapidly away, and without turning his head, the stout man said something that sounded like, "Run, you fool!"

The man in the blue uniform took something out of his pocket. It was an electric bell, which began to ring insistently and loudly. Inside the display case, the mechanism was revolving, presenting another canned ham. The young man looked at it, then at the one he held, and felt a vague alarm. The stout man was moving faster; the one in blue uniform was waving and shouting. The young man turned and began to run, although he did not know why.

At the front of the food section, another blue-uniformed man was coming toward him from the left. The young man scrambled up the five steps, holding the canned ham awkwardly to his chest. The stout man was nowhere in sight.

"Stop!" called one of the blue-uniformed men. But the young man's heart was beating in unreasonable panic. He ran across the open space, dodging back and forth between shoppers' carts, pursued by shouts and the ringing of the bell. Another bell began to ring, somewhere off to his right, then a third. Utterly terrified, unaware of what he was doing, the young man dropped the ham on the floor and ran at a woman with a full cart, who shrieked and pushed it into another cart, upsetting both and spilling oranges like quicksilver on the floor. The young man ran past her, nearly falling, and found himself between two advancing men in blue, while before him was only a decorative grille of arabesques in gold-plated metal, which reached all the way to a balcony on the second level. With a gasp of fright, the young man flung himself at this grille and began to climb it. In spite of the clumsiness of his feet, which would not grip and could not even feel the metal, he was above the men's heads in a moment, and they shook their fists at him, shouting, "Despicable ruffian, come down here!"

The young man kept on climbing. Shortly, the people on the floor below were colorful dolls, many with faces turned to look up at him. One of the blue-uniformed men had begun to climb the grille, but now the young man was almost at the top.

He arrived at the top of the grille, and reaching up, found that he could grasp the railing of the balcony and swing himself up and over. Panting with exertion, he found himself in a narrow corridor, lined on the wall side with open doorways from which came the sounds of voices and the clicking of machines. A man stepped out of a doorway some distance down the corridor and craned his neck to listen to the sound of the bells. He turned, saw the young man. "Hi!" he called, starting forward.

The young man ran again. Faces turned, startled, inside the rooms as he passed; he caught glimpses of men and women in their blouse sleeves, of desks and office equipment. The next door was closed and was marked "Stair." The young man opened it, hesitated briefly between two narrow flights, then chose the up flight and went bounding up, three steps at a time, swinging around at each tiny landing until he grew dizzy. Below, voices echoed. He kept on going up past other landings and closed, dark doors, narrower and dingier, until he reached the top. The stairs ended at one last door, lit only by a grimy skylight through which filtered a dim violet glow.

The young man paused to listen. Deep down, there were tiny voices, like the chirping of insects under layer after layer of earth.

He opened the door and went in. He was on a floor of empty rooms, dark and gray with dust. Everything was much older and shabbier-looking than the glittering aisles downstairs. In the weak light from small pebble-glass windows, he saw goods piled in the corners of one room, a neglected huddle of filing cabinets in another. There was no one here. No one had come here for a long time.

At the end of the hall, half hidden by an ancient wardrobe, was another door, another stair, the narrowest and darkest of all—plain bare wood, that creaked under his steps as he went up. It was only one short flight, and at the top he found himself in a tiny room with slanting walls.

Bundles of papers lay piled on the floor, yellow and brittle under their coating of dust. There was a length of rope, an old light bulb or two, some shredded bits of paper that might have been gnawed by small animals. All this he saw in the dim, cool light from a triangular window under the peak of the roof. It was a wide window, framed in old ornate molding that filled almost the entire wall, and from it, when he had rubbed a clear space with his hand, he could see the city spread out below him.

Silent and empty it lay under the violet sky, all the buildings peacefully ranked one beyond another out to the misty horizon. Some of the building faces were illuminated by a glow of the avenues, but no sound came up from those lower levels. It was like a deserted city, whose inhabitants had gone away leaving all the lights on. The luminous strand of a Flugbahn hung empty against the sky. In the twilight the letters of sky-signs stared coldly: MOBIL, URANIA, IBM, ALT WIEN.

The young man looked around him with calm satisfaction. He was still hungry and in bodily distress, but here he was safe and sheltered. With those papers he could make a bed, here by the window. He would look out at the world all day, as long as he wished, and no one would know he was here at all.

He sat down and let his muscles relax. After all, to be free and to have a place of one's own were what mattered most. He had been terribly frightened, but now he could see that it was all coming right in the end.

With a contented glance around at the dim, slanting walls, which already had the comforting familiarity of home, he lay down on the floor and let the slow waves of silence muffle him to sleep.

IV

The food in the tray turned out to be a steaming mess of something dark green and odorous, the consistency of mud, with chunks of fibrous substance mixed up in it.

The biped was hungry, but repelled by the unappetizing appearance and smell of the stuff, and did not touch any. Next door he heard the scrape of a spoon on a metal plate: the female was eating hers, anyhow. The keeper had removed the table from her doorway and lectured her severely. He had not heard what she replied, if anything. The biped tried to sip water from the bowl on his tray, found that his stiff mouth would not permit it, and dashed the bowl to the floor with a sudden howl of fury. Immediately afterward he grew thirsty, and filled the bowl again from the washbowl faucet. He tried lapping the water with his tongue, and got some relief that way, but not enough water to swallow. He ended by pouring water into his open mouth, half choking himself before he discovered the trick of throwing his head back to swallow.

His chest and legs were sodden, the feathery spines clumped together with moisture. He felt acutely uncomfortable until he had dried himself with a towel. For some reason, the trivial incident depressed him severely. He tried to cheer himself up by thinking of the unfinished letter hidden in the desk, but to his despair found that he no longer cared about it. He sat in the inner room and stared dully at the wall.

He was roused from his torpor by footsteps in the office space, and Grück's careful voice calling, "Fritz! Emma!" The pimpled young keeper came in, looked at his untouched tray and removed it without comment.

The biped got up, simply because it would have required more resolution to stay where he was. He followed the keeper into the office space.

The keeper was showing the tray to Grück and Wenzl, who stood side by side, Grück ample in brown broadcloth, Wenzl narrow in his white smock. "Nothing eaten, sirs."

Wenzl glared, but Grück said expansively, "Never mind, never mind! Take it away, Rudi—this morning our guest is not so hungry, it's natural! Now!" He rubbed his fat pink hands together, beaming. "But where is our beautiful Emma?" He turned. "Emma?"

The female was in the doorway of her room, peeping out, only one side of her face visible. At Grück's command she ad-

vanced a few steps, then hesitated. Her arms were raised, both
hands clasped tightly over her forehead, hiding the knob.

"But, Emma," said Grück reproachfully, "is this our hospitality?
When were we ever so impolite? And our friend's first day, too!"

She made a wordless sound, looking at the biped.

"You are alarmed, Emma, he frightens you?" Grück asked,
looking from one to another. "Ah, loveling, there is nothing to be
frightened of. You are going to be great friends—yes, you will
see! And besides, Emma, what about all the work that is here?"

The female spoke up unexpectedly, in a thin, absurdly human
voice. "Take him away, please, and I'll do it all myself, Herr
Doktor." She glanced toward the biped, then ducked her head.

"No, no, Emma, that is not right. But let me tell you something. Because you are so alarmed, so frightened, we want you to
be happy, Emma, we are going to do something to relieve this
fear. (Wenzl, some chalk.) Fritz shall stay and help you with the
work—"

"No, no."

"Yes, yes! And you will like it, wait and see. (The chalk,
Wenzl—ha!)" Wenzl had spoken sharply to Rudi, the pimpled
young keeper, who, blushing, had fumbled in his pockets and
produced a piece of pink chalk. Wenzl, snatching it, now handed
it to Grück.

"See here, Emma," said Grück soothingly, "we are going to
draw a line on the floor. I draw it myself, because I want you to
be happy—so . . ." Bending with a grunt, he began at the wall
between the two bedroom doors and drew a wavering chalk line
across the room, separating it into two roughly equal parts.

"Now," he said from the far side, straightening up in panting
triumph, "see here, Emma, on this side, Fritz stays. Correct, Fritz?"

"Whatever you like," said the biped indifferently.

"See, he gives me his promise," said Grück, with emphasis.
"And my promise to you, Emma. So long as he stays on his side
of the room, you will work on your side, and not be frightened.
But if he should cross over the line, Emma, then you have *my*

permission to be frightened again, and to run into your room and bar the door! Understood?"

The female seemed impressed. "Very well then, Herr Doktor," she said at last.

"Good!" ejaculated Grück. He rubbed his hands together, beaming. "Now, what else is left?" He looked around the room. "Wenzl, move one of those typewriters so that Fritz has one to use. And some of the work, also, on this side—not too much for Fritz, I'm sure Emma works much faster! Good, good." He started to leave, followed by Wenzl and the young keeper. "Until next time, then, Emma, Fritz!"

The door closed.

The biped made as if to sit down at his desk. At his first movement Emma flinched back, jaw gaping in fright, hands over her knob. This startled the biped, who said irritably, "I'm not going to hurt you."

"Don't speak to me," the female said faintly. She clutched her knob. Her body was trembling all over, slightly but perceptibly.

The biped, trying to ignore her involuntary starts and shrieks, moved to the desk and sat down. He took the cover off his machine, looked at the heap of dictaphone spools in the In basket, then opened the desk drawer and quickly glanced inside to make sure his letter was there. By this time, the female was in the doorway of her room, poised for further flight.

Under her horrified gaze, the biped did not dare take his unfinished letter out of the drawer. He picked up the first dictaphone spool, inserted it in the machine, put the earphones on his head and began to listen.

A sudden loud noise in his ears made him jump and tear off the earphones. After a moment he turned down the volume and cautiously tried again. A voice was speaking faintly; he recognized it as Grück's, but could not make out the words. He turned the spool back to "start." The abrupt sound came again, and this time he realized that it was Grück clearing his throat.

He turned up the volume. Grück's voice was saying, "Attention, Emma! Here is tape number two of *Some Aspects of Extra-Terrestrial Biology*. Begin. Bibliography. Birney, R. C. Bay-ee-air-en-eh-ipsilon, Emma. *Phylum and genus in the Martian biota. Journal of comparative physiology*, 1985, 50, 162 to 167. Bulev, M. I. Bay-oo-ell-eh-fow, Emma. Remember, not with *vay* again, as last time! A preliminary study of *natator veneris schultzii. Dissertation abstracts*, 1990, 15, 1652 to 1653, Cooper, J. G. . . ."

The biped irritably removed the earphones and switched off the machine. The earphones did not press hard on his small external ears, but they felt unfamiliar and made him nervous.

The female had moved out a few steps from her doorway, but when he glanced up, she backed away hastily.

The biped swore. After a moment, reluctantly, he turned the dictaphone spool back to the beginning and put the earphones on again. He rolled paper into the typewriter carriage, then switched on the dictaphone and began trying to type as he listened. But in the first few words he typed there were so many errors that he ripped the paper out and threw it in the wastebasket.

There was a stifled shriek from the female, who had advanced halfway across the room. Clutching her knob, she retreated two steps.

"Don't look at me!" she piped.

"Then don't shriek," said the biped, annoyed. He rolled another sheet into the machine.

"I wouldn't shriek, if you only wouldn't look at me."

He glanced up. "How can I help looking at you if you shriek?"

Except for another piping sound, more a gasp than a scream, she made no reply. The biped went back to work. Touching one key at a time with painful care, he managed to get through five entries in the bibliography before making an error.

He threw the page away and started over once more.

Time passed. At length he was aware that the female had crossed the room to her desk. He concentrated on his work, and did not look up. After a few minutes, he heard the clatter of her machine. Her typing was smooth and rapid; the carriage banged against the stop, banged back, and reeled off another line.

Angrily, the biped hit a key too hard and it repeated. He ripped the page out.

"You are spoiling all your work," she said.

He glanced up—her hands leaped to her knob—he looked down again. "I can't help it if I am," he said.

"Weren't you taught to type properly?"

"No. I mean yes." The biped clenched his three-fingered fists in frustration. "I know how to type, but this animal doesn't. I can't make his hands work."

She stared at him with her mouth slightly open. It was plain that she did not understand a word.

The biped growled angrily and went back to his work. After a moment he heard the clatter of Emma's machine begin again.

For a long time neither spoke. Keeping at it grimly, in the next hour the biped managed to complete a page. He took it from the machine and put it into his out basket with a feeling of triumph. Glancing over at the female's desk, he was a little disconcerted to note that her out basket was heaped with typescript and dictaphone spools, while her in basket was empty.

His back and his hands ached from the unaccustomed work. He felt weary and dejected again. How was he going to finish the letter, the all-important letter, while the female was constantly in the same room? Perhaps if he deliberately frightened her once again . . .

The thought ended as he heard the outer door open. Emma looked up expectantly. The clatter of her machine ceased. She covered the machine in two deft movements and stood up.

In walked Grück, beaming and nodding; then Wenzl, grim as ever; finally the pimply keeper with his cart.

Grück's expression changed slightly when he glanced at the biped.

"Please!" he said, making upward motions with his fat hands. Belatedly realizing what was meant, the biped got up and stood at attention beside his desk, as Emma was doing beside hers.

"Good!" cried Grück happily. "Excellent! You see, Fritz, a little politeness, and everything is better." He turned to Emma, examined the contents of her out basket, beaming with approval. "Fine, Emma, good work. Emma shall have three bonbons with her dinner! You hear, Rudi?"

"Very good, Herr Doktor," said the keeper, with a bow. He put three large lumps of some dry-looking, pale green substance on a plate which already contained a sort of gray-brown stew, and carried it into Emma's room. When he returned, Grück was staring at the biped's out basket with an expression of hurt disbelief.

"Fritz, can this be all?" he asked. "For a whole morning's work? Surely you can't be so lazy!"

The biped muttered, "I did the best I could."

Grück shook his head sadly. "No bonbons for Fritz today, Rudi. What a shame, eh, Wenzl? Poor Fritz has earned no bonbons. We are sorry for Fritz. But to give him bonbons for such work would not be fair to Emma, who works hard! Correct, Wenzl?"

Wenzl, fixing the biped with a cold and unregretful stare, said nothing. Grück went on, "But this afternoon, if there is an improvement—well, we shall see! Until then—" He picked up the single page in the biped's basket, glanced at it again, and clucked his tongue. "Not correct! Not correct!" he said, stabbing a blunt finger against the page. "Here are mistakes, Fritz! So little work, and also so bad! And where . . . *where* are the carbon copies?"

"No one said anything to me about any carbon copies," the biped replied angrily. "As for the typewriting, I've told you, this animal's body is unfamiliar to me. Let me see you type with somebody else's fingers, and see if you do as well!" He felt a little dizzy, and went on shouting without caring much what happened. "You can take your whole damned Zoo, for all I care," he said, shaking his fist in Grück's face, "and slide down my—"

The room was tilting absurdly to the left, walls, Grück, Wenzl, keeper, Emma and all. He clutched at the desk to stop it, but the desk treacherously sprang up and struck him a dull blow across the face. He heard Grück and the keeper shouting, and Emma's voice piping in the background; then he lost interest and drifted away into grayness.

"Lie still," said a fretfully reassuring voice.

The biped looked up and recognized the gigantic face of Prinzmetal, the surgeon. Prinzmetal's large brown eyes were swimming over him; Prinzmetal's soft mouth was twisted nervously.

"Shock and strain," said Prinzmetal over his shoulder. The biped could make out two or three other persons standing farther back in the room. He was lying, he now realized, on the cot in the back room of his cage. He felt curiously limp and weak.

"It's all right," said Prinzmetal soothingly. "You lost consciousness a moment, that's all. It could happen to any highly strung creature. Lie still, Fritz, rest a little." His face turned, receded.

Grück's voice asked a question. Prinzmetal replied, "Nothing—he will be as good as new tomorrow." Feet shuffled on the concrete floor. The biped heard, more dimly: "It's a good thing it isn't something organic, Herr Doktor. What do we know about the internal constitution of these beasts, after all? Nothing whatever!"

Wenzl's voice spoke briefly and dryly. "When we get a chance to dissect one—"

They were gone. The biped lay quietly, staring at the discolored ceiling. He heard the door close; then there was silence except for a faint, far-off strain of music from somewhere outside. No sound came from the inner office, or from Emma's room next door.

At length the biped got up. He relieved himself in the little bathroom, and drank some water. He realized that he was hungry.

His tray was on the folding table near the bed. The biped sat down and ate the brownish-gray stew, then picked up one of the two round lumps of dry greenish stuff which lay at the side of the tray—the "bonbons" Grück had made so much of. The biped put the thing cautiously in his mouth, then paused incredulously. The lump, which was almost as dry to the tongue as its appearance suggested, had a subtle, delicious flavor which was utterly different from anything the biped had ever tasted before. It was not sweet, not salt, not bitter, not acid. His eyes closed involuntarily as he sucked at it, causing it to grow slowly moister and dissolve in his mouth.

When it was gone he ate the other one, and then sat motionless, eyes still closed, savoring the wonder of this unexpected good thing that had happened to him. Tears welled in his eyes.

How was it possible that even in his captivity, and his despair, there should be such joy?

The central building of the Berlin Zoo, built in 1971 by the architect Herbert Medius, was a delightful specimen of late 20th-century architecture but had several irremediable defects. For example, the garden-roof dining room, used on formal occasions by Grück and his staff, was roofed with a soaring transparent dome into which arcs of stained glass had been let, and at certain times of the year the long, varicolored streaks of light from this dome, instead of dripping diagonally down the lemon-wood and ebony walls, lay directly on the diners' tables and colored what was in their plates. The canvas curtains which were supposed to cover the dome's interior had never worked properly and were now, as usual, awaiting repair. Consequently, although Herr Doktor Grück's bauernwurst and mashed potatoes had the rich brown and white tones with which they had come from the kitchen, Prinzmetal's *boeuf au jus* was a dark ruby, as if it had been plucked raw from the bleeding carcass; Rausch's plate was deep blue; and Wenzl's was a pure, poisonous green. The visitors, of course, Umrath of *Europa-News*, Purser Bang of the Space Service and the trustee Neumann, had been placed in uncolored areas, except that a wedge of the red light that stained Prinzmetal's place occasionally glinted upon Neumann's elbow when he lifted his fork.

Wenzl, as always, sat stiff and silent at his place. His sardonic eyes missed nothing, neither the strained reluctance with which Rausch lifted his gobbets of blue meat to his lips, nor the exaggerated motion of Prinzmetal's arm which lifted each forkful for an instant out of the sullen red light before he took it into his mouth. But Wenzl looked upon his dinner and found it green: he carved it methodically with his knife in his green hand, forked it up green and ate it green.

Umrath, the *Europa-News* man, was square and red-faced, with shrewd little eyes and pale lashes. He said, "Not a bad dinner, this. Compliment the chef, Herr Doktor. If this is how you feed the animals down here, I must say they live well."

"Feed the animals!" cried Grück merrily. "Ha, ha, my dear Umrath! No, indeed, we have our separate kitchen for that, I assure you! To feed more than five hundred different species, some of them not even terrestrial, that is no joke, you can believe me! Take for instance the Brecht's Bipeds. Their food must be rich in sulfur and in beryllium salts. If we put that on the table here, you would soon be three sick gentlemen!"

"Wenzl would eat it and not turn a hair," said Neumann, the aging trustee. He was quiet and dark, with a weary but business-like air about him.

"Ha! True!" cried Grück. "Our Wenzl is made of cast iron! But the bipeds, gentlemen, not so. They are delicate! They require constant care!"

"And money," put in Neumann dryly, picking with his fork at the meat on his plate, which he had hardly touched.

"It's true," said Grück soberly. "They are rarities, and they come from eighteen light-years away. One doesn't go eighteen light-years for a picnic, eh, Purser Bang?"

The spaceman nodded. He was tall and taciturn, lantern-jawed, and looked more like a doorkeeper than an intrepid adventurer. He cut precise cubes from the meat on his plate and chewed them thoroughly before swallowing.

"Why spend so much for bipeds, then, Grück?" Umrath demanded. "They're amusing, I suppose, in their way, but are they worth it?"

"My dear Umrath," said Grück, laying down his fork, "I must

tell you, the bipeds represent the dream of my life. Yes, I confess,
it's true that I dream! After all, we are alive to do something in the
world, to achieve something! That is why, dear Umrath, I
schemed and wrote letters for five years, and why I traded two
Altairan altar birds and how much money to boot I had better not
mention—" he glanced at Neumann, who smiled faintly, "for our
wonderful new biped Fritz. He is here, he is well, and he is a
mature male. We already have our female biped Emma. No other
zoo on earth has more than one. Laugh at me if you will, but it
shall be Grück, and his Berlin Zoo, who is remembered as the first
man to breed bipeds in captivity!"

"Some say it can't be done," put in Umrath.

"Yes, I know it!" cried Grück gaily. "Never have bipeds been
successfully bred in captivity, not even on Brecht's Planet! And
why not? Because until now no one has successfully reproduced
the essential conditions of their natural environment!"

"And those conditions are—?" asked Neumann with weary
courtesy.

"That we shall discover!" said Grück. "Trust me, gentlemen, I
have made already a collection of writings about Brecht's Planet
and especially the bipeds. There is no larger one in the Galacti-
cum, not even excepting the Berlin Archive!" He beamed. "And
between ourselves, gentlemen, Purser Bang has a connection with
a group on Brecht's Planet who are able to make physiological
studies of the bipeds! Depend on it, they will give us valuable
information—by way of Purser Bang, our good friend!" He
reached over and patted Bang's sleeve affectionately. The spaceman half-smiled, blinked and went on eating.

"Well, then, here's to the bipeds!" said Umrath, lifting his
wineglass.

Grück, Prinzmetal, Rausch and Bang drank; Neumann merely
raised his glass and set it down again. Wenzl, coldly upright, went
on methodically cutting and eating his green meat.

"All the same," said Neumann after a moment, "it seems to me
that a good deal depends on Fritz."

V

On the morning of his fourth day in the store, the young man climbed down as usual, very early, when the great vault was almost empty. Once or twice someone glanced at him curiously as he passed down the aisles, but he kept walking, and no one spoke to him. The clerks were busy behind the walls of glass cases, inserting new merchandise, clicking the metal doors open and shut, the cleaners in their gray-striped uniforms were pushing their whining machines along the floor. Voices echoed lonesomely under the distant ceiling.

The young man quenched his thirst at the drinking fountain between the grocery and the art gallery. Then he went into the produce section, with its mountains of fruit under glass, for his breakfast. By this time the outside doors had been opened, the music was playing and people were beginning to stream down the aisles. The young man spent seventy pfennigs for a transparent bag of oranges and a package of bananas. Alternately eating the bananas and sucking the oranges, he wandered through the store. When he finished a piece of fruit, he tucked the peel neatly into the bag under his arm.

Once, on the evening of his second day, the young man had ventured out into the avenue again, but the crowds, the noise and the lights had disturbed him and he had gone back into the store almost immediately, afraid he would be outside when it closed its doors. To be inside was much better. Here there was also noise, but it was of a different quality, not so alarming. The light was even and cool, and did not hurt his eyes. And besides, in the store he found all he needed—food, drink, entertainment. Sometimes he became lost, the store was so large. But he could always find his way again by following the moving rocket-trails of light on the ceiling.

Whenever he saw one of the blue-uniformed men, he looked straight ahead until he was past. He had learned that the men in blue would not pursue him unless he climbed the grille or took something from a case without paying, and now he always made sure to pay. As for the grille, he climbed it every night, not being able to find any other way up. Twice more he had been noticed, and the men in blue had run and shouted, ringing their bells; but no one could climb after him. So he was not really very afraid of the blue-uniformed men. But he did not like to be near them, all the same.

There were still some discomforts in his new body that constantly worried him and occasionally even alarmed him by their intensity. There was something his mouth and throat wanted to do, for example. He kept trying different kinds of food and drink, and the feeling always went away, but it came back afterward. Dark, curly hair was sprouting all over his cheeks and chin, and it made his face itch. Nevertheless, he was getting along much better than he had at first. He had found out that taking his clothes and shoes off at night made them easier to bear the next day. When his underclothes had become dirty yesterday, he had bought new ones out of a machine, and he discovered now that the smooth, clean fabric was unexpectedly pleasant against his bald skin.

Without watching where his feet were leading him, he had wandered into the women's clothing section. In the middle of the central open space, a crowd had gathered around a platform. The young man went nearer. On the platform a perspiring dark-skinned man was energetically looping a wide ribbon of violet cloth around a blond young woman who stood passively, arms raised, and stared out into space.

Both man and woman had the bright, unreal colors and the curious black outlines of the cinema he had seen on his first day, and he realized that this was another illusion.

The cloth took shape, became a dress. The dark-skinned man ran a piece of metal up the woman's side, pinching out the cloth into a ridge and tightening the dress to her body. Then he did the same thing to the other side, touched the dress swiftly here and there, cut a slit halfway down the back and began to work the finished dress up over the woman's head. Underneath, her body was shapely and cream-skinned in two brief garments of dark blue lace. Looking at her made the young man feel peculiar, and one of his discomforts suddenly became much more acute.

As he turned to work his way out of the crowd, he came face to face with a dark-haired, pale-skinned young woman who first looked startled, then smiled happily. "Martin!" she said, taking his arm.

The young man moved away nervously. "I don't know you, madam," he said.

"What?" The woman's face changed. The young man kept on moving away. She took a step after him. "Martin Naumchik—"

Thoroughly alarmed, the young man turned and dived into the crowd. He worked his way around the platform, turning his head frequently to see if he was being followed. Above him, the dark-skinned man was turning the dress inside out. When he finished, he poised it over the young woman's shoulders, then began to work it down over her body. Both seemed to revolve as he circled them. No matter how far around he got, he could never see their backs.

The young man left the crowd cautiously on the opposite side, and looked around. The dark-haired woman was not in sight. Nevertheless, he took a complicated route out of that part of the store, glancing back many times.

Crossing the elevator plaza, he saw people looking at him, and realized he had been shaking his head unconsciously as he walked. The encounter with the dark-haired woman had taken him completely by surprise. It had somehow never occurred to him before that as a human being he now had not only a name and clothing, personal possessions and so on, but also friends and acquaintances. The idea frightened him. What could he possibly say to these people? What would they expect of him?

The comfort and safety of his refuge in the store began to seem illusory. For a moment he thought wistfully of his clean, bare little cubicle in the Hamburg Zoo. But the memory was already so faded and distant that it could not occupy his attention long. The reality was this gigantic, glittering room with its unending murmur of voices, its exciting smells, its clicking elevators, its rocket-trails of red, green, amber, blue that traveled in pulses across the ceiling.

The best thing might be to go away, change his name perhaps, find a place to live in some other city where he was not known. But he had no confidence that he could manage such a trip properly. Were there stores such as this in other cities than Berlin? He was humiliated to realize that he did not know. He had lived in Hamburg for twelve years, but had no idea what lay beyond the Zoo grounds. Other cities were only names to him.

An hour later, up in the third-floor lunchroom, he was still thinking about it over buns and coffee. It was his first experiment with coffee. The flavor was unexpected and rather unpleasant, but he liked its sweetness and warmth.

It was odd how differently he felt about foods now that he was a human being. He had been going cautiously, since his bad experience of the first night in the restaurant. He had eaten only fruits and bread, and sometimes a sausage on a roll. But in time he expected to do all things human beings did, even to eating the wet brown messes he saw on his neighbors' plates.

He picked up his cup, experimentally flexed the muscles of his lips and drank. He was proud of this accomplishment, which had cost him much effort.

The last few drops rattled noisily as they went in, and one or two people nearby glanced at him with raised eyebrows. Evidently this was not a sound that one made. He set down the cup in some embarrassment, and consulted his wristwatch: it was just eleven.

He restrained himself from checking the time by his other wristwatch, which was in his pocket. He had observed that human beings did not wear two at once, perhaps because the watches were so accurate that no checking was required.

A pattern of bright lights flashed for an instant on his section of the counter. He glanced upward automatically, as he had done the time before, and the time before that, and saw only a fading starflower of red sparks in the machine overhead. They dimmed and went out. A moment later they flashed on again, making him blink and jerk his head back. The bright chrome and glass ring of the revolving display case slowed, stopped. Directly in front of him, a square black hole appeared, and a transparency lighted up. The young man read, "EMPTY PLATES, PLEASE." He pushed his empty cup and saucer, and the plate with the remnants of his buns, obediently into the hole, which closed on it with a metallic snap. The transparency blinked, shimmered, and lighted up again: "THANK YOU."

With a warm feeling for the polite machine, the young man stood up and left the lunchroom. As he passed the entrance, where a crowd was waiting to get in, he found himself once more face to face with the same dark-haired young woman.

She stared at him, apparently as shocked as he was. Neither moved for an instant. Then the young woman, without a word, raised her hand and slapped him in the face.

The blow was so unexpected and painful that the young man was unable to move for a few moments longer, while the young woman turned and walked away. People standing around were staring at him; some were whispering to each other.

No one had ever struck him before. With one hand to the curious numbness that was the pain in his cheek, the young man turned away.

He spent the rest of the day wandering the store half-blindly, shivering a little. His pleasure in the bright colors and varied shapes around him was dimmed almost to extinction. He was waiting for it to be time for him to climb to his hideaway in the tower. Beyond that he did not think.

Eventually it was eighteen-thirty. The crowds were beginning to flow toward the exits. The young man moved across the elevator plaza, vaguely aware that the crowds were heavier and somehow more anxious than usual tonight. He passed a man with a camera, then another. Two in a row. He had sometimes amused himself by counting men with cameras, or fat women, or crying children, but now he had no interest in games. There were a lot of uniforms in sight, too: not only the blue store police, but white uniforms, red ones, gold-and-white ones . . .

He passed two blue-uniformed men who were standing together, looking intently around them. One stepped forward, glancing at the young man, then at something he held in his hand. "One moment, sir."

The young man sidestepped, anxious not to be touched again. "Stop!" cried the store policeman, reaching.

The young man whirled and ran for the grille. Bells were ringing on all sides; footsteps pounding after him. He sprang, caught the grille, began to climb.

Halfway up, he glanced back. No one was climbing after him, but there was a great deal of activity at the base of the grille. Blue-uniformed men were clustered around a bundle of something gray, unrolling it. There were others, in gleaming white uniforms, with feathers on their hats: but these were not doing anything, only standing with feet apart, staring up at him.

He went on climbing. As he neared the top of the grille, two heads appeared over the edge, then a third.

The young man paused. The three men wore blue uniform caps—they were store police, not merely the clerks who lived in this upper level. While he was wondering what do do, the three heads ducked out of sight, then reappeared. The shoulders and arms of the three men came into view. Something cloudy and gray seemed to float down toward him.

The young man ducked, but it was too late. The cloudy thing settled around him with a solid thump, and he discovered that it was a net of grayish cord. It pulled tight around him when he attempted to swing away to the side. There were ropes attached to the net, and the men above were holding them.

Panicked, the young man tried to climb down. The ropes held him back, then slackened a little; but when he paused to try to remove the net with one hand, they tightened again.

Down below, two men in gray-striped uniforms were pushing up a sort of tall ladder on wheels. The plaza was full of motionless people now, and the men in white were keeping them back. The ladder was in position almost directly under him, and now a white-uniformed man began to climb it.

The young man saw that in another moment all his chances would be gone. Taking a deep breath, he swung himself violently away from the grille, tearing with both hands at the net that held him.

The great room revolved massively around him. His back struck the grille hard, knocking the breath out of him. He kicked himself away again, still tearing wildly at the meshes of the net. The man on the ladder was very near. The net gave a little; he had found an edge. His head was out, then his shoulders.

The grille struck him again. The man on the ladder leaned out and reached for him. Then he was falling.

VI

Sprawled on the couch in his room, the biped read:

"The bipeds of the Great Northern Plateau, although the most interesting life-form on Brecht's Planet, are a vanishing species. Their once numerous herds are no longer seen in the vicinity of the Earth settlements. Only scattered groups of three to five are occasionally met in the mountains and foothills to the north. These animals, prior to the development of Brecht's Planet by man, possessed a complex herd organization and communicated by vocal signals. Their mating ceremonies, held in the spring of the year, are said to have involved barbaric cruelties to the females."

He closed the book thoughtfully. That might account partly for Emma's attitude, he supposed—if she had witnessed something of the kind before being captured and brought to Earth as an infant. However—

He thumbed the book open at a different place. "The knob or crest," he read, "appearing only as a vestige in the male, is a conspicuous purplish-red ovoid in the female. The function of the crest is unknown, but it is thought to be a secondary sexual characteristic. Erhardt (6) has suggested that it functions as an organ of display in the animals' natural state, but Zimmer (7) has pronounced it to be merely a hypertrophied pineal eye. The organ is vulnerable, as attested by the large number of older females who have lost it through accident or in conflict with other bipeds."

The biped closed the book again and tossed it irritably onto the floor. He was reading *Brecht's Planet: Riddle of the Universe* for the second time, out of sheer boredom, since it was the only book he had in the back room: but the parts that were full of footnote references reminded him too much of the work he copied every day for Grück and the other staff members.

In another two hours or so it would be closing time, and he could go into the living room without exposing himself to all those meaty red faces. This time he would remember to bring some reading matter into the back room, enough to last him a few days.

Actually, there was nothing to stop him from going out there now . . . there were some magazines in the rack, he remembered, with bright covers. He could scoop them up and come straight back in. But he hesitated to make the move.

It was extraordinary how hateful a row of human faces could be, staring in at you over an iron railing, with their great fat jaws moving as they chewed.

He stood up restlessly. Hell and damnation! There was nothing to do here except read *Brecht's Planet* again, and nothing to do in the office. His work was all cleaned up, and there was no point in trying to smuggle out another letter until he found out what had happened to the first one.

Anxiety seized him again, and he began pacing back and forth. Surely nothing could have gone wrong?

When the first batch of signed correspondence had come down from "upstairs" to be folded and sealed in envelopes, the biped had simply added his to the pile. Rudi, the pimply young keeper, had carried them out on his next trip. There was no reason to suppose that stamped, sealed letters were inspected by Grück or anyone. The keeper probably took them directly to the post box.

But he had been waiting for a week. If Stein had received the letter, why hadn't something happened before now?

From Emma's living room next door he heard a faint creak, a pause, another creak. Probably she had got up from her chair for something, then sat down again . . . all in full view of the crowd, naturally.

That decided him. He looked at the open doorway, then stiffened himself and walked through it, looking straight ahead.

The first moment was even worse than he had expected. The room was enormous and empty; the window was crowded with faces. He tried to shut them out of his awareness, looking only at the magazines, which now seemed much less attractive than he had remembered them. After a moment it began to be easier to go on than to turn back, but his mouth was still dry and his heart thumped painfully. Outside, there was a steady movement along the railing as people who had been staring at Emma came over to stare at him.

Walking stiffly, the biped reached the relaxing chair and leaned past it to get the magazines. Be natural, he ordered himself. Pick up the magazines, turn . . .

Outside the wall of glass, people were waving to attract his attention. There were cries of "Ah, just look!" and "Fritz, hello!" A blond child, carried on his father's shoulder so as to see better, turned suddenly beet-red and began to cry. Several people were aiming cameras. Through the uproar, just as he turned away, the biped thought he heard his name called.

He turned incredulously.

In the front line of the crowd, wedged in between two fat matrons, was a medium-sized man in a gray surcoat with a wad of paper in his hand. His eyes, friendly and inquisitive, were looking straight into the biped's. His mouth moved, and once more the biped thought he heard his name spoken, but the noise was so great that he could not be sure.

The man in gray smiled slightly, raised his wad of paper, then wrote something on it with careful, firm motions. He held the paper up. On it was lettered, "ARE YOU NAUMCHIK?"

The biped felt a rush of joy and gratitude that almost choked him. He fell against the glass, nodding vehemently and pointing to himself. "I am Naumchik!" he shouted.

The man in gray nodded reassuringly, folded up his paper and tucked it away. With a wave of his hand, he turned and began to struggle out of the crowd.

"Fritz! Fritz!" yelled all the red faces.

The biped waited, pacing up and down, for twenty minutes by the big office clock, and still nothing happened. He knew he should control his impatience, that the gray man might be upstairs at this moment, arguing for his release; but it was no use, he had to do something or burst.

He eyed the telephone. He had been forbidden to use it except for routine calls in connection with his work. But to the devil with that! The biped strode to the phone, swung out the listening unit. The call light began to pulse. After a moment the voice of the switchboard girl spoke faintly from the instrument: "Please?"

"This is Martin Naumchik," said the biped, feeling as he spoke that the words sounded subtly false. "I want to speak to Dr. Grück. Please connect me with him."

"Who did you say you are?"

"Martin—" the biped began, and swallowed. "All right then, never mind, this is Fritz the biped. I want to speak—"

"Why didn't you say so in the first place? Is there anything wrong with the work?"

"No, the work is finished. It's something quite urgent, so if you will kindly—"

"Is anything wrong in the cage?"

"No, but I must speak to Grück. Look here, whatever your name is, kindly don't argue and just let me speak to—"

"My name is Fraülein Müller," her voice broke in coldly, "and I have instructions not to let the animals make personal telephone calls. So if there is no emergency, and nothing wrong with your work—"

"I tell you it's urgent!" howled the biped. With mounting fury, he went on shouting into the mouthpiece. "You idiot woman, if you prevent me from speaking to Grück, there will be an accounting, I promise you! Make that connection at once, or—Hello? Do you hear me? Hello, Fraülein Müller, hello?"

The empty hum of the line answered him.

With shaking fingers, the biped closed the instrument and then yanked it open again. The light call pulsed, and went on pulsing.

The female's greenish, wide-jawed head was visible beyond her doorframe as the biped turned. "Well, what are you staring at?" he shouted. The head vanished.

The biped sat down abruptly in his desk chair, kneading his three-fingered hands nervously together. It was intolerable to be shut up like this now, just when his freedom was perhaps so near. If something was about to happen, the least they could do was to let him know, not leave him in the dark like this. After all, whose life was at stake? But that was always the way with these inflated bureaucrats, they couldn't see past their own fat noses. Let the lower ranks wait and worry for nothing. What did they care?

Oh, but just let him get out, and then! What an exposé he would write! What a series! *Shocking Inhumanity of Zoo Keepers!* His nervousness, which had abated a little, increased again and he sprang to his feet. Let him once get out, that was all—just let him get out! The rest would not matter so much, even if he were condemned . . .

He paused to listen. Yes, there came the sound again. The door was opening.

The biped ran to the passage; but it was not Grück or the man in gray, only Rudi with his little cart.

"Oh, you," said the biped, turning away dully.

"Yes, me," Rudi answered with spirit. "Who else should it be, I'd like to know? Who does all the hard work around here, and gets no thanks for it?" He pushed his cart into the office space, grumbling all the time, without looking at the biped. "Does Herr Doktor Grück feed the rhino, or the thunderbirds? Who pokes the meat down the boa constrictor's throat with a broomstick, Wenzl? Does Rausch swamp out the monkeys' cages, or is it me? You bipeds are not so bad, at least you clean up after yourselves, but some of these beasts, you wouldn't believe how filthy they are! They throw things on the floor, they let themselves go just where they feel like it . . . Well, that's life. Some live on the fat of the land, and others have to work up to their elbows in monkey dirt." With a scowl, he took a small object off his cart and threw it onto the nearest desk. "There's some soap for you. You're to clean yourself up and be interviewed, and the order is to hurry. So don't be late, mind, or I'll get the blame, not you."

The biped's heart began pounding violently. "Did you say interviewed?" he stammered. "Who—what?"

"Interviewed, is all I know. Some newspaperman wants to write a story about you. All lies, I dare say, but that's his lookout." Rudi was wheeling his cart around, still without glancing at the biped.

There was a sound behind them, and the biped turned in time to see Emma come darting nervously out of her doorway.

"Rudi," she piped. "Oh, Rudi—please wait!"

But the keeper had disappeared into the passage, and either did not hear or did not choose to turn back. After a moment came the sound of the outer door closing.

Emma retreated toward her room as the biped turned, her hands going to her head in the familiar gesture. But she paused when she saw him reach for the small packet on the desk.

"Is that soap?" she asked timidly. "I heard him say it was."

The biped picked up the small paper-wrapped oblong. It had a faint aromatic scent which was oddly disturbing. "Soap, yes," he said abstractedly. "I've got to get cleaned up so that I can be interviewed."

"I had some once," the female said, edging nearer. "It was a long time ago. They said it was bad for me."

"I suppose so," the biped muttered, tearing at the paper with his blunt fingers. The paper ripped open, the soap shot out between his hands and clattered across the floor almost to Emma's feet. She bent slowly and picked it up. The fragrance had grown almost overpoweringly strong.

"Give it to me, will you?" the biped asked impatiently, walking nearer. He was at the scuffed chalk line that divided his side of the room from hers, but she took no notice. With the soap clutched in both hands, she was intently sniffing. Her mouth was half open, her eyes turned up.

Alarmed, the biped halted and stared at her. "Emma!" he said.

Her head turned. "Yes?" she said in a dreamy voice.

"What's the matter with you, Emma?"

"Nothing matter," she replied, with a vacuous grin.

"Well then, give me the soap if you please."

"Good soap," she said, nodding, but she did not move to hand it over, and seemed almost unaware that she was still holding it close to her face.

On the point of crossing the line to take it from her, the biped hesitated. It suddenly struck him as rather odd that Rudi should have given him soap to wash with at all. He had not seen any in his week's incarceration, and had not really missed it. Was soap good for this body, with its feathery spines? But if not, then why—?

Shaking his head irritably, he moved backward, away from the fascinating smell that came from the thing Emma was holding. With that insistent odor in his nostrils it was hard to think connectedly.

He concentrated. At last: "Why did they say soap was bad for you, Emma?" he demanded.

"Bad for me," she agreed, swaying as if to inaudible music. "Soap bad for Emma. No more soap, too bad. Beautiful soap."

As the biped stared at her silently, he heard the door opening again. His dulled brain began to work quickly once more. "Emma, listen to me," he whispered. "Take your soap and go into your own room. Understand? Go into your own room. Don't come out till I tell you!"

"Emma not come out." With exasperating slowness, she moved toward the door as Rudi came back in, this time without his cart.

"Ready, are you?" he asked, with a glance at Emma's disappearing figure.

The biped turned to face him, trying to look as dreamy and distant as Emma had. "All ready," he said slowly.

"Know who you are, do you?"

"My name is Naum—"

"No, no," Rudi interrupted, "don't be stupid, your name is Fritz. Now say it after me. 'My name is Fritz.' "

"Name is Fritz," said the biped agreeably. He kept his eyes rolled up, and swayed on his feet. His head was buzzing with angry surmise, but he kept his voice blurred and slow.

"That's all right, then," Rudi said, satisfied. "How much is two and two, Fritz?"

The biped pretended to consider the question at length. "Four?" he asked hesitantly.

"Good fellow. Now how much is four and four and four and four?"

The biped blinked slowly. "Four and four," he said.

Rudi smiled. "All right then, come along. You're going upstairs to meet some nice gentlemen, Fritz, and if you behave yourself— mind, I said if—I'll give you something tasty all for yourself." He took the biped's arm.

They rode up in the elevator, walked along the glass-walled corridor overlooking the Zoo grounds. It was a sunny late afternoon, and the gravel paths were full of strolling people. A few faces tilted to watch them, but there was not much excitement. They entered the main building, Rudi opened a door, and the biped found himself being ushered into the same oak-paneled office where he had been received on the first day. Beside the desk, Grück, Wenzl and the man in the gray surcoat were waiting.

"Ha!" said Grück jovially, "here is our Fritz at last. Now we shall see, my dear Tassen, how much truth there is in this fantastic story. We could have begun sooner, but our Fritz sometimes dirties himself, not so, Wenzl? Too bad, but what can one expect? So!" He rubbed his hands together. "Fritz, you are well?"

"Very well, Herr Doktor," said the biped.

"Excellent! And you have eaten a good supper, Fritz?"

"Yes, Herr Doktor."

Grück frowned slightly, glancing at Rudi, but in a moment collected himself and addressed the biped again: "Very good, Fritz. Now then, this gentleman is Herr Tassen of the *Freie Presse*. He will ask you some questions, and you will answer correctly. Understood? Then begin, Herr Tassen!"

The man in the gray surcoat looked at the biped with a faintly uncertain expression. "Well then, Fritz—" he began.

The biped took a step forward, away from Rudi, and said quickly, "How long have you worked for the *Freie Presse*?"

Tassen's eyebrows went up. "A little over a year, why?"

"Do you know Zellini, the rewrite man?"

"How is this?" cried Grück, coming forward, red-faced with astonishment and anger. "Fritz, your manners! Remember—"

"Yes, I know Zellini," said the newsman. He was scribbling rapidly on his wad of paper.

"A little dark man, nearly bald, I sat next to him at the last European Journalists' Dinner. He—"

"Wenzl!" shouted Grück. The biped felt himself seized by Rudi from behind, while Wenzl, his face a white mask, came toward him around the desk.

"They are holding me against my will!" shouted the biped, struggling. "My name is Martin Naumchik! They tried to drug me before they brought me up here!"

Grück and Tassen were shouting. Wenzl had seized the biped's arm in one hand and was gripping his muzzle in the other,

holding it closed. Between them, he and Rudi raised the biped off
his feet and began carrying him out the door.

"Outrageous!" Grück was trumpeting. "A trick!"

The newsman, almost red-faced as he, was shouting, "Bring
him back at once!"

The door swung closed, cutting off the din. Without bothering to set him on his feet, Wenzl and Rudi carried the now
unresisting biped down the corridor toward the elevator.

Emma, it appeared, had not only been sniffing the soap all the
time the biped had been gone but had eaten some as well. She was
taken to the infirmary, unconscious, and remained there two days.

Deliveries of work stopped. Rudi, the keeper, disappeared and
his place was taken by a heavy slow man named Otto. No one
else visited the cage.

Exhausted and triumphant, the biped spent most of his time in
the front room of the cage, sometimes reading or watching television, sometimes merely watching the crowds, to which he had
slowly become accustomed. He hoped to see Tassen again, but
the man did not reappear. On the day after the interview, however, a man outside took a folded newspaper from his surcoat and
spread it out for the biped to see.

He was just able to read the headline, REALLY HUMAN,
ZOO BIPED CLAIMS. Then a guard snatched the newspaper
away and led the man off, lecturing him severely.

The biped would have given a day's meals for that newspaper:
but now at least he knew that Tassen had written the story and
the city editor had printed it.

Now he could wait. Once the truth was out, they would never
be able to hush it up again, whatever they did. The biped schooled
himself to patience. For a while he had toyed with the idea of
lettering some messages on large pieces of cardboard and holding
them up to the crowd. But he was afraid that if he did so he would
be taken out of the front room, and then he could not watch for
Tassen.

On the third day, Emma was brought in after breakfast, looking feeble and wild-eyed, her spines draggled. She gave the biped a look as she passed which he could not interpret—wistfulness, a reproach, an appeal of some kind?

He found himself worrying about it and wanting to talk to her, but she did not emerge from her room.

A little later, the outer door opened again and Otto came in. He stood in the doorway and growled, "Wanted upstairs. An interview. Come."

The biped got to his feet, feeling his heart begin to pound. He asked wryly, "No soap this time?" But the keeper stared at him in brute incomprehension.

This time, instead of going to Grück's office, they passed it and entered a smaller room on the opposite side of the corridor. The room was empty except for a table and two chairs.

Otto held the door without comment, waited until the biped was inside, then went out again, closing the door.

The biped looked around nervously, but there was nothing to see: only the three pieces of furniture, the scuffed black tiles of the floor, and the mud-brown walls, which were dirty and in need of paint.

After a long time, the door opened again and a large, olive-skinned man in a red surcoat appeared. Behind him the biped glimpsed the leviathan bulk of Grück, and heard his rich, fluting voice.

"Of course, my dear Herr Opatescu, of course! We have always desired—"

"Don't think I am taken in by these games," said the visitor furiously, pausing in the doorway. "If I had not threatened to go to the Council—"

"You are mistaken, Herr Opatescu, I assure you! We only wished—"

"I know what you wished," said Opatescu with heavy sarcasm. "Go on, I've had enough of it."

Grück retired, looking chastened, and the visitor closed the door. He was carrying a pigskin briefcase, which he put down carefully on the table. Then, with a toothy smile, he advanced on the biped and shook his hand cordially.

"We newsmen have to stick together when it comes to dealing with swine like that," he said. "Allow me to introduce myself. My name is Opatescu. You have no idea the tricks they played to keep me out—but here I am! Now then, Herr Naumchik . . . one moment." He busied himself with the briefcase, from which he produced a flat, clear crystic solid-state recorder and a microphone. "Here we are. Sit down, please—so." He pushed the microphone toward the biped, adjusted the controls of the instrument and switched it on. The indicator began to crawl over the surface of the record block.

Opatescu sat down opposite the biped, leaning forward on his arms, without bothering to remove his bulky surcoat. "This recording is being made in the Berlin Zoo, June seventeenth, 2002. Present are Martin Naumchik, otherwise known as the biped Fritz, and the reporter Opatescu."

He settled himself more comfortably and began again. "Now, Herr Naumchik—for I believe that you are in reality Martin Naumchik—I want you to tell me, if you will, in your own words just how your amazing experience took place. Begin then, if you please."

The biped did as he was asked willingly enough, although Opatescu was a type he did not like—glib, assertive, the sort of reporter you expected to find working on Central European scandal sheets. But since the man was on his side, and anyhow a recording was being made—

Opatescu listened rather restlessly but without interruption until the biped had brought his story up to date. Then, with a thoroughness which made the biped wonder if his first estimate had not been mistaken, Opatescu took him over the story all over again, asking questions, eliciting more details, getting him to repeat certain points several times in different words. When he was satisfied with this, he began questioning the biped about his past life, and particularly about sources of evidence that he was actually Naumchik. They went over this ground with equal thoroughness. When Opatescu finally turned off the recorder and began to pack it away, the biped watched him with grudging respect.

"I must tell you I'm grateful to you for all this," he said. "I suppose you're a friend of Tassen's, the man who broke the story?"

"Tassen, yes, I know Tassen," said Opatescu, busily fastening his briefcase. "He's written some follow-up yarns, good stuff, you'll see when you get out."

The biped moistened his stiff lips. "I don't suppose you have any idea—"

"When that will be? Not long. You're going to have a press conference, a big one this time—newspapers, sollies, TV. They can't hold you after that. The public wouldn't stand for it. Well, Naumchik, it's been a pleasure." He held out his meaty hand.

"For me, too, Herr Opatescu. By the way, what paper did you say you were from?"

"*Pravda.*" Opatescu glanced at his watch, then swung his brief-case off the table and turned to go.

"Do you happen to know Kyrill Reshevsky, the—"

"Yes, yes, but let's reminisce some other time, shall we?" He smiled, showing large gleaming teeth. "I've got a deadline. You understand. Good-bye, Herr Naumchik—patience." Still smiling, he backed out and closed the door.

The keeper Otto appeared almost at once to take the biped back. Though usually laconic, he spoke up on the way down to the cages. "So now they are going to let you out, are they?"

"So it seems," said the biped happily.

"Well, well," said Otto, shaking his head. "What's next?"

For the next two days the biped could not read or sit still for more than a few minutes at a time. He kept the television turned on, and watched every hourly news broadcast. Once, early on the first day, a commentator mentioned his story, and a brief glimpse of him on film—evidently taken on the day of his arrival at the Zoo—was flashed on the screen. After that, there was nothing.

In between news broadcasts, he spent most of his time pacing up and down the office space, imprisoning poor Emma, who no sooner put her head out of her room than the biped, by some gesture or exclamation, frightened her back in again. He gave the switchboard girl no rest, ringing her up all day long and demanding to speak to Grück, to Prinzmetal, to anyone. On the afternoon of the second day the phone went dead. The line had been disconnected.

Shortly afterward, Otto entered. He had a bundle of newspapers and magazines on his cart.

"They send you these," he said, dumping the bundle onto a vacant desk. "Read, and don't bother Fraülein Müller." He turned and left.

The biped forgot him at once. He snatched up the topmost paper—it was the Frankfurter *Morgenblatt*—and leafed through it with trembling fingers until he found a column headed, "STRANGE STATEMENTS OF ZOO BIPED."

He read the story avidly, although it was evidently nothing more than a rehash of his interview with Tassen. Then, curbing his impatience, he began sorting out the papers in the stack by date and piling them on the floor. When he got to the bottom of the stack, to his delight, he found a scrapbook and a pair of shears.

Squatting on the floor—his old legs had never been so limber—he began carefully cutting out the stories about himself and pressing them onto the adhesive pages of the scrapbook. The culled papers he put aside for later reading.

As he worked, he discovered that the biped stories fell into three classes. First, straight and rather unimaginative reporting, like that of the Frankfurter *Morgenblatt*; second, sympathetic pieces, appearing usually in the Sunday feature sections and with feminine by-lines (an item headlined TRAPPED IN AN ANIMAL'S BODY!, by Carla Ernsting, was typical of these); and finally a trickle of heavily slanted stories and editorials, turning up in the later issues and in the newsmagazines. These he read with surprise and a growing fear. "Neurotic pseudohumanitarians, "said *Heute* in a boxed editorial, "seek to degrade humanity to the level of animals, and in so doing, strike at the very root of our civilization. Make no mistake: these sick minds would have us recognize as human every slimy polyp, every acid-breathing toad that can parrot a few phrases in German or walk through a simple maze. The self-styled Martin Naumchik, an upstart member of a vicious, degraded species . . ."

The biped crumpled the paper in a burst of anger. Rising, he circled the piles of newspaper, glaring at them. Then he squatted again, smoothed out the offending page and read the editorial to the end.

But he was too agitated to go on working. He closed the scrapbook and went into his front room to stare out at the gray autumn day. The sky had turned cold and rainy, and few people were on the paths.

He could no longer ignore the fact that people did not *want* to believe a biped's body could be inhabited by a human mind and soul. In a general way he could even sympathize with it. But surely they must see that this was a special, different case!

He pressed his muzzle against the cold glass, down which scattered raindrops were slowly creeping.

But what if they would not?

He tried to imagine himself set free, recognized as Martin Naumchik, his rights as a citizen restored . . . What then? A grotesque vision of himself, a naked biped, in the city room of *Paris-Soir*, talking to Ehrichs . . . then himself at a party, among fully dressed men and women with glasses in their hands.

It was absurd, impossible. Where could he go? Who would accept him? Where could he get work, or even lodgings?

The biped set his jaw stubbornly, gripping his three-fingered hands together. "I am Martin Naumchik!" he muttered. But even in his own ears, the words sounded false.

VII

The biped woke himself up, tossing and muttering, from a pecu-
liarly unpleasant dream. Something had happened to his body,
his face had gone all soft and squashy, his limbs stiff . . . The
horror of it was that everyone around him seemed to take this as
entirely normal, and he could not tell them what was wrong.

He came fully awake and sat up in bed, clacking his jaws and
rumpling the feathery spines along his side with his fingers. He
had been dreaming, he realized suddenly—dreaming of himself as
he had been before the change.

He sat for a moment, dully thinking about it. He felt a dim
sense of betrayal, as if he had somehow foresworn his loyalty to
that human body, once so familiar, which now seemed like an
improbable nightmare. It disturbed him a little that his feelings
could change so radically, in a matter of weeks. If that could
happen, where was there a bottom to anything?

He got out of bed, feeling his good spirits return with the
healthy responses of his body. After all, there was no use looking
backward. He was himself, as determined as ever, and—he stiffened with realization . . . how could he have forgotten?—this was
the morning of his final accounting with Grück.

Yawning nervously, he went into the living room and
switched on the television. It was not time for the news yet. He
glanced out the window, past the temporary fence, a dozen yards
away, that the workmen had put up yesterday. The lawns and
paths were empty in the early sunlight; there was a flutter of
wings in one of the distant aviaries, then stillness again.

Now that the time was so near, he was beginning to feel
anxious. He had half expected Grück to try to drug him once
more, and had slept every night with a barricade across the doorway; but except for the fence, which kept anyone from coming
near the cage, nothing had been done to interfere with him. He
dragged the table and bookcase out of the way and wandered into
the office space.

As he crossed the room, Emma's face appeared in her doorway. "Good morning," she said timidly.

"Good morning, Emma," the biped answered, mildly surprised. His attention was not on her. He was thinking about the press conference to come.

The female ventured a step or two out of the doorway. "Today is Wednesday," she observed.

"That's right, Wednesday."

"This is the day you are going to prove you are Herr Naumchik."

"Yes," the biped said, surprised and pleased.

"Then you will be going away."

"I suppose I will, yes." What was the creature getting at?

"I shall be all alone," Emma said.

"Well," said the biped awkwardly, "I expect you'll get used to it."

"I shall miss you," Emma said. "Good-bye, Fritz."

"Good-bye."

She turned and went back into her room. The biped stared after her, touched and vaguely disturbed.

From the living room sounded a chime, then a hearty voice, "Eight hundred hours, time for the news! Good morning, this is Reporter Walter Szaborni, at your service. Seven hundred are known dead in a Calcutta earthquake! Two members of the Council of Bavaria have been accused of improper conduct! These and other stories—"

Hurrying into the living room, the biped picked up the control box that lay beside the chair and pressed the channel selector. In the wall screen, the ruddy-faced announcer vanished and was replaced by a beaming elderly lady, eccentrically dressed, who sat at the keyboard of a piano. "For my first selection this morning," she announced in a heavy Slavic accent, "I shall play Morgenstern's 'Dawn' . . ." *Click!* She gave way to a muscular young man in a cream-colored leotard, who sat on the floor rotating himself on one buttock. "Just ea-sily back," he said, "and then forward—" *Click!*

". . . We bring you the latest development in a case that has all Berlin talking," said an invisible voice.

The biped caught his breath: the screen showed a view of the Zoo grounds, moving at a walking pace toward the main building. With a curious shock, turning and looking out the window, past the incurious faces of a few people who stood at the railing, the biped realized what he was about to see. Out there in the early sunshine, walking slowly across the lawn, was a man with a tiny television camera.

". . . who claims to be Martin Naumchik, a reporter for *Paris-Soir*," the voice was saying. At the same moment, the outer door rattled. The biped vacillated a moment, then left the screen and hurried into the office space. It was the keeper with his cart.

"Otto! Have you any message for me?"

"No message. Eat," said Otto, unloading trays from his cart.

"But, is the press conference really going to be held? Is anyone here yet?"

"Plenty of people," Otto grunted. "All in good time. Eat." He walked away.

But eating was out of the question; the biped pushed the food around with his fork, took a bite or two, then gave it up and walked restlessly back and forth in his inner room until, after what seemed hours, the door opened and Otto returned.

As he ran into the office space, the biped caught sight of Emma peering out of her doorway again. Ignoring her, he demanded, "Are they ready for me now?"

"Yes. Come," Otto said. The biped smoothed down his spines and followed.

There were crowds outside the gallery, and in the corridors as well; the biped glimpsed Prinzmetal going by with a harried expression. Outside the penthouse dining room, there were men wearing earphones, crouching over metal boxes covered with switches and dials. A white-uniformed Berlin policeman stood guard by the entrance. Ignoring him, Otto opened the door and leaned in for a moment, blocking the way with his body. He spoke to someone inside, then closed the door again. "Wait," he told the biped.

After a few moments the door opened again and a pale, sweaty face appeared. It was a young man the biped had never seen before. "All right, bring it in. Quickly, quickly!"

"Always in a hurry, aren't you?" Otto grumbled. "Very well, go, then." He gave the biped a push.

Inside, the pale young man seized the biped's arm. "Go straight in, don't keep them waiting!" Beyond him, past the backs of several men who were standing close together, the biped glimpsed Grück's rotund figure behind a table. "And now," the director's voice said nervously, "I present to you the biped, Fritz!"

The biped walked stiffly forward in the silence. The big room was packed with people, some standing with cameras, the rest seated at tables arranged in arcs all the way back to the far wall. Grück gave the biped an unreadable look as he approached. "Tell them your story, Fritz—or shall I say Herr Naumchik?" He bowed and stepped back, leaving the biped alone.

The biped cleared his throat with an unintended squawk, which caused a ripple of laughter around the room. Frightened and angry, he leaned forward and gripped the edge of the table.

"My name is Martin Naumchik," he began in a loud voice. The room quieted almost at once as he spoke, and he could feel the listeners' respectful attention. Gaining confidence, he told his story clearly and directly, beginning from the moment he had seen the young man with the camera outside his cage. As he talked, he looked around the room, hoping to see familiar faces, but the lights were so arranged that he could barely make out the features of those who were looking at him.

When he finished, there was a moment's silence, then a stir, and a forest of hands went up.

"You, there," said the biped, pointing helplessly at random. A woman rose. "Who told you to say all this?" she demanded. She had a sharp, indignant face, glittering eyes. A groan of protest went up around her.

"No one," said the biped firmly. "Next! You, there . . . yes, you, sir."

"You say you took a degree at the Sorbonne in 1999. Who was the head of the German department there?"

"Herr Winkler," the biped answered without hesitation, and pointed to another questioner.

"Who was your superior on *Paris-Soir* when you worked at the home office?"

"Claude Ehrichs."

Most of the questions were the same ones he had answered before, many of them several times, at previous interviews; repeating the same responses over again made him feel a trace of discouragement. When would there be an end? But the attitude of the listeners cheered him: they were respectfully attentive, even friendly.

A tall, red-bearded man stood up. "Let me ask you this, Herr Naumchik. What is *your* explanation of this incredible thing? How do you account for it?"

"I can't account for it," the biped said earnestly. "But I'm telling you the truth."

There was a murmur of sympathy as the tall man sat down. The biped opened his mouth to speak again, but before he could do so the mellifluous voice of Dr. Grück was heard. "That ends our little question period, thank you very much, gentlemen and ladies." Grück came forward, followed by two keepers who quickly took the biped's arms and started to lead him away.

The biped, at first taken by surprise, began to resist. "I'm not finished!" he shouted. "I appeal to you, make them release me!" In spite of his struggles, the keepers were dragging him farther away from the table. "Make them release me! I am Martin Naumchik!"

They were at the door. Behind them, an angry hum was rising from the audience. There were shouts of "Shame! Bring him back!" Over the growing uproar, Grück's voice was vainly repeating, "One moment, ladies and gentlemen! I beg your indulgence! One moment! One moment!"

The keepers thrust the biped outside; the door closed. The

biped ceased to struggle. "Will you behave yourself?" demanded one of the keepers, straightening his collar.

Otto appeared through the crowd, his face as stolid as ever. "Go on, if I want you I will call you," he grunted. "Fritz, come."

The biped followed him docilely, but his heart was thudding with excitement and indignation. "Did you hear it?" he demanded. "Did you hear how that man cut me off, just when—?"

"Not me," said Otto. "I don't concern myself with such things. I was sitting down and having a smoke." Avoiding the crowd, he pushed the biped toward a rear stairway. They walked down two flights, then crossed a library exhibit, threading their way between the tables and brushing through red banners that urged, "Read a book about animals!" This part of the building was almost deserted; so was the gallery.

As soon as Otto unlocked the outer door, the biped heard Grück's voice booming from within. His excitement increased again: he ran into the living room. In the television screen, Herr Doktor Grück's red, perspiring face stared wildly. "Gentlemen and ladies, if I may have your kind attention! Gentlemen and ladies!"

The voice of an invisible commentator cut in smoothly, "The hall is still in an uproar. The Herr Doktor is unable to make himself heard."

The biped danced with excitement in front of the screen, clasping his hands together. Outside, beyond the fence, a crowd was gathering, but he ignored it. The sound from the television had a curious echoing quality, and he realized after a moment that Emma must have her set turned on next door, too.

The noise was subsiding. Grück shouted, "Gentlemen and ladies—you have heard the biped's statement! Now permit the director of the Zoo to make a statement also!"

There were scattered cheers. Silence fell, broken at first by coughs and the shuffling of feet. When it was complete, Grück spoke again.

"Let me ask you to think about one question," he said. "*Where is Martin Naumchik?*"

He glanced from side to side. The silence deepened. "Where is Naumchik, this enterprising newspaperman, who has scored such a triumph?" A mutter arose; the camera swung to show restless movement in the room, one or two people rising; indistinct voices were heard.

"Is he wandering the streets of Berlin, with an animal's soul inside his body?" Grück persisted. "Then why is he not seen? Isn't this a curious question, gentlemen and ladies? Doesn't this make you wonder, doesn't it arouse your interest? I ask again, *where* is this famous Martin Naumchik? Is he *hiding*?" He stared out at the camera, eyes gleaming behind his rimless glasses.

The biped clenched his fists involuntarily.

"Suppose that I now tell you we are all the victims of a clever hoax?" Grück demanded. There were hisses, groans of protest from the audience. "You don't believe it? You are too thoroughly convinced?"

A deep voice echoed up from somewhere in the audience. After a moment the camera swung around: it was the tall, red-bearded man who had spoken before. His voice grew clearer. ". . . this farce. Why did you hurry the biped out of sight—why isn't he here to speak for himself?" Cries of approval; the red-bearded man looked self-satisfied, and folded his arms on his chest.

Dr. Grück appeared again. "My dear Herr Wilenski—that is your name, is it not?—do you realize that if *I* am telling you the truth," he carefully smote his plump breast, "this biped is a very valuable animal, very high-strung and nervous, which must be protected? Am I to endanger his health? Do you think I am such a fool?" A little laughter; scattered shouts of approval.

The red-bearded man popped into view again, aiming his finger sternly. "What about the biped's charge that you drugged him? What have you to say to that?"

Then Grück's earnest face, in close-up: "Somehow the animal got hold of a piece of soap, Herr Wilenski. The keeper who was responsible has been—"

("Soap?" echoed Wilenski's voice.)

"Yes, soap. The sodium and potassium salts in soap have a toxic effect on these bipeds. You must remember that they are not human beings, Herr Wilenski." He raised one plump hand. "Let me continue." Mutterings from the audience. "But first let me say this to you, Herr Wilenski, and to all of you—if I shall not convince you that we have to do here with a hoax, a dirty publicity scheme—if you shall have listened to me and still believe that in that poor biped's body there is the soul of a human being—then I solemnly promise you that I will release Martin Naumchik!"

Sensation in the hall. The biped closed his eyes and groped weakly behind him for the chair. His relief was so great that he did not hear the next few words from the screen.

"—we here at the Zoo were just as much in the dark as you, you may believe me! How could such a thing occur? We did not believe the biped's story for a moment—yet, what other explanation could be found? We were at our wits' end, gentlemen and ladies—until we had the lucky inspiration to search the biped's cage! Then! Imagine our shock, our horror, when we found . . . this!"

The camera drew back. Grück, half turning, was extending his hand in a dramatic gesture toward a machine that lay on a little table behind him. An assistant wheeled it closer. It was, as far as the biped could make out, nothing but a solid-state recorder, the same kind of machine Opatescu had used . . .

A cold feeling took him in the chest. He leaned forward uneasily.

"Under the blankets of the biped's bed," Grück's voice went on, "we found this recording machine concealed!"

"How did it get there?" boomed Wilenski's voice.

Grück's face turned; his expression was solemn. "We are still investigating this," he said. "And you may believe me, that when the guilty individuals are caught, they shall be punished with the full severity of the law! But at this moment, I can say only that we are highly interested in questioning the keeper who was discharged." He stepped closer to the small table, laid his hand on the recorder. "Now, I want you all to listen to what we found in this concealed machine! Listen carefully!"

He switched on the recorder.

After a moment, a man's deep voice spoke. "Listen and repeat after me. My name is Martin Naumchik . . . I was born at Asnieres in 1976 . . . I am a newspaperman. I work for *Paris-Soir*. My superior there is Monsieur Claude Ehrichs . . ."

A distant murmur came through the glass. The biped turned his head involuntarily, and saw a little knot of people clustered around the aerial of a portable TV. Fists were being shaken. Voices drifted over, faintly: "Charlatan! Hoaxer!"

With a sense of doom, the biped turned back to the screen. The camera was panning now over the faces of the listeners. He saw shock and surprise give way to cynical understanding, disgust or anger. People were beginning to stand up here and there throughout the room; some were leaving. The biped saw the red-bearded man, shaking his head, move off toward the aisle.

"Wait! Wait!" he called. But the man in the screen did not hear.

The room was emptying. The monotonous voice of the recorder had stopped. Grück was standing idly looking out over the room, with a faint smile of satisfaction on his lips. Wenzl leaned over to speak to him; Grück nodded absently. His lips pursed: he was whistling.

"And so," said the voice of the announcer breathlessly, "in this dramatic revelation, the mystery of the human biped is explained! All honor to Herr Doktor Grück for his dignified handling of this difficult situation! We now return you to our studios."

The screen flickered, cleared. The biped hit the control button blindly with his fist; the image faded, dwindled and was gone.

"Ssss! Fritz the faker! Ssss!" came the voices from outside.

The uproar in the Aviary redoubled the moment Wenzl strode in. Toucans opened their gigantic beaks, flapped their wings and screamed. The air was full of fluttering smaller birds, flash of tail feathers, red, yellow, blue. Macaws left off hitching themselves along their wooden perches, beak, claw, beak, claw, to flutter against the invisible air fence shrieking, "Rape! Rape!"

Wenzl strode past them, his death's-head face like a pale shark swimming down the green corridor of the Aviary.

At the far end of the building, two under-keepers stood to attention. All was in order here. Wenzl crossed the short open entranceway, making a path through the sluggish crowds, and went into the Primate House.

Shrieks, roars and the thunder of shaken bars greeted him as he stepped through the doorway. Capuchins hurtled forward over one another's backs, clustering at the bars, showing their sharp yellow teeth, shrieking their little lungs out. Proboscis monkeys dropped out of their tree-limb perches, blinking and chattering. The baboon, Hugo, leaped against his bars with a crash, shoved off and somersaulted in midair, flashing his blue behind; the two chimps rattled the bars and squealed together.

Wenzl moved along the row of cages, attentive and calm. He passed through another open entrance to the Reptile House.

Here all was quiet. Wenzl's glance softened for the first time. The Galapagos tortoise, big as a wheelbarrow, was slowly munching a head of lettuce in his cruel jaws. The boa constrictor was coiled sluggishly around a conspicuous lump in its gullet. Four diamondbacks hissed, clattered faintly, slithered off into their rocky den.

In its floodlighted cage, the grass snake hung in graceful festoons. Its tiny head swayed toward Wenzl; the pink tongue flickered out. Wenzl paused an instant to regard it with pleasure. Then he moved on.

In the Terrestrial Mammal House, there was a crowd around the rhinoceros wallow, where Prinzmetal was giving the rhino an injection. Finished, he climbed over the rail and joined Wenzl, mopping his brow with a tissue.

"Successful?" Wenzl demanded.

"Oh, yes, I think so," said Prinzmetal in his soft, unassuming voice. "He will be all right."

"It is necessary for him to be all right."

"It is necessary for him to be all right."

"Oh, well, he will be." They walked through the exit together, turned right, opened a door marked "No Admittance."

A slender, flaxen-haired young keeper was hurrying toward them, carrying a pail of fish.

"Schildt, why are you not feeding the sea lions?" Wenzl demanded severely.

"Just going now, sir!" said the unfortunate keeper, stiffening to attention.

"Then what are you waiting for? Go!"

"Yes, sir!"

Wenzl, as he strode along beside Prinzmetal, took a tiny notebook from his breast pocket and with a tiny silver pencil, sharp as a bodkin, made a minuscule entry in it. Prinzmetal watched him with one soft brown eye, but made no comment.

"Have you seen the papers?" Prinzmetal asked, as they rode up in the elevator.

"Yes," said Wenzl. They got out. Wenzl hesitated, then followed Prinzmetal into the latter's washroom.

"What papers did you mean, exactly?" he asked.

Prinzmetal, looking surprised, straightened up from the basin where he had begun washing his hands. "Oh—there it is, on the table. The *Zeitung*. On the third page. There's a story about a baby in Buenos Aires that understands what you say to it in French, Spanish and German. Three months old."

"Yes."

"And the curious thing—what struck my attention—"

"Is that the child's French nursemaid underwent an attack of amentia at the same time," said Wenzl, biting his words.

"Yes," Prinzmetal said, forgetting to wash.

"She is incontinent," said Wenzl.

"Yes."

"She understands nothing, must be fed, can only make childish sounds. But the child understands French, German and Spanish."

"So, you saw the paper," said Prinzmetal.

"And you, did you see this in the *Tageblatt*?" Wenzl asked, almost unwillingly. He took a folded newspaper from his breast pocket. "A man and his wife in Tasmania each claims to be the other."

"I heard also, on the television, that while laying a cornerstone in Aberdeen, the mayor changed into a naked young girl, who ran away crying," said Prinzmetal. "But who knows what those fellows make up and what is true?"

"Supposing it should be all true?" Wenzl asked, folding his paper neatly and putting it away.

"It would be interesting," said Prinzmetal, turning his attention to his soft, hairy hands, which he began to scrub with care.

"And?"

"It is our duty to report to the director anything that might be of importance to the work of the Zoo," said Prinzmetal, as if reciting a lesson.

"On the other hand," said Wenzl deliberately, "It is useless, and even has a harmful effect, to take up the Herr Doktor's time with baseless newspaper scandal."

The two men looked at each other for a moment with complete understanding in their eyes. "After all," said Prinzmetal, drying his hands, "what would be the good of it?"

"Exactly," said Wenzl, and folding his newspaper precisely lengthwise, he dropped it into the waste can.

VIII

When the young man woke up, he was in a narrow bed in a white-tiled room. Wires that came out of the bed were stuck to his head, arms and legs with sticky elastic bands. He plucked at them irritably, but they would not come off.

He looked around. There was a doorway, open, but no window. In the corner, behind a single wall that half concealed it, was a w.c. In the other corner was a flimsy plastic chair and a reading light, but nothing to read.

The young man tried to get up, pulling at the wires, and discovered they had silvery joints that would break apart. He got out of bed, trailing the wires.

After a moment a stout woman in nurse's uniform came in, and clucked her tongue at him. "Up, are you? Who told you you could?"

"I want to use the w.c.," he told her plaintively.

"Well, go ahead, then back into bed with you. Herr Doktor Hölderlein hasn't seen you yet." To his mild surprise, she stood with hands folded in front of her and watched while he used the toilet. Then she pushed him back and made him lie down, while she snicked the silvery joints of the wires together again, all around the bed. "Lie still," she told him. "No more nonsense. Here is the bell—ring if you want anything."

She showed him a plastic knob on the end of a flex cord, and went away. "Am I sick?" he called after her, but she did not come back.

The young man tried once more to pull off the elastic bands, then gave it up. His last memories were confused. He could remember falling into the net, and being held down while he struggled. Then a feeling of being carried, a glimpse of many legs walking. . . . Then nothing, until he found himself in a white-walled tiny room with bars instead of a door. His clothes were gone, and he was wearing gray pajamas. No one had come in answer to his calling, until he began to bang on the bars with a steel pot he found in the room, and then a man came and squirted water on him from a spray gun. So he did not bang any more, but sat and shivered.

He remembered falling asleep and waking up at least twice in that room. Once he had been fed. Then two men had come to fetch him, and they had given him his own clothes again, and coffee to drink, which he liked. Then they had taken him down a long corridor into a crowded room, and told him to wait. At the end of the room, behind a high counter, was a man in red robes, with a red floppy hat. The young man knew from his watching of television that this man was a judge, and that he was going to be sentenced . . .

Now, here he was in still another place. Time passed. The young man was growing hungry, but did not dare ring the bell. At last an orderly came in with a cart, and he was allowed to sit up and eat. It was almost like the Zoo. Then the orderly came back for his plate, and hooked him up to the wires again, and for a long time nothing else happened.

The young man was bewildered. Why was he here? What had the judge and that other man been whispering about, down at the end of the room, and why had the judge looked so annoyed when he glanced his way?

This place was better than the jail, it would not do to complain—but if he was not sick, then why was he here?

Bells tinkled outside. Every now and then people passed his doorway, walking rapidly, with soft soles that swished and squeaked on the tile floor.

Then the nurse came in again. "You are in luck," she told him. "Herr Doktor Hölderlein says you may see Herr Doktor Böhmer today." She yanked his wires apart briskly, then helped him up. "Come, don't keep the doctor waiting!"

She took his elbow and led him down the hall, where messages in colored letters rippled silently along the walls, to an office where a man with a bushy mustache sat behind a desk. On the desk was a card that said "Hr. Dr. Böhmer."

The doctor gave the young man a long measuring look, and unscrewed a thick old-fashioned tacrograph slowly. "Sit down, please." He began writing on a pad. "Now then. Can you tell me your name?"

The young man hesitated only a moment. If he said "Fritz," he knew very well they would send him back to the Zoo. "Martin Naumchik, Herr Doktor," he said.

"Occupation?"

"Journalist."

The doctor nodded slowly, writing. "And your address?"

"Gastnerstrasse."

"And the number?"

The young man tried to remember, but could not.

Doktor Böhmer pursed his heavy lips. "You seem a little confused. How long is it since you were in your apartment in Gastnerstrasse?"

The young man shifted uncomfortably. "I think three—or, no, four days."

"You really don't remember." Doktor Böhmer wrote something slowly, in his thick black handwriting, across the ruled pad. The young man watched him with apprehension.

"Well then, perhaps you can tell me the date?"

"June 10th, Doktor . . . or perhaps the 11th."

Böhmer's bushy eyebrows went up a trifle. "Very good. And who is the president of the High Council, can you tell me that?"

"Herr Professor Onderdonck . . . is that right?"

"No, not quite right. He was president last year." Böhmer wrote something else slowly on the pad. "Well, now." He folded his heavy arms across the pad, holding the big black tacrograph as if it were a cigar. "Tell me, do you remember being in the department store?"

"Oh, yes, Herr Doktor."

"And hiding upstairs, and coming down during the day?"

"Yes, Herr Doktor."

"And why did you do that?"

The young man hesitated, opening and closing his mouth several times.

"You can tell me, Herr Naumchik. Go ahead. Why did you do it?"

The young man said helplessly, "Because I had nowhere else to go, Herr Doktor."

Böhmer slowly unfolded his arms and made another mark on the pad. He reached without looking and touched a bell-push at the corner of his desk. "I see. Well then, Herr Naumchik, tomorrow at the same time, is it agreed?"

"Yes, Herr Doktor." The nurse entered and stood holding the door open. The young man rose docilely and went out.

"Doctor says you can sleep without the wires tonight," said the nurse briskly as they entered his room again. Breathing heavily through her nose, she stood close to him and began peeling off the elastic bands. "Don't squirm," she said.

"It hurts."

"Nonsense, this takes only a moment. There." She wadded up the bands, wrapped the wires around them and turned to leave. "Lie down now, rest."

"But nurse, why do I have to be here? Am I sick?" the young man asked.

She turned and stared at him briefly. "Of course, you are sick. But you are getting much better. Now rest." She waddled out.

After a long time there was supper, and then pills to swallow. When he woke up, it was morning again.

"Good news!" cried the nurse, entering to plump up his pillows. "You have a visitor today!"

"I have?" the young man asked. His heart began to beat faster. He could not imagine who it could be. Someone from the Zoo?

"A young *lady*," said the nurse archly.

"What's her name? I don't know any young lady."

"All in good time. Eat your breakfast now, then comes the barber to shave you, and next you will see your friend."

She left. The young man rubbed at the furry growth on his cheeks and chin. Shaving he knew, but not how it was done. It would be good to be shaved.

After breakfast the barber came in, a short, dark man in a white coat, who plugged a buzzing machine into the wall and applied it, with a bored expression, to the young man's whiskers. At first it pulled and hurt him, then it was better, and at last the hair was all gone. His skin stopped itching and felt delightfully smooth to the touch.

He waited impatiently. An orderly came and gave him a comb, and he combed his hair in the mirror, several ways, until he thought it was correct.

Then he still had to wait. At last the nurse came in again, looked at him critically, and said, "Very good! Follow me!"

She took him to a little room with windows, rather bare and clean, with upholstered chairs and magazines in a rack. In the room stood a woman in a blue dress. There was a man in a white coat a little behind her. Glancing from one to the other, the young man recognized Herr Doktor Böhmer almost at once, but it was only when the woman stepped forward that he knew her. She was the woman in the store—the one who had slapped him.

"Oh, my poor Martin, what has happened to you?" she wailed, putting out her arms.

The young man stepped back nervously. "They say I am sick," he muttered, watching her closely.

"You identify our young friend, then, Frau Schorr?" asked the doctor amiably.

"He doesn't remember me," she said in a tight voice. "But it's Martin, of course it's Martin."

"And you are his—"

The woman bit her lip. "His sister. Will they let me take him away, Herr Doktor, do you think?"

"That depends on many things, Frau Schorr," said the doctor severely. "Come into my office when you are finished, and let us discuss it in detail."

"Yes, in a moment," she said, turning back to the young man. "Martin, you would like to go with me?"

He hesitated. It was true that she did not seem so excitable as before, but who knew when the mood might not take her again?

"To get away from this place?" she asked.

The young man made up his mind. "Yes, please, I would like it."

She smiled at him and turned to the doctor. "Very good, Herr Doktor, now I am at your service. Until very soon, Martin . . ." They both went out. In a few moments the nurse came to lead him back to his cubicle.

Then, although the young man waited expectantly, nothing happened except lunch. After the meal was cleared away he waited again, growing indignant, but hours went by and still no one came.

The orderly brought his dinner. He began to feel frightened. Suppose something had gone wrong, and the woman was never coming back at all?

The nurse could not answer his questions, but kept repeating stupid things like, "Wait and see. Don't be so impatient. Why are you in such a hurry?" She gave him pills to take, and insisted on hooking him up to the wires again. Then he woke up, and again it was morning.

"Good news!" cried nurse cheerily, entering the room. "They are going to release you today!"

"They are?" the young man asked eagerly. He tried to clamber out of bed, but was brought up short. "Devil take them!" he shouted, tearing at the wires. "Nurse, get me my clothes!"

"Temper, temper!" she said, raising her hands in mock dismay. "Can't you wait even till after breakfast? Such impatience!" She disconnected the wires at the joints and tucked them neatly away. "Nothing was ever done in a hurry," she went on. "There, go, wash yourself. All in good time." She bustled out.

The young man cleaned himself and combed his hair again. It was hard to sit still. Breakfast came and he ate some of it, thinking, "Now she is almost here."

But more hours passed in the same endless way as before. What could have gone wrong? He stood in the doorway and waited for the nurse; at last she came.

He held out his hand. "Nurse, when are they going to let me out?"

"Soon, soon," she said, slipping past him. "Go and comb your hair—don't worry. It won't be long."

"But you said that this morning!" the young man shouted after her. It was no use. She was gone.

When he had been sitting for a long time, staring blankly at the floor, an orderly came in. "Your hair is a *fright*," he said. The orderly himself had carefully waved hair, gleaming with oil. "Here, use my comb," he said.

"When are they going to let me go?"

"I don't know. Soon," the orderly said indifferently, and went away.

Lunchtime came. Now the young man realized that it was all a cruel joke. He lay down on the bed, leaving his dishes untouched.

There was a clatter at the door. The orderly entered, pushing a metal rack on which some clothes were hung. Watching incredulously, the young man recognized the trousers and surcoat he had been wearing before; the coat was ripped up the side, and the sleeve was grimy with some sticky, odorous mass.

"Put them on," said the orderly. "Orders." He went away again.

The young man dressed himself awkwardly. His heart was beating very fast, and he had trouble deciding which way some of the things went on. At last he was done, and he combed his hair carefully all over again.

Then he waited. Footsteps came and went hurriedly in the corridor; white-jacketed figures passed and repassed. A bell jangled, and a boy in a purple robe went by carrying a candle in a glass bowl, followed by a man in black robes, head down, mumbling something to himself. The bell dwindled in the distance.

A burst of laughter sounded from somewhere not far away. "Well, you know what I would have told him!" a hearty male voice exclaimed. Then two voices began speaking together, in lower tones, and the young man could not make out any more of the words.

Footsteps approached the door again. In walked a woman.

At first he did not recognize her as Frau Schorr. She was more formally dressed than the day before, in a puffed skirt and overdress under which the shape of her body could hardly be made out. She looked pale and nervous and did not meet his eyes.

"Martin, they promised they would release you at nine-thirty this morning," she said at once, "and here it is almost—"

"Madame Schorr," the orderly interrupted, putting his head in at the door, "they are blinking for you to come down to the office at once."

"Oh, my God!" said the woman and, turning around, she walked out again.

The young man waited. At last Frau Schorr entered, walking rapidly. This time she looked flushed and energetic. "Come, quickly," she said, taking his arm, "before they change their minds."

"I can go?" he asked.

"Yes, it is all arranged. Hurry!"

She led him down the white hall, past the blinking colored letters on the wall. There were potted plants at every intersection of corridors—always the same plant, with shiny saw-toothed leaves.

They got into a rapid elevator of the kind the young man had seen in the store. It opened for them, clicked shut and with a dizzy swoop they were hurtling downward; then another swoop in the reverse direction, a click, and they were standing on the gray tile floor of a large lobby, with enormous windows of clear glass through which the young man could see the central tower of the Flugbahn, glittering in the sunlight against the sky of pure blue.

"Hurry!" said the woman, leading him to another elevator. This one was the spiral kind. They dropped through a glass tube, past dark walls at first, then, startlingly, into the daylight.

What had happened to the building? The young man craned his neck, saw the titanic slab of masonry receding above his head. They had emerged from the bottom of the hospital, which was supported high in the air on concrete legs. Around them bright green lawns and flowering shrubs were visible. Only one other building could be seen in the middle distance, and that was a single, carelessly carved block of pink stone, without windows or visible entrances. Beyond, the rooftops of a few buildings showed over the treetops.

The elevator went underground without pausing, and a moment later they were in the white, flat light of a subterranean tunnel. As they left the elevator, an oval car drifted up on two fat wheels. It stopped, and the transparent top swung open. There was no driver.

The young man hung back, but Frau Schorr urged him in. They sat down on the deep cushions; the top hesitated, then slowly dropped and latched with a click. The woman leaned forward. "Take us to the Fiedler Platz exit, please."

After a pause, a mechanical voice spoke from the grille facing them. "That will be two marks ten, please." The woman fumbled in her purse, found a piece of paper money and put it into a slot beside the grille. "Thank you," said the voice; coins clattered into a metal cup. The woman picked them out carefully and put them away as the car glided into motion.

They did not seem to be moving fast, but the young man felt himself pressed back into the cushions, and the white lights of the tunnel whisked by at a dizzying rate.

Other cars were visible far ahead and behind. Now the tunnel forked, the left-hand branch turning downward, the right-hand one up. Their car whirled to the left without losing speed. At a second fork, they turned right, rising again.

The car glided to a stop beside an elevator, identical to the one they had taken from the hospital. The top swung back.

A little dizzy from so much rapid motion, the young man followed the woman into the elevator. As the car rose in the tube, another car with two men and a child in it whirled down past them in the counter-spiral. It made the young man feel ill to watch them, and he shut his eyes.

Now they were aboveground once more. The street was full of cool blue shadow, but over their heads the sun was still warm on the façades. Taking his arm again, the woman led him across the empty pavement to one of the entrances, over which the young man read the number "109" in silver letters.

In the lobby, she paused, one gloved hand going to her mouth. "You have your key?" she asked.

"Key?" The young man explored his pockets, brought up the key on the gold ring. "Is this it?"

She took it with relief. "Yes, I'm quite sure. Come."

They entered another elevator, an ordinary straight-up one this time, and the woman spoke to the grille. "Three."

They emerged into a narrow hallway carpeted in beige and green. Frau Schorr led the way directly to a door numbered 3C, opened it with the key.

Inside, they found themselves in greenish dimness. The room was small, with a narrow bed, a table with some coffee things, a typewriter on a desk. There was no dust, but the air had a stale, bottled-up smell.

The woman crossed to the windows and threw back the green drapes, letting in the sunlight. She touched a button on the control panel over the bed, and at once fresh air began to whisper into the room.

"Well, here you are then!" said the woman happily. "Your own little room . . ." She paused. "But you don't remember this, either?"

The young man was looking around. He had never seen the room before, and did not much care for it. "Isn't there any television?" he asked.

The woman studied him for a moment, then went to the control panel again, touched another button. A picture on the wall opened and folded back, revealing a TV screen, which instantly bloomed into life. A man's smiling face loomed toward them, gigantic, all-swallowing, while laughter roared from the wall. Then the sound died, the open-mouthed face shrank and disappeared as the woman touched the controls again.

The halves of the picture jerked, flapped, slid together.

"What's the matter?" asked the woman.

"I didn't know it was going to do that," said the young man, quivering.

She looked at him thoughtfully. "I see." She put the tips of her gloved fingers to her lips. "Martin, you know this is your own room. It doesn't remind you at all? I thought perhaps when you saw it— No. I think it's better that you don't stay here, Martin. Come, help me."

She crossed briskly to the opposite wall, slid back a panel, took out two pieces of luggage. She laid them open on the bed, then crossed the room again, pulled a drawer out of the wall, scooped up a pile of clothing. "Here, take these." She dumped the clothing into his arms. "You put everything on the bed, I'll pack."

"But where are we going?" he asked, carrying his burden obediently across the room.

"To my apartment," she said. She picked up the clothes, straightened them neatly, began to pack them into the larger of the two suitcases. "Go, get more."

The young man went back, found another drawer under the first. There were nothing but socks in this one. He brought them dutifully over to the bed.

"And if Frau Beifelder doesn't like it, let her choke!" said the woman, punching shirts down into the open suitcase with brisk, angry motions.

Understanding nothing, the young man did as he was told. All the clothing, including two sets of overgarments, went into the larger suitcase. The other case, which was very flat and narrow, was filled with papers from the desk. Frau Schorr took both suitcases, and the young man carried the typewriter in its case. They went down again in the elevator, across the street, down the other elevator, and got into a cab exactly like the one that had brought them.

This time they emerged into a more populous street. Carrying their suitcases, they crossed the open area past a group of strolling girls, a tall boy on a unicycle, a flower vendor.

There were shops on either side, with interesting things displayed in their windows, but Frau Schorr would not let him linger. They turned the first corner to the left, entered a building faced with blue stone. In the lobby sat a little white-haired old lady with a face full of wrinkles. "Good afternoon, Frau Beifelder," said

Frau Schorr stiffly. The old woman did not reply, but stared after them with tiny, red-rimmed eyes.

"It's good for her to be shocked a little, after all," muttered Frau Schorr as they crowded into the elevator. She looked distressed. The young man would have liked to comfort her, but did not understand what was the matter, so he said nothing.

Upstairs, the hall was tiny, with only two red-enameled doors. "Well, here we are at last!" said the woman brightly, opening the first of these.

Inside was a sunny and comfortable-looking room, with bright colors in the upholstery and rugs. As they entered, a tawny cat leaped down from the window seat and came toward them, pale blue eyes staring from a masked face.

The young man looked at it in surprise. He had never seen a housecat before, except in pictures—only the big ones in the Zoo, and those from a distance.

"Is it fierce?" he asked.

"Maggie?" said the woman, looking puzzled. "Whatever do you mean?" She stooped to pick up the cat, which was staring at the young man with its back arched, making a low wailing noise. When she lifted it, it hung limply from her hand for a moment like a furpiece, then writhed once and leaped to the floor. The wailing sound grew louder. The fur along the cat's back was ruffled.

"Oh, dear!" said the woman. "Maggie, don't you remember Martin?" She turned to him in bewilderment. "She is upset. Sit down, dear, everything is going to be all right. Take off your surcoat and rest a little. You shall have some coffee and sandwiches in a moment." The cat was advancing, stiff-legged; she pushed it away with her foot. With an angry screech, it retreated to the window-seat again and tucked itself together into a ball. Its blue eyes grew narrow, but whenever the young man moved they widened and its mouth opened in a sharp-toothed smile.

"I can't imagine what is the matter with her," said Frau Schorr from the next room. A cupboard door banged shut; a pot clattered. "She is such an affectionate creature, and she always liked you, Martin."

Wanting to examine a picture on the opposite wall, the young man took one or two steps toward it, watching the cat out of the corner of his eye.

The animal stared back at him and made a faint hissing noise, but did not move. Emboldened, the young man crossed the room and looked at the picture closely, but still could not decide what it represented.

Baffled, he turned away, just as something squat and dirty-white waddled into view from the hall doorway. It looked up at him out of tiny red eyes and made a wheezing sound. Spittle hung from the loose lips of its enormously wide mouth, and two discolored fangs stuck up from the lower jaw. It stared at the young man in astonishment for a moment, then the gray-white hair on its shoulders rose stiffly and it made a menacing noise. The young man raised a hand. The animal began to bark, dancing about in the doorway, its eyes bulging insanely to show the yellowish, blood-shot whites. The young man backed away as far as he could go.

"Churchill!" called the woman from the kitchen. The dog turned its head toward her voice, but went on barking. "Churchill!" she called again, and in a moment came hurriedly into the room, wiping her hands on her apron. "Shame!" she said, glancing at the young man. "Churchill, what is the matter with you?" The barking continued.

"Now then!" said the woman, slapping the infuriated animal on the snout with her palm. The dog hiccoughed, shook its head and stared up at her with a surprised expression. It barked once more. The woman slapped it again, more gently. "No, Churchill—shame! This is Martin, don't you remember? He has forgotten you," she said apologetically over her shoulder. "Go on now, back to your rug, Churchill. Bad dog, go on!" She herded the dog through the doorway. It moved stiffly backward, then turned reluctantly and disappeared, wheezing and snuffling. A final bark sounded from the next room.

"Oh, dear," said the woman. "I'm so sorry, Martin. Excuse me a moment—the coffee." She went back into the kitchen, and the young man, slightly unnerved, began trotting back and forth beside the low bookshelves, looking at the titles of the books.

At the far corner of the room he came upon a tiny cage suspended from a polished brass stand. There was a beige cloth cover on the cage. Curious, he plucked up the edge of the cloth and peered inside. In the dimness, a tiny bird with green and violet feathers was perched on a miniature trapeze. One pin-sized golden eye blinked at him; the creature said, "Weep?"

The young man closed the cover again. "It is just like the Zoo," he thought.

The woman returned, looking flustered, with a tray in her hands. On the tray were sandwiches and coffee. She set it down on the table in front of the sofa. "Now come, eat, Martin, you must be hungry." She made him sit on the sofa, and while he dutifully ate the sandwiches and drank the good coffee, she sat opposite him in the upholstered chair, hands clasped in her lap, smiling faintly as she watched him eat. Her cheeks were flushed with exertion. A few strands of dark hair had escaped from her coiffure and hung over her forehead.

"Yes, eat, that is good," she said. "Would you like some music, Martin?" The young man nodded, with his mouth full. The woman rose, went to a machine in the corner and punched several buttons. After a moment the machine began to emit music, something slow and soothing, played by an orchestra with many violins. The young man listened with pleasure, waving his sandwich.

The woman sighed, then smiled. "No. You don't remember, do you?" she asked.

"Remember what?"

"The music. We used often to dial it . . . never mind." She crossed to the machine again and touched it; the music stopped. "But it's really true, then, that you don't remember anything?"

"I think I do," said the young man, lying cautiously. "You are my sister—"

"No!" said the woman vehemently. "That's not true at all. You don't remember." Her mouth was compressed and her eyes were closed.

"But then why did you tell the doctor that you were my sister?" the young man demanded, bewildered.

"Because I had to be a member of your family, or they would not have let me sign you out."

The young man swallowed, thinking this over. He laid his sandwich down. "But if you are not my sister—"

"Yes?"

"Then what are you?"

The woman's face colored, and she glanced away. "Never mind, Martin . . . just a friend. We are just friends."

She roused herself and stood up after a moment. "Have you had enough to eat, Martin? Would you like some cake? No? Another cup of coffee? . . . Well, then, let me see: would you like to play a game of chess? You would?"

She reached into the cabinet behind her and pulled out a small folding table with a chessboard in the top, and a box of chessmen.

"I don't know if I am good enough," said the young man, staring at these preparations eagerly. "I've never played a real game with anyone, only the problems in the Hamburg newspapers. . . ."

The woman was looking at him oddly, her hand poised over the open box of chessmen. "In the Hamburg newspapers?" she repeated.

"I—that is to say . . ." said the young man, realizing he had made a blunder.

"But where was this? In the store?" she asked.

"In the store, yes," said the young man gratefully. "You see, there were some newspapers up there—where I slept—and to pass the time—"

"Oh, of course. I see." She spilled the pieces out onto the board. "Still, it's odd that they were from Hamburg."

"Yes, that is odd, isn't it?"

"Well." She took two pieces in her hands, held them behind her back, then offered her two closed fists. "Choose."

The young man touched her left hand; she opened it, showing a white pawn. "Such luck," she said cheerfully, pushing the white pieces toward him. "Hand me those cigarettes, won't you, Martin?"

He followed her glance; there was nothing on the low table beside him but an ashtray and an enameled box. He lifted the lid: Correct, there were cigarettes inside.

She took one, lit it with a tiny rose-quartz lighter, tilted her head back to puff out a long streamer of smoke. With her left hand she was absently setting the black pieces in their places.

"Don't you want one?" she asked.

The young man looked dubiously at the white cylinders. He had never tried to smoke a cigarette, but doubtless it was one of the things he should learn.

He put one gingerly between his lips, took it out again and looked at it, then replaced it and touched the other end with the lighter. He sucked cautiously; the cigarette glowed. Cool, bitter-tasting smoke ran into his mouth. Before he realized what he was doing, he breathed some of it into his lungs, where it felt astonishingly good. He took another pull at the cigarette. He realized with grateful delight that the smoke was somehow soothing one of the urgent discomforts he had been feeling all this time, ever since he had left the Zoo.

"How good that is!" he said, staring at the burning cylinder.

The woman's eyes filled with tears. She leaned forward and put her cheek against his. Her arms went around him convulsively.

"Oh, darling, had you forgotten that too?" she said, weeping.

IX

The biped awoke. The room was flooded with pale, colorless morning light. He got slowly out of bed, clacking his jaws. What day was this? He could not remember. But what did it matter, anyhow?

He could hear Emma in the office space, already clattering away at the orthotyper. The biped got a drink of water, glanced into his outer room—no one was at the railing as yet, the Zoo was not open so early—then wandered into the office space and sat down at his desk.

The basket was piled with work he had not finished yesterday, but it was only accounting forms. Nowadays they gave him nothing else to do. He picked up the top one, then set it down again without even trying to read it; it was too much trouble.

The female said something in a low voice. In his surprise at hearing her speak, he missed the words.

"What?"

She said, without pausing or looking up from her work: "Do you think you are the only one who is unlucky? I don't."

The biped gaped at her. "What do you mean by that?"

"Some others, also, have a difficult life." She whipped the page neatly out of her machine, added it to the stack beside her. She inserted another page, spaced down, began typing again.

The biped felt vaguely insulted. He snorted. "What do you know about it?"

Before she could reply, the outer door clicked. Emma stopped typing. They both turned to watch Otto come in with his cart. "Breakfast," said the man gruffly. "Here, take it, eat, don't waste my time." He dumped a basket of work on the biped's desk, then another on Emma's.

Blinking angrily, the biped picked up his covered plate and carried it into his own room.

What did the creature mean by it? Who was she, to speak to him that way?

His anger grew; he could hardly eat. He put the plate aside half-finished, went back into the office space. Emma was not there.

He walked aimlessly around for a while, kicking at the gray

tiles. Here was the scuffed mark, almost invisible, where Grück had drawn a chalk line across the room. There was irony for you! To protect Emma from him, as if he were some sort of crude beast, whereas in reality it was just the other way around.

He heard a noise, and turned to see the female coming out of her room. She paused. Her hands went to the knob on her head.

"Look here, Emma," the biped began a little uncertainly.

"You are on my side of the room," she piped.

"Oh, hang that! What does it matter, any more?" The biped took a step toward her, growing excited. "Look here, just because you've lived in a Zoo all your life, I suppose you think—"

She snapped something, and moved past him to her desk.

"What was that?" the biped demanded irritably. "Speak up."

"I said, I have not lived in a Zoo all my life." The female put on her earphones, rolled paper into the machine, began to type.

"Well, perhaps not in this Zoo, but you were born in a Zoo somewhere, weren't you?"

Emma glanced up. "I was born on Brecht's Planet. They came and took me away when I was a baby." Her typing resumed.

The biped felt he had somehow been put in the wrong.

"Well, of course that's too bad and so forth, but don't you see the difference?" He began to speak more vehemently, warming to his subject. "My God, I should think it's obvious enough. Here you are, an animal that's spent most of its life in one Zoo or another—you're used to it, you can put up with it. And here am I, a man shut up in an animal's body, kept in this stinking cage day after day!"

While he was speaking, the female had stopped her work, and now sat looking quietly down at her three-fingered hands on the keyboard.

After a moment, she got up from her chair and began to walk past him. Her eyes were closed. The biped saw that her throat was working convulsively.

"Oh, now, wait a minute," he said, stricken.

She kept on walking. When a desk got in her way, she maneuvered around it by using her hands.

"Look here, Emma," the biped said, "I didn't want to hurt your feelings or anything. The fact is, I got carried away. I didn't mean the cage is actually stinking, it was just an expression."

The female disappeared into her room. Irritated again, the biped followed as far as the doorway. "Come out, Emma!" he shouted. "Haven't I said I was sorry?"

Emma did not reply. Although the biped hung sulkily around the office space for hours, she did not come out for the rest of the morning.

"But tell me," Neumann was saying at lunch that afternoon, under the shifting colored lights of the rotunda, "in all serious-ness, my dear Grück, what was the truth of the matter? You managed it so cleverly that I am still confused. Is the biped really this Herr Naumchik, or not?"

Herr Doktor Grück laid down his knife and fork, his eyes turning sober behind their rimless glasses. "My dear Neumann," he said slowly, "what does it matter? In either case, the result is just the same—we have, as before, two bipeds. One is male, the other female."

"But if the male was a human being before?"

"Still he is a biped *now*." The good doctor stuffed a bite of liver sausage into his mouth and chewed vigorously. "If I take any credit to myself in this whole affair, gentlemen, and really, allow me to say this in passing, my success has been due to the excellent cooperation of my staff—"

"Too modest," murmured Neumann.

"Not at all!" cried Dr. Grück happily. "But if, and I emphasize *if*, I take any credit to myself, it is precisely because I alone perceived this one small fact from the beginning. Who or what our Fritz was, before, is not of the slightest consequence. If we are to believe the Hindus, our Wenzl here might have been a beetle in some previous incarnation."

Here Grück paused to let the laughter subside. "But this makes no difference. Beetle or no, at the present moment he is still Wenzl. Our Wenzl understands this, I am confident. As for our

Fritz, he does not understand it as yet. But when he does, trust me, you will see a much healthier and more contented animal."

A gawky young keeper appeared at his elbow, holding out a package. Grück turned in annoyance. "Yes? What is it?"

"Pardon me, Herr Doktor," said the young fellow, blushing and stammering, "but Freda, that is, your honored secretary, asked me to bring this straight up. She said you would want to see it at once."

Grück accepted the parcel with a humorous shrug and a glance around at the company, as if to say, "You see what my life is!" He turned the parcel over once or twice, glancing at the inscriptions.

All at once he gave a start of interest. "By the packet from Xi Bootes Alpha! From Purser Bang! Excuse me, gentlemen, this really may be important." He began to tear open the wrappings impatiently. Inside was a sheaf of papers. Grück examined the first sheet intently.

"Yes, the report of the research team on Brecht's Planet. Now we shall discover something!" He turned a page, then another. "Yes, they have dissected three bipeds, a male and two females. . . ." He fell silent, reading on. After a moment, his jaw dropped in surprise. He glanced up at the curious faces around the table.

"But . . . it says that the males are females, and the females are males!" Grück frowned. "But it's impossible!" he muttered.

"What's that you say?" Neumann demanded. "The females are males, and the males females? That doesn't make sense, Herr Doktor. What, are they hermaphrodites? Then why not say so?"

"No . . . no . . ." answered Grück abstractedly, still reading. "My God, we have all made a serious mistake! Just look here, see what it says!" He held out a page, pointing to one paragraph with a thick, trembling finger.

Neumann took the paper, held it to the light and read slowly, " 'The inguinal glands, previously thought to be male gonads, have been found to be without connection with the reproductive system, and their function remains unknown. It has been suggested that they are merely organs of display, analogous to the wattles and comb of the terrestrial cock. However, it must again be emphasized that the bearer of these organs is the female, not the male of the species. It is she who carries the young in a placental sac and gives live birth. Impregnation, however, is achieved by an extremely unusual method. The male gametes are carried in the purplish-red frontal organ which appears in developed form only in the adult male. During rut, the female . . .' Good heavens, Grück, just listen to this . . ."

Fritz and Emma were sitting side by side in the cot in her inner room—Emma tensely, with her hands tightly covering her knob, the biped leaning toward her, an arm around her body, speaking earnestly into her ear.

"You know, Emma, that I didn't mean any harm. You do believe it, don't you?"

"It isn't that," she said in a muffled voice. "It's the way they all treat me—as if I were only an animal. They say I am not human, and so it is correct to keep me in a cage all my life." She looked up. "But what is it to be human? I think, I have feelings, I talk. I even type their letters for them, and still it's not enough." Her slender body shivered. "It's bad enough to hear them talk about me as if I were some creature that couldn't speak or hear. But when *you*—"

"Emma, don't, please," said the biped, overcome by tenderness and remorse. "Of course you're right, you're as human *really* as any of them. What does it matter if you have a different shape? It's the mind inside, the soul that counts, isn't it? Why can't they understand that?"

She looked up again. "Do you really—"

"Of course," said the biped, hugging her closer. Warm, new emotions were coursing through him. "Some day they must all see it, Emma. We'll make them listen, you'll see. There, Emma. It's going to be all right. We're friends now, aren't we?"

She looked up again, timidly. Her body stopped shivering. "Yes, Fritz," she said.

The biped hugged her still closer. Along with the protective-
ness he felt, there was a fierce joy, a sense of rightness. For some
moments they did not speak.

"Emma?"

"Yes?"

"We're really friends now? You're not afraid of me any more?"

"No, not any more, Fritz."

"Then why keep your hands over your knob? Isn't it uncomfortable? Don't you trust me?"

She shook her head. "I don't know why ... it's just— Of
course, I trust *you*, Fritz."

"Well then."

After a moment's hesitation, she dutifully lowered her hands
to her lap. Her knob was large, purplish-red, and had a faint spicy
scent.

"Now isn't that better? Has anything dreadful happened because you uncovered it?"

"No, Fritz," she said. She laid her muzzle against his shoulder.
"I feel so much better now."

"So do I, Emma. Oh, so do I." Bursting with emotion, the
biped bent his head closer, and with an instinctive deftness which
took them both by surprise, he bit her knob off.

X

The young man was afloat, all sensation. Gigantic rustle of
cinnamon-scented taffeta, endlessly unfolding. The whisper and
crinkle of satins as the two bodies strained titanically together,
lips seeking ... pressure, a stab of sweetness. (Groans around him
in the theater.)

Lips parting, gasp for breath; snow-white face swooning on
the satin shoulder, beauty spot startling against her cheek. Her
high-piled wig, whiter than her skin, obscures his face. Sweetly
and sadly: "Forever?"

"Forever!" His triumphant baritone.

"Oh, *Stephen* . . ." The two bodies massively receding, as if
trundled away into the distance; her face turns up to his.

He: "What is it?"

She: "Look!"

Their bodies swinging apart like celestial orbs, all lace and
shimmer, to reveal a long blue perspective of the Cyclopean
room. Down there, so huge and yet so distant, the dark man in
sweaty scarlet, pointed black beard glistening, blazing the dark
eyes. His oily voice: "So, my young lovers, we meet again?"

Afloat in the void, the young man sighed, shifted. (This was
where he had come in.)

Harsh words hurled back and forth down the long room: the
woman shrinks back, breast heaving. See the dark man's hand go
to his sword hilt, see the murderous steel sweep out.

(Gasps.)

Now the combat of titans: clang of steel on steel, sparks, swish
of blades in air. A table goes over with a world-ending crash; a
candle is sliced in two, falls, flaming; a jug explodes into a hundred spinning shards.

"Ha!"

The pale man's hand clapped to his shoulder: blood leaking
between the fingers. Now the blades are clanging again. Over the
dark man's shoulder, see the pale face gone grim. A whirling
thicket of blades: then the pale man's sword thrusting up, looming
gigantic (and the flash of light to the left, above, that warned the
young man to let go the arm rests, but his time, daring, he hung
on). Oh! A stab of bright pain to the heart. God in Heaven—

Limp, half-fainting in his chair, heart thumping, he *was* the
dying man—saw the room darken slowly, saw the ceiling reel
above him—saw, dimly, the two enormous figures rush into each
other's arms. Then blackness.

Light flares up, bathing the two happy lovers. Joyful music fills
the air as the two faces grow, become impossibly huge, then drift
out of focus, until all that is left is the fading ghost of a smile.

THE END.

The world vanished, leaving a greenish glow. The young man

became aware of his body, cramped into the cushioned seat. Around him in the great bowl, other figures were stirring. His buttocks were numb and his head ached. He struggled to his feet. It was hard to become used to the silence, and the smallness of things.

Reeling, dizzy, he came out into the hot afternoon sunlight. He passed the bakery with its gigantic, fragrant stereo-loaf forever swelling over the doorway. Three dark-skinned men in funny white hats and baggy white trousers came toward him, all talking at once in a foreign language.

A cat ran across the plaza, pursued by something small and green, with many scuttling legs. The sun was hot on the paving stones; heat waves swam in the air.

At the next corner, a crowd had gathered around a little man in green and a gigantic, barrel-chested creature with sparse pinkish feathers, which the little man held by a leash. Coins tinkled in a cup. Prodded by its owner, the huge creature did a clumsy, shuffling dance. Its face was part human, part jellyfish, moronic and blank. "Thank you, sir, thank you, lady," said the little man, tipping his cap. *Tinkle.* "Thank you, sir."

The young man kept walking. After all, in the cinema one saw bigger monsters than that.

He paused at the newsstand at the end of the plaza, bought the *Berliner Zeitung* and the *Hamburger Tageblatt,* folded the crisp sheets pleasurably under his arm. The next stall was a fruit stand. The young man passed it nearly every day, and sometimes bought bananas or oranges. But today it was different. In the middle of the stall was a mound of greenish-yellow ovoids, bigger than pears, with a sign: "Special! Just arrived from Brecht's Planet! Unusual! Try one!" The price was 1 mark 10.

The young man's mouth went dry with excitement. From Brecht's Planet! He fumbled in his pocket. He had just enough.

The bored attendant took his money, handed him one of the greenish fruits. The young man held it carefully as he walked away. It was heavy, warm and waxy to the touch.

A phrase from his lost book came back to him: "Certain green-ish fruits, which the bipeds eat with avidity . . ."

Never before had he felt so close to the planet of his birth. It had always been a little unreal to him, something one read about in books. Now, for the first time, he felt that it really existed, that it was made up of real stones and dirt, and had real trees on it bearing real fruit.

Catching sight of Frau Beifelder in the building lobby, her little red eyes watchful and suspicious as always, the young man instinctively slipped the heavy fruit into his pocket, but he kept his hand on it.

"Good afternoon, Frau Beifelder," he said politely, crossing to the elevator. The old woman did not reply.

The young man stopped the elevator at every floor, as usual, peering curiously at the closed red doors. Julia's door stood ajar, but instead of stopping, he went on up in the elevator, fourth floor, fifth, sixth. He got out, trotted over to the little stair, climbed to the roof.

Berlin lay spread out around him in the hot summer sunlight. The curved threads of the Flugbahnen glittered against the blue. Over there, rising out of a cluster of lower rooftops, bulged the golden dome of the Konzertgebaude.

A cool breeze was blowing steadily across the roof, making the newspapers flap against his arm. The young man gripped them in annoyance, not wanting to relinquish the warm fruit in his hand. A few meters away, a ventilator was turning rapidly under its little black hood. The young man turned his attention to an airplane soaring over the blue-gray horizon. He sniffed the air with interest. Diesel fuel, ozone, hot concrete.

On the parapet a large butterfly or moth was lying feebly moving its blue-and-purple wings. The young man examined it curiously. It did not seem able to fly. When he prodded it with his finger, it merely went on with the slow, spasmodic movements of its wings.

Something landed with a faint thud behind him, and he

turned to see another butterfly, identical to the first. It lay quivering for a moment, then began the same slow, feeble motions. Suddenly the young man realized that the air was full of them: tiny dark shapes drifting down, landing on the rooftops all around. There were half a dozen at his feet, then twice as many. One struck him a limp, soft blow on the neck before it dropped to the roof.

Annoyed, the young man turned to leave; but although he picked his way carefully to the stair entrance, he could not avoid crushing several of the brittle bodies under his feet.

He got off at the third floor again and opened the door cautiously. Julia kept it unlatched now, usually, because he had had so much trouble with keys. Inside, all was quiet.

Maggie, the cat, strolled up to greet him with a querulous sound. The young man dropped to all fours to touch noses with her. Her nose was wet and cold. She rubbed her face against his, arching her back and twitching her tail.

A moment later there was a sound from the bedroom and Churchill came out, looking dangerous. When he saw it was only the young man, the mad glare left his eyes. He waddled up and sniffed, then caressed the young man's face with his ill-smelling tongue.

The young man got up and wiped his face with a tissue.

"Martin?" came a sleepy voice from the bedroom.

The young man went down the hall and peered in through the doorway. Julia was looking sleepily at him from the bed. "What time is it?"

The young man glanced at his wristwatch. "Nearly three o'clock. Are you feeling better, Julia?"

"Yes, I think so. Would you mind bringing me a drink of water?"

"Not at all, dear Julia." The young man trotted into the kitchen and filled a glass.

He sat on the bed to watch her drink it, feeling rather peculiar. It was the first time he had ever been invited into her bedroom. Once before, he had happened to look in while she was undressing, and had seen her naked breasts, which interested him very much, but made him feel so odd that he had run out of the apartment. Now he could see their round shapes under the thin white nightdress she wore, and out of curiosity he touched one. It was soft and swinging, but had a hard protrusion of another color in the middle.

"Oh!" she said, looking startled; her hand went up to grasp his.

"Did I hurt you?"

"No . . . no, it's all right, Martin. Touch them if you like." She set the glass down and taking both his hands, guided them to her breasts.

"Dear Martin," she said. He saw her eyes were bright with tears.

"Dear Julia." Leaning over, he kissed her. For a first attempt, it was not at all bad; the noses went to one side of each other, which he had always thought would be very difficult.

The woman's breath caught; after a moment her arms went around him, held him tightly. The kiss continued, and after a short time, other interesting things began to happen.

When it was over, the young man lay on his back, exhausted and astonished. Julia was sitting up, brushing her hair and humming quietly to herself.

Suddenly the door-light flashed. They looked at each other. "Oh, dear, who can that be?"

"I'll go and see."

"Darling!" said the woman, holding out her hand to stop him, half weeping, half laughing. "First put your clothes back on."

"Oh." The young man kissed her again, because she looked so rosy and contented, then got dressed. The doorlight flashed repeatedly. "All right, I'm coming, I'm coming," he muttered.

In the hall stood a medium-sized man in a gray summer surcoat, puffing a cigar. "Well, Naumchik?" he said, smiling.

"Yes?" asked the young man uncertainly.

"Don't you know me? Tassen, of the *Freie Presse*—remember?"

"No. Herr Tassen? What do you want?"

"I was passing by," said Tassen, looking him over with shrewd, friendly eyes. "So this is where you're holed up? Mind if I come in a moment?"

"Well—I suppose not." The young man backed away uncertainly, and Tassen followed him, looking around the apartment with interest.

There was a bellow from the bedroom, then the sound of claws scratching frantically against the closed door, followed by Julia's muffled voice: "Churchill, stop it! Bad dog!"

Tassen cocked an eyebrow toward the sounds but made no comment. "Well, this is a cozy place, Naumchik. I won't keep you a moment. You won't mind if I sit down, I suppose?"

"Please."

"See anything of Zellini lately?"

"Please?"

Tassen frowned, tapped his cigar into an ashtray. "Have you been back to Paris at all—since the—?" He raised his eyebrows again.

"To Paris?" asked the young man, confused. "No."

"I suppose you know they've tied a rocket to you?"

"Pardon?"

"Discharged you—given you the sack."

"Oh. No, I didn't know it."

Tassen drew on his cigar, staring at the young man. After a moment he asked, "Just what happened to you, anyhow, Naumchik? One moment, as far as I understand, you were a perfectly regular young newspaperman—then that biped business, and next you were swinging from the ceilings in Elektra. I gather you're all right now."

"Oh, yes, perfectly."

"Well?"

"Well?"

Tassen looked baffled and faintly annoyed. "Of course, if you don't want to discuss it with me—"

"But I don't remember."

"Oh?" Tassen blinked. "What don't you remember?"

"Anything—before Elektra."

"I see. So that's it. Then you're not likely to tell me what you were up to with that biped, are you?"

"No."

"I see that. Well, anyhow, Naumchik, it's good to know you're on your feet again. I take it you haven't been doing any journalistic work lately?"

"No."

"Want to do any?"

"I haven't thought about it," the young man said.

"Not too easy for you to get a job on any of the Berlin papers, after that stunt, probably," said Tassen. "But you might get some free-lance work. Do a feature on your experiences in Elektra—why not?" He stood up, took a card from his surcoat pocket. "Here's my address. If I can be any help—"

With a cheerful wave, he was gone.

On the following day, the young man remembered the fruit from Brecht's Planet, and decided to open it before it should spoil. The greenish-yellow rind was quite thin; inside was a rather sickly-looking yellow pulp. Julia ate a slice and pronounced it interesting. The young man, however, took one bite and immediately spat it out: the pulp was soft and unpleasant, with a distinct rancid flavor. The disappointment was so acute that he mourned for days.

The good weather lasted until October; then it turned blustery and cold, with snow and occasional flurries of sleet. On an evening in late November, the young man entered the bar of the Correspondents' Club. He stood for a moment, shaking melted snow from his hat. The long mahogany bar was half deserted; the hooded bar lights were reflected in the mirrors, and the little green telephone lights glowed down the bar.

Emile, the bartender, a red-faced Saxon, raised an eyebrow in greeting as the young man approached. "Good evening, Herr Naumchik. We haven't seen you in some time."

"No, I've been in Westphalia, Emile. Give me a double Long John."

"Yes, sir." Emile reached behind him for the bottle, poured a glass brimming full. He leaned nearer to remark, "There was a call for you earlier, Herr Naumchik. A lady."

"Oh? Did she give her name?"

"No, sir. If she calls again, shall I say you are here?"

The young man reflected. "Might as well. I wonder who it is, Nina? Olga? What sort of looking woman was she, Emile?" he asked, but the stout bartender had already moved away and was cupping an ear toward another customer.

"Hello, Naumchik, when did you get in?" A tall man wearing tweeds and a Tyrolean hat edged in beside him at the bar. He spoke in a thick English accent. By a short leash he held a slim, silkenhaired greyhound with great mournful eyes. The dog nudged his cold nose into the young man's palm.

"Oh, hello, Potter." The young man slapped absently at the dog's muzzle. "Just this morning. Down, Bruno. Should have been two o'clock last night, but we were stacked up five hours over Tempelhof."

"Terrible weather," said Potter. "Anything to that regeneration story?"

"No, it was a frost, but I got a couple of columns out of it anyway. You look all right. I heard you'd broken your arm at Riga."

"No, that was Merle," said the man, motioning with his chin to a corner table, where a blond young woman sat with one arm in a sling. She lifted her glass and smiled.

"Oh, too bad," said the young man, returning the gesture.

"It's all right. Makes her more manageable. Sometimes I wish they'd all break their arms, or legs, or something."

A perspiring young man in black came by and clutched the Englishman's arm. "Look here, Potter, do you know where I can find Johnny Ybarra?"

"No, no idea—have you tried the brothels?"

"All of them?" asked the sweating man despairingly over his shoulder as he hurried out. "Hello, Naumchik," he added just before he disappeared.

Emile, who had been speaking into the hooded telephone at the end of the bar, looked up and raised his eyebrows. The young man nodded. Emile pressed a key, and the handset in front of the young man lighted up.

"Excuse me, Potter. Hello—oh, it's you, Julia!"

The tiny face in the screen looked up at him with a smile. "How lucky to catch you, Martin! I called just on the chance of finding— Can you come for dinner?"

"Let me think. Yes—no, confound it, I've got to have dinner with Schenk. I'm sorry, Julia, I forgot."

"It's a pity. I'd love to see you, Martin." She looked up at him wistfully.

"So would I. Maybe I could meet you somewhere tomorrow for cocktails . . ." The young man reflected that although Julia was a bit old for him, and he had no intention of starting that up all over again, still there was no getting around the fact that he had many pleasant memories of that little flat on the Heinrichstrasse, where he had written his first story on Julia's portable—*I Was Elektra's Climbing Enigma*, by Martin Naumchik. How proud they had both been when they saw it printed in the paper! Everything since had stemmed from that . . . "How is Churchill?"

"I had to give him away, Martin. He was becoming so surly; he bit a good friend of mine."

"Too bad. But you still have Maggie?"

"Yes, Maggie is fine."

Down the bar, three men in plastic surcoats were tossing coins into a metal tub which stood before a stereo of a plump young woman in Bavarian peasant costume. Each time a coin fell into the tub, the girl turned slowly around and lifted her skirts, displaying her bare bottom; each time this happened, the three men burst into roars of coarse laughter.

Potter touched him on the shoulder and mouthed, "Good-bye"; the young man turned, waved.

"Well, Martin, do call me if you can."

"Yes, I'll do that. Tomorrow, sometime in the afternoon. You're still at the Ministry?"

"Still there."

"Fine, I'll call you. Good-bye."

The pathetic face in the telephone screen winked out. Sighing with regret and relief, the young man replaced the handset.

A plump young man in a brown jacket took Potter's place at the bar. He had a bristly, unkempt mustache and protruding blue eyes, and somehow managed to look both innocent and dissolute.

"Hello, Naumchik, how are they hanging?"

"Hello, Wallenstein. One high, one low, as usual."

"And the third?"

The plump man signaled to the bartender. "Emile, a Black Wednesday. Listen, Naumchik, you may be just the man I want. You know Kohler, the fellow who runs that string of provincial weeklies?"

"Yes, what about him?"

"Well, it's ridiculous—I owe the man a favor—I promised I'd cover that Zoo story for him tomorrow. Then what should happen but UPI offers me a plush assignment in Oslo. Two months, all expenses, best hotels. Well, I mean to say! But I've got to leave in the morning or it's no go. You wouldn't mind, would you, Naumchik—take you just half an hour—I'd even throw in a bit out of my own pocket."

"Hold on a minute, I've lost you. What Zoo story?"

"Oh, one of their bipeds has given birth, and Kohler wants to play it up for the farm audience. What do you say?"

"Well, I suppose there's no reason—" the young man began, then suddenly stopped. What a curious sensation! Out of the depths of his memory floated the picture of a two-legged creature scrabbling against the glass wall of a cage, while he, outside in the cold air, looked with amazement at his pink, five-fingered hands. How odd. It was the first time in months he had even thought of it.

"Well? It's agreed?"

"No, on second thought, I don't believe it would be advisable," said the young man.

"Not advisable? What do you mean? Come on, old fellow, I'll

put in ten of my own on top of Kohler's twenty—now how's that?"

Naumchik drained his glass quickly, set it down. "No, I'm sorry," he said. "I've just remembered, I've got to be somewhere else tomorrow." He clapped the plump young man on the back. "Well, you'll find someone, I'm sure. So long, Wallenstein."

The plump man pouted at him. "Well, then, if you want to be a bastard."

"I do," said Martin Naumchik cheerfully. "Aren't we all? Keep it clean, old man." He walked out, whistling. On the threshold he paused to breathe deep. The snow had stopped. The stars were crystal bright over the rooftops.

GOOD-BYE, DR. RALSTON

····················
····················
····················
····················

This story resolves to my satisfaction the puzzling question of fashions in female beauty. Why is the sex goddess in 1990 so different from her counterpart in 1770?

I once incautiously raised this question with a dear friend, telling him that I couldn't see why Marie Antoinette was considered a beauty. He told me that he thought she was a beauty, in fact, and then I remembered that his wife strongly resembles Marie Antoinette.

The visitor got out of the hyperport shuttle, looking haggard. He was a large man in his thirties, sandy-haired and blue-eyed, with a strong jaw and a cleft chin.

"There it is," said one of the volunteer escorts to the other. They had met for the first time an hour ago. They stepped forward, smiling brightly. One of them was nearly seven feet tall, spidery thin, with big eyes, sharp features, and a corona of flaming red hair; the other was shorter, white-haired, and more or less egg-shaped.

"Dr. Ralston?"

He peered at them doubtfully. "Yes, hello, uh, ladies?" His accent made him hard to understand.

"Whatever," said the spidery one. "I'm Kim Glashow, and this is Leslie Watt. Welcome to New York! Did you have a tiring trip?"

"Oh, no, the trip was all right," Ralston said vaguely. He could not seem to keep looking in any one direction for very long.

"The zipway is right over here," said Watt, taking his arm. "Let's get you settled into your hotel, and then we can *plan.*"

Ralston looked at the people who were boarding the zipway: they were getting on through a sort of revolving door that came up behind them and then flung them onto the moving strip. "Oh, ah, no thanks," he said. "Could we, ah, just walk?"

"No mess," agreed Glashow. "Right this way."

They got him into the hotel and, after some persuasion, into the uptube. He looked around at the hotel room as if he had never seen one before. "Is that the bed?" he asked.

"Yes, that's the bed, and your crapper's over there. And here's the holo tank—why don't we see if they've got anything about you?"

Glashow went to the control pad and tapped in "RALSTON," then "NEW TERRA." At once the tank came to life with an image of Ralston nervously smiling, and the anchorvoice said, "Dr. Edmond Ralston, the envoy from New Terra, arrives in Manhattan today. The lost colony, cut off for seventy years by subspace turbulence, was rediscovered earlier this week by Navy scouts." A person with bright yellow hair came into the volume and said, "Dr. Ralston, what is your number one emotion when you think about returning to the world of your forebears?"

"Turn that off," said Ralston hoarsely. "Listen, are you all— Is everybody—"

The two waited for him to finish.

"Are you all *women?*" he said, and looked frightened.

"Oh. Oh, no. Didn't they explain to you?" Glashow asked. "About the genetic engineering?"

"Genetic engineering, yes."

"Well, you've probably noticed that our faces are flatter than yours. No sinuses. And no hair on the face. Of course, *you* don't have any, either, but probably you depilate it? Is that the word?"

"Shave," said Ralston faintly. "I shave."

"Burma Shave!" said Watt. "I remember."

"Right, and then some other things that don't show, like no vermiform appendix, and a stronger spine. Then they got ecto-genesis, and after that it was really a question of what people *wanted* to look like. I mean, if breasts look good on a woman and give it pleasure, why shouldn't a man have them too? And, you know, both sets of organs for everybody, that's fair. Am I going too fast?"

"No," said Ralston, and sat down on the edge of the bed.

"All right, the next part is real interesting. After we got ecto-genesis and omnisex, and, you know, longevity and all that, the next thing was beauty. I mean, that was all that was left."

"Beauty," said Ralston.

"Right, and the first generation, they all looked like old-timey holo stars, didn't they, Leslie?"

"My parents," said Watt, rolling its eyes. "Farrah *Fawcett.* You want me to get some pix on the holo?"

"That would be purfy." Glashow turned to Ralston. "See, what nobody thought about at first, beauty is a norm that's a minority. It's an hourglass-shaped curve instead of bell-shaped, with 'beauty' in the middle. So if you make people look all alike, that stops being beauty anymore. Nowadays—well, for instance, I'd say Les-lie here is an exceptionally good-looking person. So *unusual.*"

Watt smiled delightedly. "You too, Kim—I really think you're great-looking."

In the holo tank, a row of smiling people appeared. They were broad-shouldered and strong, with finely chiseled features; they looked, in fact, a little like Dr. Ralston. Then another row, all shapes—spidery like Glashow, pillowy like Watt, bald, big-eared, steatopygous.

Glashow was saying, "Beauty is like the stock market. If you want your kids to be beautiful, you have to bet against what other people are betting *on.* They're even saying the Farrah look might come back next season. So it's really exciting."

"Yes, exciting," said Ralston.

"Well. Now, the next thing is the press conference, then the reception," said Glashow briskly, "and then the Mayor's ball tonight. Would you want to wear what you have, or should we take you shopping?"

"No," said Ralston, with a look of pain. "In fact, if you could find out when that ship leaves, the one I came on—"

"The hyper? I think they said it's going back this afternoon, didn't they, Leslie?"

"Let me check." It turned to the control pad, punched buttons. "Yes, that's right—fourteen-thirty today."

"Could you get me a ticket?" Ralston asked.

"You want to go back home? And miss the reception, and the keys to the city, and everything?"

"Yes, I really think— If you wouldn't mind."

"Well—" Watt punched more buttons. "Done. Your luggage is still on board, so I just told them to hang on to it."

After they had delivered Ralston to the hypership, Kim looked at Leslie and Leslie looked at Kim.

"You know, that room is paid through the weekend, and so are we."

"I was thinking the same thing."

"By the way, are you male or female?"

"Biologically male, but I've always been better at fem. What are you?"

"Male, but listen—the reason I asked—I have a little trouble getting it up and I usually go fem too."

"Well, what's wrong with that? Don't worry about it, sweets— we'll work something out."

LA RONDE

*All I had better tell you in advance about this one is that it has the same
form as "On the Wheel," although the substance is completely different.
The old house described here is The Anchorage in Milford, Pennsylvania,
where I lived for fifteen years. It has since burned down, as white
elephants in Milford tend to do; Tom Disch, who also lived there for a
while, tells me that day lilies have covered the plot.*

    *I found the stuff about cat's cradle, which my parents never taught
me properly, in a children's bookstore in Paris.*

He felt that he was gone a long time, and when he came back
from wherever it was, he found himself sitting on a stone, gazing
at a wrecked automobile that was tilted upside down against a
tree. One of the front wheels was lazily turning. The door on the
driver's side hung open; below it the whole top of the car had
been crushed flat, and it seemed to him a miracle that anyone had
got out alive.

    There was a buzzing in his head, but he stood up and went
closer to the wreck to see if anyone needed help. The car was
empty. What could have become of the driver?

    For that matter, what was he himself doing here? Perhaps it
would come back to him in a minute, when he was rested. He
went all around the car with a kind of dumb obstinacy, through
brush that whipped his legs under his coat. No one was there.

    Above him there was a broad muddy swath, littered with

glass, bits of chrome, and more incongruous things—scattered pieces of white tissue, sunglasses, a pack of cigarettes. He climbed, helping himself up from one sapling to another, until he reached the highway, where he stood looking uncertainly around him. There were long black skid-marks on the macadam. The road made a curve here, and on the opposite side the slope resumed, rising another hundred feet against the gray sky. It was very cold.

He peered down the slope again, thinking that from this elevation he might be able to see the body of the driver, but he could barely make out the wreck itself through the screen of branches.

Although he could not think very clearly because of the continuous dull buzzing in his head, he knew that he ought to report the accident, and he trudged out around the curve in the direction the car had been going. The road straightened here for a distance of half a mile or so; it was empty and gray under the sky, with the gloomy forested slope on one side and the ravine on the other. There were no highway signs, no billboards, nothing to tell him where he might be.

He kept on walking down the road. Sooner or later, no doubt, a car would come along, but it was too cold to stand and wait. It was very strange that his memory was so bad, and that the accident had happened, apparently, right in front of him where he sat on the muddy hillside; and this, together with the strangeness of the missing driver, nagged at his tired mind.

The road ran on, empty and cold under the gray sky. The forested hill was behind him now and on either side were bare fields. A few flakes of snow came drifting along; they melted at once on the highway. Then the snow came more thickly and made a white film in which he left a trail of glistening footprints. For some reason this alarmed him, but when he looked back after a few minutes, he saw that the prints were rapidly being covered.

He went on, with the snow whipping into his eyes, until at last he came to a private road with a chain across it. He ducked under the chain. The road went up steeply, covered with dead leaves and fallen branches. Over the crest of the rise, it ran straight between fields grown up with tall weeds to a white house on a hill. While he was climbing the slope he had been sheltered a little from the wind-driven snow, but now it flew at him again. As he approached the house he could see that the windows were boarded up. The big front door had a padlock on it. He went around the house and found the back door padlocked too.

As he stood under the eaves to get out of the wind, he noticed an oblong pit covered by a framework of metal bars next to the foundation. He crouched over it and tugged at the framework; the metal was rusted and heavy, but it came up. He laid the framework aside. When he had cleared out the dead leaves and spruce needles underneath, he found, as he had guessed, that the pit was a light-well for a cellar window. He pulled up the hinged window, crawled through and dropped into musty darkness.

The light from the cobwebbed glass was water-gray, but it was enough to show him the wooden steps that led up to a trapdoor. When he raised the trap, he found himself in a long gray room illuminated only by a watery glow at one of the windows. It was cold—colder, it seemed, than the outdoors. His ghostly breath rose in the air.

There was firewood and kindling in a box beside the old-fashioned cookstove, but not a scrap of paper, though he opened one drawer after another and lighted matches to look in. In one of the drawers he found the stub of a candle, and with this in his shivering hand he went through a pantry into a dining room, and from there into a library. Even here there were no newspapers, only the moldy apricot-colored leather books in the glass-fronted bookcases. He retreated into the kitchen, and this time opened the doors of cabinets, where he found brittle shelf paper under the heavy old plates and tumblers. He pulled out a few pieces of this, and presently had a blaze going in the stove.

The tall wooden icebox was empty, but he found peaches in a glass jar in the pantry. The jar was like none he had ever seen; it had a glass top held down by two jointed handles, and a red rubber gasket between jar and lid. He stood beside the stove, which was now radiating an almost imperceptible warmth, and ate the peaches with a cold metallic-tasting spoon.

There was a kerosene lamp on the kitchen table; he filled it from a can he found in the pantry and lighted it. It smoked at first, blackening the inside of the glass chimney, until he found out how to adjust and trim the wick. Carrying the lamp, he mounted the back stairway and found two bedrooms. The beds had been stripped, but the mattresses, covered with coarse gray-striped twill, were still there. He dragged one of them down the stairs to the kitchen; there, in front of the stove, he stretched out in his clothes and fell asleep.

The cold woke him early in the morning; the fire had gone out. He built it up again, ate the rest of the peaches for breakfast, and then set out to explore the house. All the furniture was Victorian, even the pieces that looked almost new. Under the high cross-beamed ceiling hung a black wrought-iron chandelier with candles in it. Kerosene lamps with painted china shades were on all the tables. The living room, dining room, and library had fireplaces, red brick in the living room, green tile in the other two; there were fireplaces in two of the upstairs bedrooms as well. Two other upstairs rooms had doors which he could not open.

He went down again to forage in the pantry. He found sacks of flour and corn meal, cans of condensed milk, oil and lard, and jar after jar of preserved fruit and vegetables. There was plenty of wood stacked on the porch and in the yard. He understood now that he was intended to live in the house always, and he began to make preparations. With tools he found in the cellar he pried loose the staple that held the padlock on the back door, so that he could go in and out freely while leaving the door apparently still locked. Gray smoke ascended from the kitchen chimney; he could not help that, but the sky was so overcast, although it was no longer snowing, that he thought the smoke would not be seen.

With flour, water, and condensed milk he mixed a batter and made pancakes; there was even a whole cheese, not very moldy; he cut off the bad part and ate a wedge with his pancakes.

Afterward he made fires in all the fireplaces downstairs. He fed them until they roared in the chimneys, but the stubborn cold of the house yielded slowly. Even when he sat in a wing chair, under the landing of the great living room staircase, with his feet on the hearth, he could feel the insistent chill probing at his back.

All through the house, the firelight sent shadows racing up the walls. These shadows disturbed him, and he went to work filling the oil lamps, trimming and adjusting their wicks.

Nowhere in the house was there any electrical appliance: no lights, no television, not even a radio. There were no newspapers, and no magazines except for the bound volumes of *Harper's* and *The Century* in the library. Even the bathroom fixtures were old; the shower (which did not work) was a vast sunflower-head of metal suspended on a stalk over the clawfooted bathtub. In the mahogany medicine cabinet he found bone toothbrushes with black hog-bristles, and medicines in plain brown bottles with paper labels: ipecac, calomine. Yet he knew that the house could not have been abandoned for more than a year or two; there was dust everywhere, but only a light film, not the accumulation of a century. Moreover, it was curious, in a house with so much food in it, that there was no sign of rats.

He was reluctant to damage anything in the house, but in the end his curiosity won out, and he forced the two locked doors upstairs. Behind one of them was a lumber room, choked with bedsteads, sofas, chairs, all dusty and soiled, but modern in appearance. The second room had been fitted out as an office, with an oak desk, a leather armchair, and an ancient Royal typewriter, the kind with a little glass window in the side through which part of the works could be seen.

Beside the typewriter lay a sheaf of manuscript. The first few words caught his eye, and he sat down to read.

My maternal great-grandfather built his house on a terrace at the foot of a wooded hill in Potamos Township, near the New York and New Jersey borders of Pennsylvania in what they now call the "Tri-States" area. Behind the house there are seven Norway spruces, of which the tallest is about eighty feet; the ground beneath them is carpeted with brown needles, and the wind moves quietly through their branches. Farther up the hill are Scotch pines, native spruces and firs, maples, and birch. Still farther up, a mile or so above the house, there is an old logging road, now grown up in maple saplings, and above that the foundations of a settler's cabin, the stones barely visible in the underbrush. Except for these, and a power line that crosses the hill, there is no sign of human habitation.

The house itself is of white-painted frame and shiplap construction, three stories tall, with dormers, a verandah, and an Italian slate roof. Over the years it has settled somewhat, having been built without footings, as the custom then was, but the frame is sturdy; I remember that an electrician who was called in to wire the house, when I was a boy, complained that he had to drill through innumerable "cats," diagonal framing members which united the studs.

The downstairs rooms are paneled in golden oak; the floors are parquet. All the rooms, even the old servants' quarters on the third floor, are ample in size; the living room ceiling is eighteen feet high, and the rest fifteen. These high ceilings make the house "hard to heat," as the local expression has it, but they give a sense of spaciousness and a quality of sound entirely different from that in "modern" cheapjack houses. It is a soothing and relaxing ambience, a feeling of permanence and safety, which must be experienced to be appreciated.

When I saw the house again, after the death of my aunt Margaret in 1978, the silences of the vast rooms seemed to speak of boyhood pleasures. I am half convinced that houses somehow soak up the psychic experiences of their inhabitants; there are certain houses that have a mean-spirited or discouraged air, and there are city apartments which seem to radiate a sense of irritability, as if the walls still contained the last echoes of an angry shout.

My aunt Margaret, who had lived in this house since I was a boy, and to whom my parents willed the possession and use of the property during her lifetime, was, I now think, a kindred soul; we were alike at least in that each of us was happiest in a state of non-matrimony. When I was a child, however, I disliked and feared her, because she sometimes seemed aware of my existence and sometimes not.

It was she who had redecorated the house and covered all the sofas with chintz, hung "modern" pictures and strewn the coffee tables with cigarette boxes and French novels. Yet even her old age and illness seemed to have left no psychic traces in this house. The walls, the cornices, the mantelpieces seemed to say, "Here we are, as we have always been. Why have you stayed away so long?"

I must add that although there were no ghosts in the house itself, the cellar was another matter. It was irregular and low, angling around a huge stone that had been too big for the excavators to remove; one went down through a trap in the kitchen and then had to walk stooping along a sort of cobwebbed passageway to reach the farther room where the furnace was. In this chamber, so long as the light was on, I felt no uneasiness, but in the stifling dark something was there, some malevolent and incoherent impulse that was older than the house.

Against the well-meant advice of my friends, I settled my affairs in New York, retired from my practice, sold most of my furniture, and disposed of my lease. In September I moved into the old house. A local woman, Mrs. Beveridge, helped me set the place to rights. I gathered that she was a recent widow, in straitened circumstances; I asked her to stay on as my housekeeper, and she agreed.

Mrs. Beveridge was a woman of perhaps fifty, sturdily built, with pale skin and dark hair which she wore in an old-fashioned bun. Her husband, whom she rarely mentioned, had been a carpenter or roofer or something of that sort; she herself had had little education, but she had a high degree of native intelligence and had formed her mind by reading. I felt myself lucky to have her, not only because of her efficiency in caring for the house, but because there was no suggestion on either side of any sexual innuendo between us. She spoke little, in a quiet voice, and adapted her habits perfectly to mine. When I wanted her for any reason she was there; when I wished to be alone she was invisible. In the evenings she retired to her room on the third floor, where I sometimes heard her radio playing softly.

In November an early storm knocked down power lines and left us without light or heat. Mrs. Beveridge kindled fires in the fireplaces and kept the wood range going in the kitchen; I got out the kerosene lamps which were kept for such emergencies, and we ate by candlelight. During the four days of the storm, I became accustomed to the soft light of lamps and candles and grew to like it. When the power came on again, I discovered that I was actually disappointed. The electric lights seemed cold and impersonal; they revealed too much. I preferred the warm brown darkness, the mystery. I continued to use the lamps; Mrs. Beveridge appeared to have no objection.

With her help, I carried down some pieces of furniture abandoned years ago in the attic. The marble-topped dressers and tables were as sound as ever; the chairs and loveseats, of course, were upholstered in horsehair, impossibly hard to sit on, and the leather was cracked and peeling. As soon as I was able, I got an upholsterer in Stroudsburg to come out and take these pieces away for refinishing. I had them done in rose and blue plush, or rather mohair, a deep-piled fabric. When they were brought back and arranged in the living room, the remaining modern pieces looked all the more out of place. One by one I got rid of them. At the Auction Barn, so-called, on the Port Jervis road I found a huge icebox and two large copper washtubs. I consulted Mrs. Beveridge about each of these changes, half expecting her to demur since they involved more labor for her, but she expressed her entire satisfaction, and indeed, I often heard her singing quietly at her work. At last, more than nine months after I had begun, I was able to look about me and see nothing whatever that had been made later than the year nineteen ten. I had, of course, canceled my subscriptions to all newspapers and magazines. Our supplies were delivered in bulk by a Mr. Thomas and stored by Mrs. Beveridge.

From a dealer in Stroudsburg I acquired a parlor organ in fair condition. It had not been converted to motorized operation, as so many old organs have; the bellows was cracked, however, and some of the padding under the keys was worn away. When it was restored, it functioned perfectly. The organ had a keyboard of two and a half octaves, and with the use of various stops ("Tremolo," "Celeste," "Vox Humana," and the like) it could produce an astonishing variety of pleasant sounds. I made some effort to learn this instrument, and amused myself with it sometimes when Mrs. Beveridge was at her work, but she was so much better at it than I that in the evenings I merely sat and listened to her play. We had a music book, published in the eighteen eighties, which contained some charming things of Schubert's, as well as some sacred music and even a few popular songs.

I discovered in myself an insatiable appetite for Victorian literature—novels, miscellanies, journals. That spring I haunted the antique shops and second-hand stores around Potamos; one of my prizes was a leather-bound set of Dickens, published in eighteen seventy-eight, with the original illustrations; another was a work entitled *Dr. Hood's Plain Talks and Common Sense Medical Adviser*, a quaint heavy volume which recommended prussic acid for stomach ulcers, and cocaine for heroin addiction. As for health care, I knew quite well that if I became seriously ill I should have to seek modern medical treatment, but my health was good apart from an occasional cold, and Mrs. Beveridge was never ill.

I was aware that the Victorian life I was attempting to recreate within these walls was not the reality. The songs of Victorian men and women were not all decorous, nor were all their habits nice. A real Victorian bachelor in my situation would long before now, in all probability, have undone the laces of his housekeeper's underwear. Bastards were a commonplace then, and indeed, although the book is not in my house, since it was—or will be—published in nineteen twenty-one or thereabouts, I remember from the reading of Rafael Sabatini's *Scaramouche* that it was still possible even then to titillate the public with the murder, or attempted murder, of a man who, unknown to either, is his assassin's father. Parricide, not incest, was the ultimate horror, because it was all too possible. No, it was not the real Victorian world that I was attempting to recreate, but my boyhood's imaginary world of safety, serenity, and gentleness.

I confess that I was as much alarmed as pleased by the alacrity with which Mrs. Beveridge fell in with my scheme. Never once did she suggest even by a smile or a gesture that what we were doing was absurd. She seemed to take it all as perfectly normal, and it was this that alarmed me. Either we were falling together into a *folie à deux*, or she was humoring me, with consummate skill, for some motive of her own which I could not guess.

At any rate, the life we now began to lead was so pleasant that I ceased to question it. In the mornings, in fine weather, I worked in my garden or chopped wood; in the afternoons I worked in my study, and in the evenings Mrs. Beveridge and I decorously diverted ourselves. On fair days the house was sunny, and the porch pillars, which I could see through the glass pane of the door at the far end of the living room, gave back the pure essence of light. But it is the winter evenings that I remember with most pleasure, when the whole world was shut out in darkness, and the lamps were surrounded by a brown gloom. With the aid of an old book of parlor tricks and games, Mrs. Beveridge and I relearned the art of the cat's cradle, forming more and more intricate figures with a loop of string. Beginning with the Cat's Cradle, we went on to the Calm Sea, the Upturned Cradle, the Mattress Turned Over, the Cat's Eye, the Pig on the Pegs. We also played at making hand shadows on the wall: the Bird in Flight, the Tortoise, the Goose a Prisoner (in which one hand grips the wrist of the other which forms the goose), and so on; we played word games, at which Mrs. Beveridge was very good, and sometimes Anagrams, Skat, or Old Maid.

I counted, I say, on the fact that I was completely aware of my own deepening obsession, but this belief was shaken one morning, when, arising earlier than usual, I went down to the kitchen to see if there was any coffee. It was about seven o'clock; the day was clear, and the sunlight reflecting from the white snow gave a shimmer to the atmosphere. Mrs. Beveridge was nowhere in sight, but a man in a long coat was carrying a sack up the steps of the back porch to the pantry. At first I thought he was Mr. Thomas; then I saw that he was an older and stouter man, and when he shifted his burden I noticed that he was wearing a long brown apron under his coat. He turned and stumped down the stair again, and as I went to another window to watch him, I distinctly saw him get up on the driver's seat of a wagon drawn by two massive horses. I saw the wagon move off down the driveway; then it was gone.

When Mrs. Beveridge came in a few moments later, I asked her, "Who was here just now?"

"Why, Mr. Thomas," she replied, and gave me such a puzzled look that I could not say any more.

One of our evening amusements was the ouija board, named by its inventor by combining the French and German words for "yes." Mrs. Beveridge was very adept at this, and under her fingertips the planchette swept rapidly about the board, spelling out ambiguous communications from various defunct notables (Napoleon informed us, for instance, that he did not like fish).

I soon noticed that she could manipulate the planchette all by herself, and it was not long before I discovered that she often went into light trance while doing so. This gave me the notion of trying to deepen the trance, to which she readily assented, and I found her to be an excellent subject; after a few sessions she exhibited all the classical signs of deep trance: catalepsy, glove anesthesia, amnesia, hallucination, and all the rest. I was able to suggest to her that her hand would write automatically, a procedure less tiresome than the ouija board. While she sat with her eyes closed, the pencil in her fingers traced large, childish letters, only a dozen or so to a page. When her pencil slipped off the edge of the paper she seemed to know it, and after a moment's hesitation would begin a new line; when she reached the bottom of the paper I lifted her hand, put a fresh sheet under it, and she began where she had left off, even if it were in the middle of a word.

When I say that her writing was childish I mean to be understood literally; not only were the letters large and painfully formed, but the *t*'s were often uncrossed and there were many misspellings, "annd" for "and," for example, and "pulleded" for "pulled." The lines sloped more and more downward as she wrote, and that seemed curious to me, because she was right-handed. When something agitated her, as when I asked her to describe a dream she had had the night before, her writing grew more irregular and the lines sometimes ran into each other.

These sessions were tiring to her, but she was as interested by their results as I was, and we performed them at least two or three times a week for a considerable period. We had been able to dispense with hypnotic induction entirely, by the use of a post-hypnotic suggestion; after having settled herself comfortably, on a word of command, she would go promptly into deep trance and begin to write. Ordinarily I would suggest a topic, but on several occasions she produced rather surprising things without any prompting from me. Her most elaborate effort was a narrative which she produced in the course of five consecutive sessions. In each case I woke her after three-quarters of an hour, and on the following evening I suggested to her that she would go on with the narrative until it was done. I put this down here for whatever it may be worth. The transcript which follows is verbatim except for the correction of errors in spelling, the elimination of repetitions, etc.

Certain persons appear to have an inborn taste for violence. Among these was Norman Edwards, who lived with his wife Sally in a hillside house in a suburb of Newark, New Jersey. The living room and master bedroom were upstairs, the kitchen, family room and spare bedroom were down. Edwards, who worked as an insurance underwriter in Newark, was a man in his thirties, pale, horse-faced, deceptively slender. His hands were large, and he enjoyed using them. One Saturday morning in early October he was taking down the screens on the side of the house when he heard the water hiss in the upstairs bathroom. Sally had slept late that morning. Edwards raised the window quietly and put his head in. He saw her body moving against the blue shower curtain in the tub. He leaned in over the windowsill, stretched as far as he could and grabbed her leg. He heard a shriek and a thump. He waited, but the water kept on running. "Sally?" he said. She did not answer.

He climbed in the window and twitched the shower curtain aside. She was lying in the tub with her yellow shower cap on. A little blood from her nose was washing away in pink trails. He turned off the water and pulled her upright. Her eyes were open, but she looked stuporous.

He had her dressed by the time the doctor came; by then her nose was beginning to swell. It was broken, as it turned out, and they kept her in the hospital overnight to see if she had a concussion. When he saw her the next day there was a red and purple bruise spreading out from under the bandage, and she had two beautiful shiners. "It was just a joke, Sally," he said, but she turned her head away.

That afternoon her sister Wanda came over. "Sally sent me for some things." She walked past him up the stairs.

"They going to keep her? I thought she was getting out today." Edwards followed her.

"That's it. Some complications," Wanda said. She opened a suitcase on the bed and began pulling things out of bureau drawers. When she finished packing the suitcase, she started on another.

"She doesn't need all that in the hospital," Edwards said.

"She might," Wanda said. She lifted the two suitcases and walked past him.

He caught up with her downstairs and crowded her against the wall. "You're lying, aren't you?" he said. "She isn't coming home."

"That's right," Wanda said, "and *listen to me*, you bastard, if you lay a hand on me, Morris will kill you. Now get out of my way."

After a moment he stepped back, and she carried the suitcases down to her car, got in and drove off.

When he thought about the incident, Edwards realized that

he was hearing in his mind the sound Sally's nose had made when it hit the water faucet, a sort of crunching click. He had not actually heard the sound, but it was perfectly clear to him, and he found himself playing it over and over, each time with the same little stab of pleasure.

It was not a complete surprise to him that he felt this way. Once, as a boy, he had hit his older brother Tim with a baseball bat, and he had heard the same sort of sound—a thud, with a sharp little crack in the middle of it when Tim's collarbone had broken.

Edwards called Wanda's number several times, hoping Sally would answer the phone, but it was always Wanda or Morris, and they told him Sally did not want to speak to him. Twice he went to their house and made a nuisance of himself. On the day after the second of these visits, when Wanda had threatened to call the police, Morris Hollander came to see Edwards. Hollander, Sally's sister's husband, was a prosperous man who had business interests up and down New Jersey. He was much older than Wanda, at least sixty, but he was still trim and erect. His sleek hair was not white, not grey, but something in between, and he wore emerald cufflinks.

"Hello, Morris, what do you want?" Edwards said.

"You can't invite me in? We have to talk on the doorstep?"

"All right," said Edwards, and led the way upstairs to the living room.

Hollander laid his hat carefully on the sofa, but he did not sit down or take off his black overcoat. "Norman," he said, "I'll put the whole thing in a nutshell. You're making Sally nervous, she don't want to see you, so what good is it? Save yourself the aggravation."

"Sally is my wife," Edwards said.

"Okay, why not treat her like a wife? Arguments I understand, believe me, and even to hit someone I understand, but to break your wife's nose—this I don't understand."

"It was an accident."

"So? A woman is taking a shower, you reach through the window and grab her leg—this is an accident? If you're walking down the street, I throw a banana peel under your foot, you fall and break your hip—this is also an accident?"

The old man took a turn around the room. "I was married to my first wife, she should rest in peace, twenty-seven years. To me a divorce is a shame. But I wouldn't say to Sally, go back to him, your place is with your husband. It's better she shouldn't have more accidents."

He turned and gave Edwards one level look. "So, now I said what I came to say. Don't make no more trouble. Good-bye, Norman."

Edwards was thinking about the phrase, "fall and break your hip," and in the plosive of the last word he seemed to hear the faint sound of a breaking bone. As Hollander started down the stairs, he said, "Morris."

The old man half turned, taking his hand off the banister. "Yes?"

"Go to hell." Edwards kicked him hard in the chest. The old man fell backward and clattered down the stairs. When Edwards got to him, he was lying against the wall with his neck bent, and he was dead.

Edwards knelt, got his arm under the body, hoisted it to his chest with an effort, and stood. As he carried it through the kitchen, the phone began to ring. He put his foot on a chair, steadied the body with his knee and one arm, picked up the receiver. "Hello."

"Norman, this is Wanda. Excuse me for calling, but is Morris there?"

"Morris? No," he said, speaking over the dead man's face. "Why would he be here?"

"Well, he said he was going to stop by on his way home from Sparta. Anyway, if he comes over there, would you please ask him to call me?"

"Sure. 'Bye."

He put the receiver down, hoisted the body chest-high again, and went out to the driveway where Morris's big blue Lincoln was parked. He toppled the body gently into the trunk head-first, moved the heavy arm that seemed to want to cling to him, then folded the legs. He explored the pockets gingerly for car keys, found them, and stepped back. The body lay on its side, one arm underneath. By the time he got where he was going, it would be stiff; it might be harder to get out of the trunk. He bent the legs upward as far as he could, folded the arm. The other one was too hard to get at; this would have to do. What else? The hat. Where was the hat?

He went back through the kitchen, glancing at the phone, but it did not ring. He found Morris's hat under the little table at the foot of the stairs, hiding there like a black animal. He put it on top of the body in the trunk, closed the lid, and went back inside for his jacket and topcoat. When he pulled out onto the street, it was just after two o'clock.

The day was cold and bright, the road clear; most of the traffic was coming the other way. According to the map, there were three or four lakes and reservoirs not far from route thirty-one. Edwards drove steadily north, keeping just under the speed limit. The car handled well. At Netcong he turned northeast to have a look at Hopatcong Lake. The approaches were too shallow, and there were too many trailers parked on the shore. He kept going around the lake, then northwest again to Lake Mohawk, but it did not suit him either. He drove through Newton, Lafayette, and Augusta. North of Branchville there was a turnoff marked "Culvers Lake." Edwards kept on going. He realized now that the Jersey lakes would not do. He was close to the state line already; somewhere along the Delaware there would be a private place where he could tip the car down into deep water. Then he would walk or hitch-hike to the nearest town, stay in a motel overnight, and take the bus home in the morning.

North of Dingmans Ferry the map showed the highway running close to the river, and he glimpsed it, or thought he did, occasionally through the trees, but there was no good approach. The sky had turned gray; there were a few flakes of snow. He turned on his headlights. A curve came up, too fast. As he swung around it, braking, two yellow-white eyes leaped into view, the headlights of another car. He turned frantically, saw the lights blaze up, felt a hammering jolt. Then things began to become very queer.

THE TIME
EXCHANGE

This one is dedicated to Dean A. Grennell, who thought of the title before I did, and wondered aloud, "Wouldn't that make a great Damon Knight story?"

When Grennell told me about that, I had already written the story. Whether this demonstrates that great minds think alike, or just that events occur in synchronous patterns, I don't know. Anyhow, here is the story, which I extracted from the title just the way you pull the fortune out of a fortune cookie.

By the way, the story was not quite right as I wrote it first; Alice K. Turner, the fiction editor of Playboy, patiently helped me to mend it.

She was half his age, a cool young woman whose green eyes he could not read. He had never known anyone remotely like her.

His name was Bryce Cromartin—Bryce Cromartin III, in fact, though he had dropped the Roman numeral, as too ostentatious, years ago. He had a house in Marblehead, a condominium on Beacon Hill and a summer place on the Cape. Her name was Vicki Mahoney; they had met in his lawyer's office, where she was a typist.

She would never allow him to take her home; she said she lived with her invalid mother. They met once a week, on Fridays, for an hour: It was the only time she could get away, she said. He gave her little presents, nothing in bad taste—a slim gold chain with a ruby, a diamond clip. Then somewhat larger presents, but she refused to meet him more often.

In his usual foursome on Wednesday, Jack and Larry were talking about a new place called The Time Exchange. "It seems they can really make the time go by faster or slower," said Jack. "Ed Vandermeer told me he tried it for a dentist's appointment. A root canal. He said it was all over before he knew it."

"But can they really give you *more* time?" Cromartin asked.

"Yes, they bottle it somehow."

The image that rose in Cromartin's mind was that of Vicki, sprawled in delicious abandon. He looked up the place in the phone book and went there the next day. The Time Exchange was in a seedy part of town, but the establishment itself looked modern and new. Around the corner, at another entrance, a line of derelicts stood waiting.

Inside, it was like a doctor's office—potted shrubs in redwood boxes, chrome and brass. A young man came forward alertly. "May I help you?"

"Well, I'm not quite sure. Those men I saw around the corner—are they—"

They were time donors, the young man said, but *that* was not for Cromartin. The best plan for him, he thought, would be the deposit-and-withdrawal system: Cromartin would deposit unwanted time by means of a little canister taped behind his ear, which he would bring back to The Time Exchange for processing; then, when he wanted time, he could withdraw it from his own account.

"No—well, perhaps later—but I was thinking of, ah, having it for tomorrow."

In that case, said the young man with an understanding smile, the Exchange had certain clients, perfectly respectable people, who left time on deposit for sale to others, and that time, which was of the highest quality, could be purchased at a very reasonable rate.

He spread out a schedule for Cromartin's inspection. The fees were graduated according to a factor system that Cromartin at first found confusing.

"Then you mean," he said, "that if I spend an hour somewhere and the factor is five, it will actually seem like *five hours?*"

Exactly so, said the young man. The fee was a little stiff, as a matter of fact, but Cromartin paid it. Thereupon a smiling young woman in a nurse's uniform took him into a back room and showed him how to attach the gleaming little canister behind his ear and how to work the little slide that turned it on. Another employee wrapped the canister for him, and the young man bowed him out.

All day Friday, Cromartin was in a sweat of anticipation. Evening came at last; he picked Vicki up at the usual place and drove her to his condominium. While she undressed, he went into the bathroom with the canister. He attached it behind his ear, as he had been instructed, and carefully pressed the slide to the ON position before he brushed his hair over it.

Vicki was lying on the black-satin sheet, arms and legs spread, looking at him with her green eyes in the dimness as he approached. And it was just as the young man had promised; his delight went *on* and *on*, and when her body convulsed, the waves of pleasure rippled through him as if they would never stop.

Afterward, as they lay together, he ran his fingertips up the side of her neck, then behind her ear, and his heart swelled with sudden joy when he encountered a little canister there. What sacrifices she must have made to buy this time with him! How could he ever repay her?

Cromartin put his trousers on. Vicki, on the edge of the bed, yawned delicately as she picked up her watch. "Is it nine o'clock *already?*" she said. "How time flies."

THE MAN WHO
WENT BACK

It is hard to talk much about this story without giving away its secret, so I will tell you only that the setting is the Newport of my boyhood, a wonderful place that no longer exists except in memory. In this story I was able to go there again. Writing is magic, for the author as well as for readers.

Early in the morning he walked from his parents' house toward the beach, past the excavation on the corner, the library that looked like a lighthouse, the movie theater, and then the boardwalk just as it used to be, the agate-jewelry store on one side and the candy store on the other, with the gleaming nickel arms of the taffy machine endlessly revolving around one another. The light, the air, were as luminous and pure as ever. It was the summer of 1948, and he was seventeen years old.

When he saw her coming toward him, his breath stopped for a moment. It was Erica George, just as he had last seen her, with her trousers rolled above her knees and her ash-blond hair blowing against her face.

"Hello, Dick. Going over to the bay?"

"I am if you are."

He was intensely aware of her hand in his as they walked

together. She was nineteen, as beautiful as he remembered. He had a curious double vision of her: she seemed so young now, the first of his four lost loves. All his life he had felt the hopeless ache to see her again. This was the time, the summer when the change had come between them. He knew that she felt it too, but he had never dared express it by a touch or a word.

"When are you leaving?" he asked.

"Tomorrow morning. I hate to go."

"You'll be back, other summers."

"Maybe not. It's a long way from Massachusetts."

"It's a long way from Massachusetts," he sang, "it's a long way to go . . ."

She laughed. "You goof."

"Is that why you love me?"

"I don't love you at all."

"Sure you do. Want to take the boat out one last time?"

"Yes, let's."

The boat was his parents' old cabin cruiser, the *Betty*. Erica cast off the lines while he started the engine, and they cruised through the channel into the September sky and sea. An hour later they anchored off a little cove where they had often picnicked before. "Let's swim ashore and look for periwinkles," he said.

"It's too cold."

"One last time?"

"Well—don't look."

Harvey stripped off his shirt and pants. When he turned, she had just taken off her brassiere. "Oh, Dick."

He stepped up to her with a confidence he had never felt before; her body was cool against his when he kissed her. After a moment her lips turned warm.

He spread the life jackets on the deck of the cockpit and pulled her down beside him. "Dick, this isn't good," she murmured. "I'm going away to college—we may never see each other again."

"I know. That's why. I'll never forget you, Erica."

"Oh. Oh. Me too."

On the way home they stopped at the soda shop and he bought five comic books. "What do you want those for?" she asked mournfully. That night, after his parents had gone to bed, he took the other magazines out of the big carton in his closet and looked them over. One or two were dog-eared, copies he had got from other people. He discarded those, and wrapped the others very carefully. He went to sleep, and awoke in his own bed in New York, in the year 1996.

After his mother died, Richard Harvey spent a week cleaning out the house in Newport. That was in June, 1984; the weather was warm for that time of year on the Oregon coast, but there was a chill in the old echoing rooms. The furniture was full of dust, the springs sagging. The will was in probate; the lawyer told Harvey not to expect much. "Your mother made some unwise investments in her later years, against my advice. The house is over sixty years old, and on today's market—"

In the back of the lumber room on the top floor he found an ancient steamer trunk. He emptied it layer by layer: brown photographs in wooden frames, a pair of golf shoes, a Mah-Jongg set. Halfway down, under a pile of yellowed summer dresses, there was a package wrapped in brown paper.

He opened it. Inside, between layers of white tissue paper, he found stacks of comic books, the kind he had collected when he was a kid: *Action Comics*, *Batman*, *Superman*, *All-American*, and dozens of others. The covers were still bright and glossy; the pages were only faintly yellowed. There was a note on top, in a handwriting he recognized as his own. "These are worth a *lot*. Don't take less than $80,000."

He had no recollection of putting the magazines in the trunk, or of writing the note. The latest magazines in the stack were dated Fall 1948, meaning they had been published in the summer of that year. That was when he had had his first episode of amnesia, the one that had worried his parents so much. They had sent him to a psychiatrist in Portland. He had tried drugs and hypnosis, but nothing had brought the memory back. Now, for the first time, he knew something he had done that weekend. But why this?

Over the years there had been other episodes, once in the week before his marriage to Janet. Another time it happened during a trip to Mexico with Linda. Each time, he had waked up with no perception that a day had passed. It was as if a piece of his life had been snipped out and the ends spliced together.

His interest in his own problem led him to study brain physiology. There was an area in the brain stem, he learned, that seemed to govern perception of time. "You might have some very small lesion there," a brain surgeon told him. "Maybe congenital, or some childhood injury. There's no way to find out without cutting you open, and frankly I wouldn't recommend it. You're better off learning to live with this."

He read articles and books about time. The physicists seemed to be saying that the passage of time was an artifact of consciousness. What was it, then, that fixed your mind to this one moving instant? He saw a glimmering of a gigantic discovery, but he had neither the training nor the money to pursue it.

He wrapped the magazines up again and took them back to New York with him. The dealer whistled when he saw them. "Listen. I'm going to be honest with you, I haven't got enough cash to pay you what these are worth."

"What are they worth?"

The dealer touched the magazines spread out on the table. "First issue of *Action*, near-mint, that's eight thousand right there. First three *Batmans*, seven thousand. For the lot, I can give you sixty-five thousand, but I'll have to get a couple of other people to go in with me."

"Make it eighty, and you've got a deal."

"You're a shrewd bargainer, Mr. Harvey. You must have spent a long time collecting these."

"No, I inherited them. I really don't understand why they're worth so much, frankly. They sold for a dime apiece; now they're worth more than their weight in gold."

"Supply and demand," said the dealer. "This one issue, this *Action* Number One with the first *Superman* strip in it, in this condition, there's only about five copies known to exist. You can buy gold anywhere."

He handed Harvey a certified check a week later, and packed the magazines with reverent care into a suitcase. They shook hands.

"Well, Mr. Harvey, what are you going to do with all your money?"

Harvey smiled. "I'm going to invent time travel," he said.

THE VERY OBJECTIONABLE MR. CLEGG

....
....
....
....

Usually I can tell you where a story came from, but there are some ex-
ceptions, and this is one. I have no idea where Mr. Clegg was before he
popped into my consciousness and started doing the things he does.

I had another name for him at first; it was even better than this one,
but unfortunately it belonged to one of my students at Clarion, who
would not have been amused.

Mr. Lionel Clegg said good-bye politely to the stewardess when
he left the airplane at O'Hare. Her bright smile slipped a little;
what an awful person how can he said one of the cricket voices in his
skull.

Mr. Clegg walked heavily up the ramp and emerged into the
concourse. There was something wrong, evidently, with his
appearance—his torso was too bulky, perhaps, his arms too short,
his lipless mouth too wide; but it was too late to change now.

Mr. Clegg looked with interest at the candy bars displayed at
the magazine stand. He bought three and ate them, wrapping and
all, as he moved on. A man with a push-broom gave him a startled
glance.

Mr. Clegg stopped at a wall of lockers and watched a man in a brown suit opening one: first he put in two quarters, then he opened the door and lifted in two Samsonite suitcases and a garment bag. Then he closed the door, took out the little key and put it in his pocket.

The lockers without keys, then, were those that had luggage in them. Mr. Clegg chose one and pressed the tip of his index finger to the lock. After a moment he turned his finger with a metallic sound and opened the door. There were three pieces of luggage inside. Mr. Clegg set them on the floor and opened another locker. This one contained a large soft-sided suitcase and a small train case. Mr. Clegg put the luggage from the first locker into the second locker and vice versa. He went down the row in this way, exchanging the contents of the lockers; then he sat down in a black vinyl seat with a briefcase which he had kept for himself. He watched the people going by and listened to the cricket voices.

A large man in a pinstripe suit walked up to one of the lockers and opened it with a key. He stared at the three brown suitcases inside. He tugged one of them partway out, shoved it in again and tried to take the key out of the lock. Then he closed the door and opened it again. He turned, scratching his head, and saw Mr. Clegg. "Not my luggage," he said.

"No."

"Somebody else's suitcases in there."

"Yes."

"I don't understand it."

"No."

The large man turned, opened the locker and looked in, shut it again. "Listen, will you watch this locker a minute?"

"Yes."

The man went away. When he was out of sight, Mr. Clegg got up and locked the door again, removing the key, which he ate. Then he sat down and opened the ash receptacle beside him. It was half full of cigarette butts, gray ash, crumpled papers. Mr.

Clegg ate three of the cigarette butts and a chewing-gum wrapper.

Presently the large man came back with a man in a blue jacket. While they were arguing, a woman in a green dress came up, opened a nearby locker, looked at the suitcases inside, and joined the discussion. Mr. Clegg sat and watched until the man with the blue jacket took them away. Then he got up and went out into the concourse.

At the United desk a tired-looking woman in a nubbly brown coat was holding a folder toward the blue-jacketed man across the counter. "But I have the ticket," she said. "I don't understand, it says right here 'Flight seventeen.'"

"We don't show a seat for you in the computer," said the man. "If you'll just wait over there—"

Mr. Clegg stepped up and said, "Perhaps I can be of assistance, madam. What seems to be the trouble?"

She turned to him. "Oh—well— It's just that I have to get to Cleveland this afternoon, and now they say I don't have a seat on the airplane."

The blue-jacketed man had turned away to talk to a young woman, also wearing a blue jacket. "Sir," said Mr. Clegg, "may I have your attention for a moment?" The blue-jacketed man went on talking. Mr. Clegg reached over the counter with an extraordinarily long arm and took the man by the necktie. "Am I right in thinking that I have your attention now?" he asked. The man gurgled.

Mr. Clegg released him and straightened his necktie. "This lady tells me that she has a ticket on Flight Seventeen for Cleveland. Is that correct?"

The man massaged his throat. "Yes," he said. Behind him, the young woman was speaking quietly into a hand-held telephone.

"And she also tells me that you have no seat for her on the airplane."

"We're overbooked."

"Therefore you have sold her a ticket which is worthless to her?"

The man glanced at the young woman, who was putting down the phone. "We'll try to get her a seat after the other passengers have boarded."

"They're boarding *now*," said the tired-looking woman, looking toward the end of the room.

"Now I suggest this," said Mr. Clegg. "Either you will give this lady a boarding pass, or you will be extremely sorry." He opened his jaws partway. The blue-jacketed man turned pale. He looked at the tired woman. "Give me your ticket," he said hoarsely. "Smoking or nonsmoking?"

"Nonsmoking, please. But I don't care, just so I get on that plane."

The man slipped the ticket into a new folder, scrawled something on it, and handed it to the woman. "Oh, thank you," she said, and looked at Mr. Clegg. "Thank *you*, Mr.—"

"Clegg," he replied, tipping his hat. "Lionel Clegg, at your service."

As he watched her join the departing passengers, Mr. Clegg became aware that two large men in blue uniforms had appeared, one on either side of him. "Will you come with us, please?" said one.

"Certainly. Are those revolvers you are carrying on your belts?"

"Yes, sir." They began to move down the hall. "This way, please." One of the blue-uniformed men opened a door marked "Security."

"One moment." Mr. Clegg reached out and plucked the revolver from the nearest man's hip, holster and all. The other one stepped back and drew his weapon. Mr. Clegg stretched out his arm and took that one as well. He ate the two guns, one after the other. *Oh jesus* said a cricket voice. Mr. Clegg tipped his hat again and walked away.

The cab driver turned in his seat. "Where to?"

Mr. Clegg was opening the briefcase on his lap. The driver

looked unhappy when he saw the gleam of metal at the end of his finger. *Why do I get all the weird ones* said the cricket voice. Mr. Clegg took out a bundle of folded papers and sorted through them until he found a business letterhead with a Chicago address. He read it to the driver, and settled back to look through the window.

The taxi deposited him in front of a large marble-faced building. Mr. Clegg took the elevator to the tenth floor. "Yes, can I help you?" asked a young woman at a desk. She wore a brown jacket and a blouse with frills all the way down the front.

"Get me the office manager," said Mr. Clegg. He strode past her down the corridor. "Sir! Sir!" she was calling after him. Mr. Clegg found himself in a maze of cubicles with transparent plastic walls. In the first empty one he came to, he sat down at the desk, pushed some papers onto the floor, and opened his briefcase. While he waited, he ate a red plastic rose and some paper clips.

A bald man with glasses came in. Mr. Clegg looked at him. "Are you the office manager?"

"Yes. I'm Ed Thorgeson, the office manager. Who—"

"Lionel Clegg. Where's the biggest office you've got?"

The cricket voice was saying *now what, did Graham send him from New York*—

"Graham sent me from New York," said Mr. Clegg. "Let's not waste time."

"Well, there's a corner office—"

"I want it ready to move into by one o'clock. Meanwhile get me the personnel files."

"The personnel files? All of them?" He swallowed. "Yes, Mr. Clegg, right away."

As the bald man turned, a red-haired young woman entered and looked at Mr. Clegg in surprise. The bald man took her by the arm and led her off.

After a few minutes a young woman in a white blouse came in with a metal cart stacked with file folders. "These are A to F, Mr. Clegg," she said. "Do you want—"

"Put the others in my new office. What's your name? How long have you worked here?"

"My name is Edith Fellowes, Mr. Clegg. I've worked here for a year and a half."

"Okay. Now beat it."

Mr. Clegg opened the first file folder and looked at it, flipped it over and looked at the next. Every now and then he removed a folder and laid it aside.

A tall dark-haired man came in, smiling nervously. "Mr. Clegg, I'm Bill Eberhard, vice president in charge of sales. Is there anything—"

The bald man looked in behind him. "Oh, Mr. Clegg, that office is ready for you now."

"Okay. Get this junk carried in there and send me a stenographer." Mr. Clegg marched past the dark-haired man without looking at his outstretched hand, and followed the bald man to a large office with windows on two sides. The desk was large, bare and gleaming; behind it was a tall padded vinyl chair, and beside it were four more carts stacked with file folders. Mr. Clegg began going through them.

A tall blond woman came in carrying a ring-bound notebook. "I'm Gloria Rickart, Mr. Clegg. Can I get you some coffee?"

"No. Sit down over there and shut up."

The blond woman turned pale and sat down at the desk in the corner. The telephone rang; she picked it up. "Mr. Clegg's office." She listened a moment. "Mr. Claverty would like to see you; he's our vice president in charge of marketing."

"Tell him when I want him I'll send for him." Mr. Clegg continued to go through the file folders. When he had a stack that threatened to topple over, he said to the blond woman, "Type the names on these folders, four copies."

"Yes, sir." She staggered away with the folders. When she returned, Mr. Clegg had another pile ready for her.

An hour went by pleasantly. Miss Rickart laid the last of the typed lists on his desk. Mr. Clegg scanned it, and made sure the names Fellowes, Eberhard, Rickart and Claverty appeared on it. "Get me Thorgeson," he said.

When the office manager appeared, Mr. Clegg handed him one copy of the typed list. "Make out dismissal notices for these people," he said. "I want them out of here by five o'clock." He folded the other three copies and stuffed them into his pocket. He rose and walked to the door. "I'm going to lunch," he said. "Call a meeting of all heads of departments for three o'clock."

"Yes, Mr. Clegg."

There was a little knot of people in the corridor. *Firing a hundred and seventy-three people* said a cricket voice.

Around the corner from the office building, he found himself in a street of small shops. The day was turning windy and cool. A ragged man came toward him, clutching his overcoat together and weaving a little. "My good man," said Mr. Clegg, "will you kindly trade coats with me?" He took off his grey cheviot topcoat and held it out.

"Uh, sure," said the ragged man, whose eyes did not quite focus. He struggled out of his coat and gave it to Mr. Clegg. "Uh, thanks."

"Not at all." Mr. Clegg tipped his hat and walked on. He draped the ragged man's overcoat across an overflowing trash basket at the corner. At a florist's in the next block he bought a dozen yellow roses, which he gave to a man in a black leather jacket who was coming out of a tobacconist's. A block farther down, he took a large paper-wrapped package away from an old man, and threw it into the middle of the street, where a taxi skidded around it.

In his cheap hotel room that night, Mr. Clegg removed his jacket and shirt, opened a large door in his chest, and took out the things he had eaten during the day: guns, paper clips, candy bars, the plastic rose. He dumped them all into the wastebasket; they had already been analyzed, along with everything he had seen and heard, and the information beamed toward the approaching fleet, now thirty days away. When his masters arrived, they would have all the knowledge they needed; the conquest would be a piece of cake.

Mr. Clegg lay down carefully on the bed, which groaned under his weight but did not collapse. He turned off the bedside lamp, then unscrewed his head and laid it on the nightstand. The cricket voices stopped. It had been a good day.

A FANTASY

....
....
....
....

"A Fantasy," like "The Very Objectionable Mr. Clegg," popped into my head all in one piece. This doesn't happen often; when it does happen, it is exhilarating, and very hard to explain.

The stuff about Cosmopolitan, the barn, and my stepson Richard Balmann Wilhelm is all true.

The gray-faced little man came up to me in the Mall; he was wearing a costume like that of the Messenger in *Through the Looking-Glass*: that is, tunic, tabard, tights, and a close-fitting hood, the difference being that the Messenger's hood was pierced for his rabbit ears, and this little person had, instead, plastic-topped antennae made of coil springs that wobbled as he moved. His face was the bluish gray of calsomine; it looked painted on, an impression heightened by the pink rims of his eyelids and the faint yellowness of his teeth. "Sir," he said, holding out a microphone, "would you be kind enough to answer a few questions? What is your opinion of the magazine *Cosmopolitan*?"

"It hit its peak in the thirties," I said.

"Why was that, sir?"

"It had an editor who was interested in fiction and willing to pay for it."

"Who was that editor, sir?"

"His name was Ray Long."

"Are you sure? Do you want to change your mind?"

"No, I'll go with that."

"You're *right!*" the little man shrieked. "For one hundred dollars! Congratulations, Mr.—"

"Knight," I said, as he pressed a crisp new bill into my hand.

"Mr. Knight, how did you happen to know the answer to that question?"

"I knew it because my stepson, Richard Wilhelm, found a nineteen twenty-nine issue of *Cosmopolitan* in a barn and gave it to me."

"Your *stepson* Richard Wilhelm found it in a *barn* and gave it to you? Mr. Knight, do you realize what you have just done? You have just said two of the secret words, 'stepson' and 'barn,' for two thousand dollars! What is your stepson's full name, if I may ask?"

"His name is Richard Balmann Wilhelm," I said.

"Balmann!" cried the little man in ecstasy. "Oh, you're not going to believe this, folks. 'Balmann' is the *third* secret word, and you, Mr. Knight, have just won a trip around the world for two and an income of fifty thousand dollars a year for life!"

Thus in the just world, which is hard to find even when you know the way. What the "real" world is like I need not remind you.

FOREVER

When I showed another story in this collection to my friends (you will know which one if you have read the stories in order), I got general approval except for the last line, which read "Forever." I took out the last line, and then became stubborn and put it back. I was so stubborn, in fact, that I wrote another story and gave it that title.

In 1887, in Wiesbaden, Germany, Herr Doktor Heinrich Gottlieb Essenwein discovered the elixir of life. The elixir, distilled from pigs' bladders, was simple to manufacture and permanent in its effects. After taking one dose of the clear reddish liquid, colored and flavored with cinnamon, one no longer aged. It was as simple as that. A chicken to which the Herr Doktor fed a dose of the elixir in January, 1887, was still alive in 1983 and had laid an estimated 25,860 eggs, of which 7,000 had double yolks.

An unfortunate side effect of this discovery was that Essenwein's son Gerd, to whom the good Doktor gave a dose of the elixir in 1888, remained twelve years old for the remainder of his life. Gerd, a talented piccolo player, had a sunny disposition and was loved by all, but he was pimply and shy.

Once the Herr Doktor had discovered his error, he recommended that the elixir not be taken until a suitable age, which varied according to the talents and wishes of the individual: an athlete, for example, might take his dose at twenty-three, when he was at the height of his physical powers; a financier perhaps at forty-five or so, and a philosopher at fifty.

Encouraged by Essenwein's example, the British physicist John Tyndall discovered penicillin in 1895. Three years later, Louis Pasteur announced his so-called universal bacteriophage, one injection of which would destroy any marauding germ whatever, at the cost of making the recipient feel out of sorts for about a year and a half.

As a result, the population of the world expanded dramatically during the years 1890–1903, the birthrate remaining the same or even advancing a trifle, while the death rate had fallen to a negligible figure. Fortunately, in 1897 the American physician Dr. Richard Stone perfected an oral contraceptive, which worked on both men and women, and also slowed down cats and dogs a great deal.

Partly because of the unbearable crankiness of children who had had their bacteriophage shots, the new contraceptive was adopted with enthusiasm all over the world, and the habit of having children fell into disrepute. Occasional infants still came into the world, by accident or inattention, but so rarely that as early as 1953, when a year-old infant was displayed to Queen Victoria as a curiosity, she started in horror and exclaimed, "What is that?"

As a consequence, a number of famous people were never born. These included Yogi Berra, George Gershwin, Aldous Huxley, Leonid Brezhnev, and Marilyn Monroe. On the other hand, a number of famous people *were* born, such as McDonald Wilson Slipher, the founder of the Church of Self-Satisfaction; the songwriter Sidney Colberg ("I'll Be Good When You're Gone"); and Harriet Longworth Tubman, the first woman president of the United States.

Early in the twentieth century, armies all over the world were plagued by mutiny and desertion; hardly anyone was crazy enough to risk a life which might last for centuries, or even, with luck and reasonable care, for thousands of years. When the Archduke of Austria-Hungary was killed by an assassin at Sarajevo, Emperor Franz Josef wanted to declare war on Serbia, but Conrad von Hötzendorf told him he would merely embarrass the nation by doing so. Kaiser Wilhem consulted von Moltke and was told the same thing. Both rulers gloomily assented to an international conference to resolve the issue; the war never took place.

Thus the world entered an era of lasting peace and prosperity. A network of electric railways covered the earth; Count Zeppelin's airships, which went into service in 1898, carried freight and passengers to the farthest parts of the globe. Thomas Edison, the wizard of Menlo Park, together with Nikola Tesla, Lee De Forest, and other giants of modern invention, poured out a steady stream of scientific marvels for the enrichment of human life.

Albert Einstein, of the Kaiser Wilhelm Institute in Berlin, published his equation $E = mc^2$ in 1905, demonstrating that the release of nuclear energy was possible, but the world already had abundant electrical power, thanks to Edison and Tesla, and nobody paid any attention.

In 1931 the astronomer Schiaparelli persuaded Guglielmo Marconi to attempt communication with the planet Mars. Marconi built a signaling apparatus, in effect a giant spark coil, in the Piedmont near Turin, and during the opposition of 1933 he fired off electric impulses into space every night; the sounds he produced were so terrific that sheep and cattle lost their bowel control for miles around. Marconi's message, repeated over and over, was a simple one: "Two plus one are three. Two plus two are four. Two plus three are five."

At the end of six months the hopes of the two Italians were realized when they received a return message: it said, "Eight plus seven are fourteen." Critics pointed out that this was not quite right, but the achievement captured the world's imagination nevertheless. The popular author Jules Verne, in collaboration with the German Hermann Oberth, immediately began to draw plans for a cosmobile in which to visit the Martians. The task proved difficult, and more than two decades passed before the designers were ready to test their first cosmic vehicle. Because of technical difficulties, no attempt was to be made to reach Mars at this time;

the vehicle was to swing around the Moon and take photographs, then return to Earth. Even so, the rocket could carry only one passenger, who must weigh no more than one hundred pounds. Gerd Essenwein, the son of the discoverer of the elixir of life, volunteered to go, and so did a double amputee named Brunfels, who had lost both legs in a streetcar accident in Berlin, but a midget was selected instead. This midget was Walter Dopsch, a popular circus performer; he was a perfectly formed little fellow who stood only three feet nine inches tall and weighed seventy-five pounds. Because this was twenty-five pounds less than the allowed weight, Dopsch was able to take along on the voyage a large supply of cognac, cigars, paperbound novels, and the bonbons to which he was addicted.

The flight took place on April 23, 1956; the space vehicle was raised to a height of thirty miles by means of a balloon designed by the Piccard brothers; then it was cut free and ascended by rocket power. The whole world listened to Dopsch's radio transmissions as he soared through space and looped around the Moon, which he described as "like a very large Swiss cheese." On the return journey, however, the parachute which was to lower the vehicle to Earth proved defective; it collapsed in the tropopause and Dopsch plunged flaming into the North Sea. His last radio message was, "I love you, Helga." Helga, it was later ascertained, was the fat lady in the circus in which Dopsch had been employed.

This tragedy put a damper on space exploration, and, since no further messages were received from the Martians, the whole enterprise was forgotten.

Public opinion, anyhow, was turning against such dangerous pursuits. The internal combustion engine, for example, which had enjoyed a brief vogue early in the century, was everywhere replaced by safe, quiet electric trains and interurban trolleys. The Safety Prize, instituted in 1944 by Count Alfred Nobel, was awarded every year to such inventions as no-slip shoe soles and inflatable pantaloons.

In 1958 a syndicate headed by John D. Rockefeller and J. P. Morgan constructed a graceful steel and glass enclosure, 225 feet tall, over the entire island of Manhattan. By an ingenious use of wind vanes and filters, fresh air was kept circulating inside the enclosure while smoke and grime from the industrial areas of Queens and New Jersey were kept out. Inside this enclosure, dubbed "The Crystal Matterhorn" by journalists, ever taller and more fanciful buildings were constructed throughout the sixties; beginning in 1970, many were joined by spiral walkways. All vehicular travel in Manhattan was by subway and electric cars; horses, gasoline engines, and other sources of pollution were strictly banned. In the winter, the enclosure was kept at a comfortable temperature by electrical heaters and by the calories generated by the island's 300,000 inhabitants. Thus, winter or summer, the Manhattanites could stroll the pavements in perfect comfort and safety.

In literature and the arts, unwholesome innovation was forestalled by the taste of the public, who knew what they liked, and by the survival of many of the great figures of the late nineteenth century. In 1983 the sensations of the opera season were Enrico Caruso in Puccini's *I Malavoglia* and Lillian Russell in Tchaikovsky's *Nicolas Negorev*; the best-selling novels were Mark Twain's *Life in an Iceberg*, *The Borderland* by Robert Louis Stevenson, and *The Society of Ink-Tasters* by Arthur Conan Doyle. A traveling exhibition of new works by James McNeill Whistler, at the Metropolitan Museum, was seen by hundreds of thousands.

A man in East Orange, New Jersey, found a painting by Paul Cézanne in his grandmother's attic; it was obviously old, and he took it to a dealer, who informed him regretfully that it was worthless.

Centuries passed. In 2250 it was discovered that the population was declining, but the world took little notice at first, although it mourned the increasingly frequent deaths of great men and women. The elixir and the bacteriophage, although one kept people from aging and the other made them immune to disease, could not protect them against fatal ailments such as cancer, heart failure, and hardening of the arteries, or against poison, fire, drowning, and other accidents.

By 2330, when the decline became alarming, it was too late; the youngest living women, although they were as little as nineteen years old in appearance, had a chronological age of more than two hundred, and they were no longer fertile.

One by one, the smaller inhabited places of the world were abandoned and their former citizens moved into the great domed cities. Eventually even these became depopulated. Forests again covered the continents, effacing the works of man; for the first time in two thousand years, there were bears in Britain and giant elk in Russia. Six centuries after the discovery of the elixir of life, there were only two human beings left on the surface of the planet.

One of these was Gerd Essenwein, the Herr Doktor's son, who was then living in a villa overlooking Lake Lucerne, where he had collected all the sheet music for piccolo in the Lucerne and Zürich libraries. The other was a Japanese woman, Michiko Yamagata, who at the time she took the elixir had been sixteen years of age. The two got into communication with each other by shortwave radio, and although they could not understand each other very well because of static, they agreed to meet. Michiko found a serviceable small boat in Takatsu, crossed the Sea of Japan, and made her way across Asia and Europe by bicycle, stopping frequently to rest and replenish her stocks of dried food. The trip took her eleven years.

It was an emotional moment when at last she appeared on Gerd's doorstep. Neither had seen another human face, except in photographs and films, for over a century. Gerd played his piccolo for her and showed her his collection of autographs of famous musicians; he took her on a walking tour around the lake, and then they had a picnic in the country. It was a warm day, and Michiko took off her dress. Speaking in German, which was their only common language, she said, "Essenwein-san, do you rike me?"

"I like you very much," said Gerd. "However, what you have in mind is not possible." In turn, he removed his clothing, and she saw that although he had lived for more than six centuries, his body was still twelve years old. They looked at each other ruefully and then put their clothes back on. The next day Michiko got on her bicycle and started home. This time she was not in a hurry, and the trip lasted fifteen years.

After her return, they continued to communicate by shortwave radio on their birthdays for some years. In 2510 Michiko told him that she was about to leave on a visit to Fujiyama; that was her last message.

A few years later, Gerd put a few prized possessions in a handcart and made his way into the mountains of Unter Walden, where he found a herd of Hartz Mountain goats, a hardy and affectionate breed. When he discovered that the goats liked his piccolo playing, he built a hut on the mountainside and moved in. Besides his sheet music and his autographs, he had a small harmonium, which he also played, but not as well; also, the goats did not care for it.

It was here, one morning in the spring of 2561, that the Arcturians found him. The Arcturians had received Marconi's signals, intended for Mars, and they had also received radio transmissions of voices singing "Yes, Sir, That's My Baby," stock-market reports, and "Amos 'n' Andy."

Three of the Arcturians disembarked from their landing vehicle and approached Gerd, who was sitting beside his hut, dressed in goatskins. The Arcturians were large gray worms, or, more properly, millipedes. They wore hemispherical dark covers over their eyes to protect them from the unaccustomed glare of our sun, and looked like bug-eyed monsters.

During their long voyage they had had plenty of time to learn Earth languages from radio and television broadcasts, but they didn't know which one Gerd spoke. "¿Es Usted el último?" they asked him. "Are you the last? Etes-vous le dernier?"

Gerd looked at them and played the opening bars of the Fantasia for Unaccompanied Piccolo by Deems Taylor.

"We come from another world," they told him in Hindi, Swedish, and Italian. Gerd went on playing.

"Do you want to come with us? Doni të vij me neve? Wollen Sie gehen mit uns?"

Gerd lowered the piccolo. "Nein, danke," he said. "Glück auf," said the Arcturians politely, and went away forever.